CLOUD RIDERS

Nick Cook completed his degree in sculpture and then moved into the computer games industry. For more than 21 years Nick worked as a graphic artist and creative director, helping to produce over forty titles, including many chart-topping hits. Nick has a passion for science and astronomy, often blogging about the latest mind-blowing discoveries made in quantum physics. He once even soloed a light aircraft, an experience he's tapping into now for the Cloud Riders trilogy.

CLOUD RIDERS

Nick Cook

To Max,

May Cloud Riders capture your imagination and take you on an amazing journey!

Nick Cook

THREE HARES PUBLISHING

Published by Three Hares Publishing 2014

This is a work of fiction. The characters, incidents, and dialogues are products of the author's imagination and are not to be construed as real. Any resemblance to actual events or persons, living or dead, is entirely coincidental.

First published in Great Britain in 2014
www.threeharespublishing.com

Three Hares Publishing Ltd Reg. No 8531198
Registered address: Suite 201, Berkshire House, 39-51 High Street, Ascot, Berkshire, SL5 7HY

ISBN 9781910153048

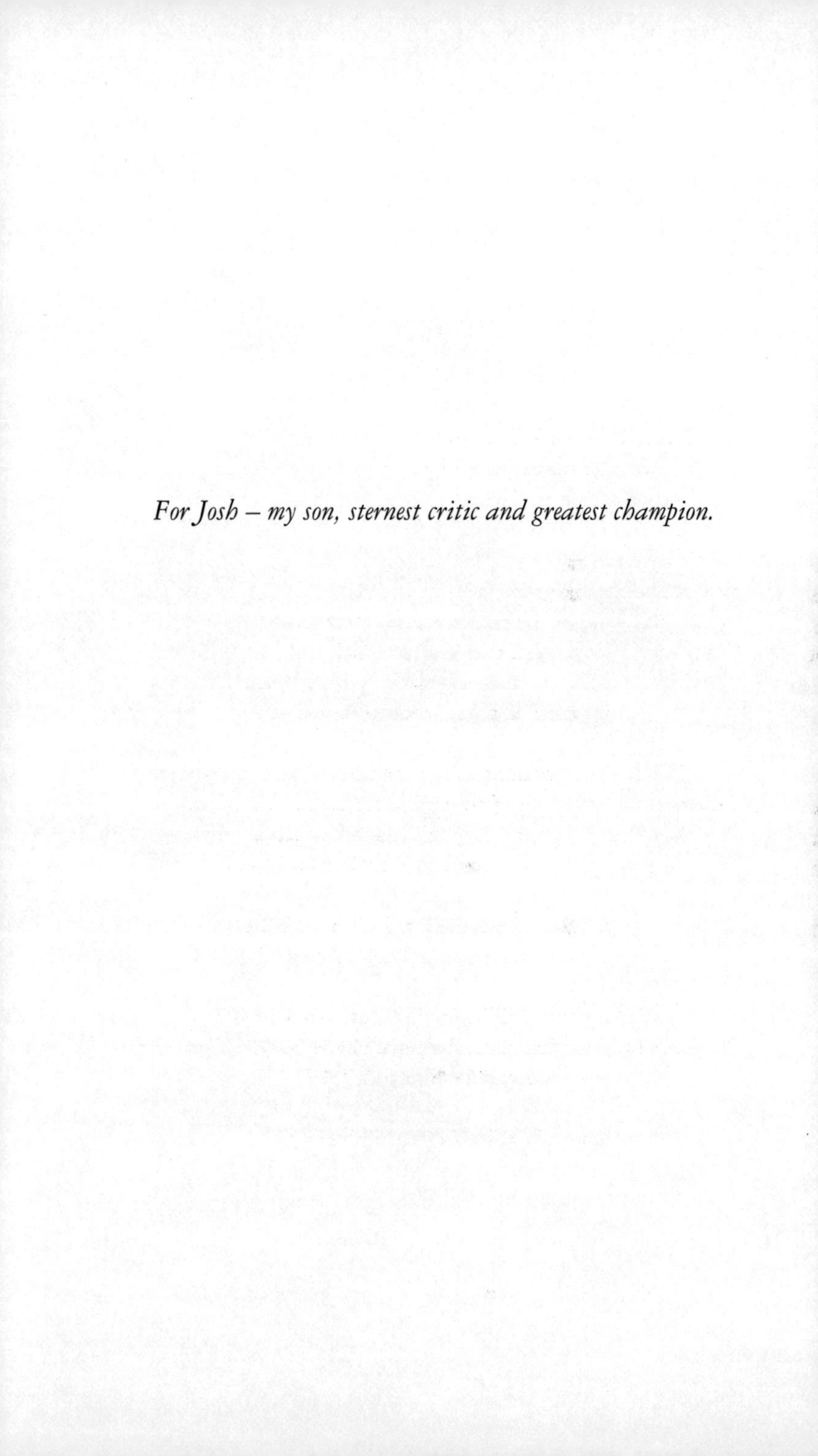

For Josh – my son, sternest critic and greatest champion.

‘I am a being of Heaven and Earth, of thunder and lightning, of rain and wind, of the galaxies.’

Eden Ahbez

Chapter One
TAUNTED

The air boiled inside the school bus and a trickle of sweat ran down my back. I tipped my gaze towards the sapphire sky and traced the aircraft vapour trails with my forefinger. It squealed across the glass.

Not even a hint of a storm cloud.

Something smacked into the back of my head, causing a spasm of pain. My gaze locked onto the coke can clattering to the ground and rolling towards the driver, trailing glistening brown liquid.

'Touchdown,' a voice called out.

I jerked round to see one of the backseat jocks leering at me, a Neanderthal with a square head and squashed nose. His adoring female fans sniggered. The familiar anger surged up through me, hotter than the air in the bus. I shot to my feet, ready to tear the guy to pieces. I seemed to do that a lot these days.

A hand with oil stained fingernails clamped onto my wrist. Jules stared up at me from her seat across the aisle, brown eyes wide.

'Dom, he's not worth it,' she said.

'That's right, listen to your pet grease monkey,' the jock said.

The back of the bus erupted with laughter.

The anger burned hotter inside me, but Jules strengthened her grip. 'Please, Dom, for me.'

God it would so easy, so easy to let go, but… I thought of Mom getting that phone call from school the last time I'd done that. Guilt surged through me, cooling my guts like water on a forest fire. I turned and sank back into my seat.

The hoots and whistles thundered. Jules crossed her arms and shot me a frown. I pressed my forehead against the vibrating window.

Could life get any worse?

As we approached the edge of town, I peered out at the big white gleaming houses with their massive double garages and sweeping driveways. The bus slowed and I heard the scrabble of feet.

'See ya, loser,' the blonde-haired cheerleader said, a clone of all the others, smirking at me with her too white teeth. She flounced down the steps to link arms with the jock who'd thrown the can.

The bus pulled away and I watched the group saunter away along the sidewalk, golden arms draped around each other, fake designer shades reflecting gleaming light; fake people off to lead fake lives.

Jules' reflection across the aisle turned towards me. 'Don't let them get to you, Dom.'

'They're just real good at pushing my buttons.'

She shrugged. 'Shallow people with nothing better to do.'

'Is that what you thought about me when I hung out with them?'

Jules' image slumped back into her seat. So that answered that then.

The driver shifted up and the engine's hum pitched down. The wannabe mansions slid away as we passed the edge of town, replaced by endless scorched cornfields under the bright sky.

The bus bumped along the old potholed highway and I dropped my gaze. I noticed my expensive jeans had started to fray around the knee. There'd be no replacing them now.

A pinging sound came from somewhere. I peeled my forehead off the window and looked over at Jules as she hunted through her bag. She fished out her cell and pursed her lips at the screen.

'Problem?' I asked.

'Nothing.' She started to shove her phone back into her bag, bright blossoms staining her cheeks.

'Jules?'

She hitched her thumb over her shoulder towards town. 'Just one of the cheerleader bimbos back there.'

'Getting hassled?'

'You so don't want to know.'

'Show me.'

Jules' face deepened to a colour somehow way beyond red. She swivelled the phone towards me.

'So Dom's dropped to your league now! LOL.'

'What's that girl code for?'

She shrugged.

Her phone pinged again.

'The Twister Loser and the Grease Monkey – match made in heaven!"

My jaw clenched. 'Ignore her.'

Jules nodded and fumbled with the phone. The screen went dark.

I turned back to the view. On the horizon a green metal monster shimmered through the heat-haze. I could just make out a thin stream of corn spraying from a nozzle and into the trailer of a tractor trundling alongside.

Jeez, just one combine.

Jules' sigh punctured my thoughts. 'Hardly a harvest, and early too.'

'You're telling me.'

In the distance a wail cried over the hum of the engine, a single note that rose and fell back to silence. I glanced at my watch. Three pm – the daily test of the storm sirens.

'Don't know why they even bother anymore,' I said.

Jules hunched her shoulders. 'The rain and twisters will be back. Gotta be.'

A brief fantasy swept through my imagination: a vast tornado reducing the mock-mansions to matchwood. If only. Twelve months and no twisters, just cloudless skies and dust storms since he'd died. I swallowed down a sudden lump in my throat.

Jules' eyes searched mine. 'You alright?'

I shrugged.

She bit her lip, angling her body towards me. 'Dom?'

'I just feel invisible some days.'

'Do you really want to hang around with people just interested in you because your dad was famous?'

'Yadda yadda yadda,' I replied, using my hand as a glove puppet.

Jules blinked, the blush spreading to her ears.

A squirming sensation went through my guts. Jules might be annoying sometimes, but she was my only real buddy. 'My bad – shouldn't be taking my crap out on you.'

She gave me a teeth-flashing smile. 'S'okay.' She grabbed her bag and dropped into the seat next to me. 'Want to talk about it?'

'Not a lot to say, is there?'

Jules peered at the floor, her shoulder length hair forming dark curtains on either side of her face. 'If you hadn't noticed, I'm not exactly running with the in-crowd either. In the meantime guess you'll have to do. Just two loners hanging out. And anyway, we're way too cool for the rest of them.' Her smile sharpened into a pixie grin.

I snorted. 'Thanks.'

'Anytime.' She nudged my shoulder. 'So, still planning to see the world?'

I raked a hand through my hair. 'Going nowhere fast as usual. Looks like I'm trapped here for another summer, just like you.'

She pulled at the corner of a smiley sticker on her bag. 'You see, Dom, that's where you and I differ.' She raised five fingers and started ticking them off. 'I love our bit of Oklahoma, the way a sunset makes the cornfields look like they're on fire, working with Dad in the garage, how friendly people are—'

I shook my head at number three. 'Well, apart from that lot, right?' I said, gesturing towards the back seat.

Jules sighed and nodded.

'I envy you,' I said.

'In what way?'

'You always seem so chilled.'

She swung her legs. 'Yep, I'm definitely a glass half-full sort of gal.'

'And I'm just a miserable jackass.' Some of the tension eased across my shoulders.

Jules laughed. 'So, about what she said…'

'What?'

She started picking at the smiley sticker again. 'You know, about us being an item?'

'What a jerk.'

She tore the sticker in two. 'Isn't she.'

The gasoline station rumbled into view. Through the doors of the open workshop, I spotted her dad, Roddy, half buried under the hood of a rusting Buick. He looked up from the engine. Jules grabbed her bag and stood up, marching to the front. The driver pulled up in a flurry of dust.

'See ya later,' I called out.

She waved a hand over her shoulder without saying her usual alligator reply, and I knew right then I was in trouble.

Without looking back, she jumped down the stairs and I filed the question under 'don't-even-go-there'. She was my best friend and, well – Julia was Jules – the person who helped me fix up the Mustang when she wasn't busy with her dad in the garage. The thought of anything else was just way too out there.

I watched as she strode right past Roddy, arms wrapped tight around herself, and headed towards the trailer.

Scratching his neck, Roddy glanced my way.

The bus rumbled into motion and I gave him an exaggerated shrug, spreading my hands wide. 'No idea,' I mouthed back.

Roddy shook his head and, wiping his hands on a rag, strolled after her. Jules was all he had now after his wife, Jules' mom, had died from cancer. Despite the heat I shuddered, remembering her funeral on a wet slate day, umbrellas floating over the mourners like black flowers bobbing on water. Jules had sobbed in my arms, while I'd patted her back. Then a year later it had been my Dad's turn, except there'd been no body to bury.

I pushed the memory away and stared out of the window.

The bus sped up and the landscape levelled out, pressed flat by the blue hand of the sky. A lone red farm sped past, a 'For Sale' sign stuck on its closed gate.

I tapped the seat in time to the song in my head. Another one bites the dust.

The bus began to rock over the uneven surface. The road stretched ahead, a shimmering line of asphalt disappearing into the distance with not another car to be seen.

I pulled my shirt away from my sweaty chest and saw the familiar flash of light on the horizon – the silver hangar and oak tree standing sentry over our house, and Twister diner. My heart squeezed. The 'T' looked like it had shifted again. One good gust of wind and it would be history. I wasn't crazy about the idea of clambering up and fixing it back on, either.

Shouldering my bag, I dragged my way to the front of the bus. The driver glanced at me in his mirror.

I tried to hold his gaze and saw my crooked smile reflected in his sunglasses. 'You got time to grab some coffee? My mom's made some great cherry pie.'

He shook his head, cutting me off like he always did. It never stopped me asking. As Mom kept telling me, 'Any business is good business right now.'

The only car I could see parked in the lot was our prehistoric station wagon – old enough to be in the Smithsonian – and covered in a fine layer of soil from the dust storms. No cars meant no customers.

The bus shuddered to a stop and the doors clunked open. Through the window I could see Mom working in the kitchen. I could just stay on the bus...escape my life.

She glanced up and waved. I put on a smile for her and squashed the idea like a cockroach.

Jumping off, I raised my hand to the driver. 'See ya after the summer—'

The engine roared and the bus lurched forward, throwing up a cloud of dirt into my face.

'Vacation,' I finished, coughing.

The vehicle swung through the lot and sped back towards town. I dropped my hand and watched until the bus shrank to a dot. I listened to the moan of the telephone lines in the gentle wind. Loneliest sound in the world when it was this quiet.

Taking a deep breath I thrust my hands into my pockets and slouched towards the entrance.

A smell of something delicious, hints of spicy meat, mom's special chilli, wafted from the kitchen extractor duct and pulled at my nose. I quickened my pace and felt the heaviness lift just a bit from my limbs.

Twelve months and it was just Mom and me against the world now.

Chapter Two

THE TWISTER DINER

I stepped into the diner and the welcome chill of the air conditioning wrapped around me. Despite the fact we could barely afford the electricity bill these days, Mom said we had to keep it cool for when a customer turned up. Made sense, I guess.

Out of habit, I tapped the ancient barometer mounted on the wall. The needle remained stuck on 'Fair'. So much for a storm coming.

Mom came out from the back, wiping her hands on a towel. 'Good day at school, hun?'

I painted on my best cheery 'I really don't feel like a social leper' smile. 'Yeah, all cool.'

Her eyes flicked straight down to the hole in my pants. 'Oh, Dom, your best jeans. Your dad bought those for you, too.'

They'd been way too long but I'd grown into them since. I glanced away. 'They've just worn out.' And anyway, the odd rip was still cool.

'We can't afford to buy you another pair like that.' She bit her lip.

I kept the groan in like always when she talked about cash, met her eyes, and nodded.

Her face softened. 'Let's see what we can do with them. If I don't darn the rip it will get bigger and they'll fall apart.'

Mom was great like that. She knew how much they meant to me. I couldn't bring myself to throw them. Not yet. They were the last thing dad had bought for me.

She disappeared behind the counter and pulled out a faded metal candy tin. 'Come on then, hand them over and I'll patch them for you.'

'Here?' No way could she be serious.

Mom raised an eyebrow. 'We're hardly being run off our feet. You might be all grown up now you're seventeen, but you're still my boy.' She reached out, waggling her fingers.

Jesus, she was serious. Sighing, I kicked off my shoes, slipped my jeans off and handed them to her.

She began rooting through the tin. 'You hungry?'

'Starved.'

Mom dug out a cotton reel and needle. 'Help yourself to some chilli, there's a big pot on the stove.' She hooked her reading glasses onto her nose.

I padded around to the kitchen, feeling self-conscious, and grabbed a white bowl with a twisting blue spiral snaking up its side – an abstract tornado I'd helped design – and heaped it to the brim. Grabbing a hunk of fresh sourdough, I sat at the counter.

Mom huddled over my jeans, her needle flashing in the afternoon sunlight angling through the window. As I took the first mouthful, I caught her watching me from the corner of her eye.

An explosion of spicy melting beef filled my mouth. 'Wow, Mom, this is fantastic.'

She smiled over the top of her glasses. 'There's plenty left if you want seconds.' Her mouth drew into a thin line.

'Another slow day?'

She blinked. 'Even slower. Down from three hundred covers to a dozen in just over twelve months – and one of those was a rep trying to sell me a top-of-the-range coffee machine. I thought things were bad enough when we lost the storm chasers and their fans, but it keeps getting worse.'

'Your cooking's still the best, Mom.'

She waved her hand around the empty silver diner. 'Well, if it's so great, where are all my customers?'

'It's not your fault that the weather screwed everything round here.' I gestured with my spoon towards the series of framed certificates above the cash register. 'Twister Diner – Gold Medal.'

She smiled at that. 'Best diner in Tornado Alley...' She blinked again, crunching the jeans between her fingers.

My eyes fixed on the photo of Dad pinned to the wall over her head, me sitting on the wing of his yellow crop dusting bi-plane – his other job when he wasn't storm chasing. Why had he even tried? I screwed my eyes shut and was back there in the roar of the storm. I'd run out of the house early that July morning, and seen his plane heading straight towards a massive twister. We'd found the note pinned to the refrigerator door later.

'I'm going for the shot!'

The old pain crept out. Dad, an experienced pilot, had talked about nothing else – video from within a tornado funnel for the storm chasing show he starred in. I remembered how he'd used our blue mop bucket to represent a twister, and one of my old yellow toy cars, swooping in his hand, the bi-plane. He'd demonstrated – complete with sound effects – how he was going to drop down into the spout for just a moment, grab the footage, and climb out again.

'Simple,' he'd said.

They'd found the mangled section of the yellow tail-plane the following day, with its cartoon of a pilot riding a tornado scratched like it'd been raked with claws. They'd also found a Saint Christopher medal that Dad had kept in the cockpit, which Mom still wore to this day. But that was all they'd found.

A rumble of tyres pulled my thoughts back and a battered rust-red pickup with an engine block roped onto it chugged into our lot.

'It's Roddy and Jules,' I said.

'Bless them, that's the third time they've come over for supper this week.'

Jules jumped out of the truck, her face one big smile.

I sighed to myself. Her mood changed direction quicker than a twister.

Carrying a cardboard box, she hurtled towards the door. Mom nudged me and held out my jeans, grinning. 'I'll finish mending them later.'

'Shit!'

She laughed. 'Language, Dom.'

I snatched them from her and yanked them up my legs as the diner door crashed open. Jules' smile morphed into a smirk.

As I fumbled with my zipper, my face burned up like a volcano. 'Don't say a word.'

She twisted her head to one side. 'Oh go on – just one comment about your Bart Simpson boxers.'

'I do not wear Bart Simpson boxers.'

'Wouldn't know – wasn't looking.'

Mom chuckled and I glowered at them. The door swung open. There stood Roddy, framed in sunlight.

He beamed at us and wiped his hands on his overalls. 'Hi, y'all.' His nose twitched. 'Something smells mighty fine.' He strolled in, blond hair flecked with oil, hands stained black like Jules'.

Mom zipped out back and began ladling two bowls with chilli.

Roddy's sharp blue eyes zeroed in, reading me. 'You okay there, Dom?'

Jules nudged my shoulder. 'Been giving him a hard time.'

He shook his head. 'Give the boy a break, huh?'

'He loves the attention really, don't you, Dom?' Jules said.

I rolled my eyes at her, grabbed the coffee pot and filled a cup.

Mom breezed out of the kitchen and placed two bowls on their regular table by the window. 'How does a Hurricane Chilli Special sound?'

'A starving man's fantasy,' Roddy replied. He retrieved a clean cloth from his overall pocket, flapped it over the chair and sat down. I'd watched him do this ritual for years, regular as a heartbeat.

He took a large spoonful of the food, jaw moving slow and deliberate, and beamed at Mom. 'Sue, I swear you make the best chilli in the whole damned state.'

Mom's smile threatened to reach her ears and she ran her fingers through her hair.

'Roddy, stop, you'll make me blush.'

Jules raised her eyebrows at me. Mom and Roddy had been like this with each other for months now.

'Don't know why they don't just get on with it and start dating,' Jules had said to me a while back.

They did seem made for each other. But I seriously couldn't deal with the idea of Roddy replacing Dad anytime soon – that was a step too far for me.

I placed the coffee cup next to the themed salt and pepper pots, designed like a spiralling tornado spout. 'See, Mom, everyone loves your food.'

'I appreciate the compliments, but I'm not sure that's really enough to pay the bills any more.'

Roddy gave her a straight look. 'Money that tight, Sue?'

Mom blinked at him and turned my way. 'There's a big bowl of cherries in the house. Why don't you take Jules over and help yourselves.'

I could take a hint. 'Okay...'

Jules grabbed her chilli and placed it on top of the box. 'Thanks, Sue – love cherries.'

'What's with the box?' I asked.

'Oh, you'll see.'

I followed her out through the kitchen. Just as she pushed the screen door open with her foot, my stomach growled. 'Hang on, forgotten my food.'

'Hurry up.' Her grin widened as the door closed.

I walked back into the kitchen. Through the hatchway I spotted my bowl of chilli steaming on the counter.

'I don't think we can carry on much longer,' Mom whispered.

I froze, heart beating fast.

'But you've worked so hard to build this place up,' Roddy replied.

Mom let out a long sigh. 'But the business is dead now. Roddy, it's time for me to face facts and sell.'

My stomach lurched. I'd known things were tight – but this bad?

'Look, Sue, I could always lend you the money.'

'If I could be sure I'd be able to pay you back, I'd take you up on that in the blink of an eye – but we're finished,' Mom said, her voice shaky. 'We've tried everything, but nothing's worked. You know, Roddy, I even find myself praying for an actual twister to hit to drum up business – how sick is that?'

I pressed my head against a tiled pillar. You and me both.

'Then let me give you the money,' Roddy replied.

'No, you need all you have for Jules' college fund. It's bad enough she's growing up without her mother. You've both been through so much already without having to worry about that as well.'

The pause seemed to go on forever, until the silence felt fit to burst the diner's walls.

Roddy's voice cracked. 'Yeah.'

I didn't need to look to know that Mom was hugging him by now.

'You've done a great job raising that gorgeous daughter of yours, and as my dad always taught me, there's no point throwing good money after bad.'

'Sue—'

'Forget it, Roddy. Look, I appreciate it, really I do, but it's time for Dom and me to move on. Maybe I could do some waitressing in the city.'

My pulse sped up. Anywhere would be better than being stuck in the middle of nowhere… And hey, a city was a city, although it would be hard on Mom after owning her own place.

I pulled the door quietly closed behind me and stepped out into the heat of the yard. Thoughts rattling like our old tumble dryer, I ambled across to our house via the oak tree – my thinking place – and stepped under its dappled light. I placed my hand against the trunk.

A thought snuck out from the back of my head. The diner was Mom's whole life.I looked towards the hangar at the end of the field where the bleached orange windsock hung limply outside.

What would you do, Dad?

Taking a deep breath, I ambled into the house.

Jules sat hunched at the table over the picture. She glanced up. 'Where's your food?'

I grabbed a handful of cherries. 'Thought I'd start with dessert first.'

'Really? Your mom's chilli is—'

'Great – yeah, I know.'

She gave me a questioning look, but I ignored it and pulled up a chair. I jutted my chin towards the box.

Her face lit up brighter than a spotlight and she shoved the box towards me. 'Go on, open it.'

Seeing her expression, I knew what it was. 'You finished it?'

She nodded and my heart missed half-a-dozen beats. I ripped open the box and pulled out a polished piston cover with 'Mustang' stamped onto it. It felt like Christmas, New Year and Easter had all merged into one. I ran my finger over the raised lettering.

'It looks amazing, Jules.'

'Yep, polished it myself – thought you'd appreciate the finishing touch.'

'God, do I ever.' It looked as good as new – better even. The last part of the engine and now the Mustang rebuild would be complete. No more bus. No more jerks on the way home. Freedom. At least if I could persuade Mom to let me drive it.

If we did hugs I would have given her a massive one right there. Instead I just gave her a shoulder nudge with my fist. That did for affection between us. Her smile dimpled.

Jules might be a bit kooky, but being able to fix up any engine made her one of the coolest people I knew. Period.

'We can get it fitted when we've finished up here,' she said.

'Sounds like a plan.' I grabbed dad's old laptop from the dresser, placed it on the table and flipped open the screen for my daily post school ritual.

Jules smile slid away. 'You're not still checking that site?'

'Yeah...'

She gave me that look of hers, gaze narrowed. She could so read me. The site was Dad's old world, a storm chasers bulletin board. But these days the equivalent of internet tumbleweed blew across it. No one had posted anything in six months. But Jules knew the real reason why I logged on every day... to read dad's old messages. And I knew every word of every entry of his off by heart, and of his team's, the Sky Hawks. Their adventures lived on for me in those old posts.

The computer boot-up seemed to take forever, almost steam powered compared to the slick laptops and tablets other students had at school these days, but by the time Jules had finished half her chilli I had the internet browser up and running. I clicked on a link and the Sky Hawks' bulletin board filled the screen. Straight away I spotted the message in bold text at the top, titled 'Have you seen this, guys?'

'Someone's actually posted something new on the board,' I said.

'Really?' Jules scooted round to my side of the table to look at the screen.

'Mr Howard,' I said looking at the posts details.

'What, from the farm next to here?'

'Yeah, he's into astronomy – always been a Sky Hawks' fan.' I opened up the message and an image filled the screen, a crescent moon just visible over a handful of stars above the flat cornfields of Mr Howard's farm. I recognised the cross of the Cassiopeia constellation to one side that Jules had once pointed out to me. 'So what's so interesting about that? It's hardly a NASA image.'

'Look at the message underneath,' Jules replied.

My gaze flicked to the text.

'Took this shot last night of the sky. But the reason for posting it is there was pressure drop way off the scale – 24.2 inches. Weird thing, there was no storm, just everything went real still, then the pressure rose back to normal.'

'But that's impossible,' I said. 'The lowest ever pressure recorded for a storm was 25.69 inches. I remember Dad telling me.'

'So where's the storm to go with it? Something that big should be ripping the sky in two,' Jules said.

'Not to mention that this happened only a couple of miles away.'

She blew her cheeks out. 'Think we would have noticed if the mother of all storms had blown through here.'

I peered closer at the screen. There was something about the stars, something not quite right. In the middle the sky actually looked a bit darker. I pulled up the contrast control and began adjusting it.

Jules leant close to me and I smelled a girl smell; the sort of thing that the cheerleaders at school always smelt of and that numbed your brain if you got too close. Since when had Jules started wearing perfume?

'Stop,' she said, breaking into my thoughts.

A familiar inverted triangular shape filled the middle of the screen.

'Jeez, it's a storm spout – a massive one – but almost invisible,' I said.

'But I've never heard of a storm behaving like this. I mean, where's all the badass wind and lightning?'

I scratched the back of my neck and frowned. 'Okay, wonder what caused it?'

'Weird, huh?'

'Hey, I've got an idea.'

'What?' Jules popped one of the cherries into her mouth and began chewing.

I opened up a new message window and began typing. 'Hey, Hawks, if you want to come and check this out, it would be cool if you came and stayed here. Cheers, Dom.'

'Do you think you'll get a response? Mr Howard hasn't and he posted yesterday.'

'Well, unless we score some big rain soon, everything's going to turn to rat shit in our own backyard. And the Hawks are the real experts in this stuff, so it's worth a shot.'

It was weird though that I hadn't heard from them before now. Considering how close we'd all been, it was like the Sky Hawks had dropped off the surface of the planet since dad's funeral.

Jules gave me a sympathetic look, almost like she knew what I was remembering. I turned away.

Like always, thinking about the funeral pushed me over the edge. One kind word now and I'd lose it right there in front of my best friend.

Chapter Three
THE STORM

I worked inside the hangar, wrapped in Dad's bomber jacket and tightened the last of the bolts of the engine piston cover for the Mustang. Jules had helped me until she had to head home with Roddy. Secretly I'd been grateful, as I'd wanted to finish the job by myself. Seemed only right.

Thing was, this had been our project first, Dad's and mine restoring a rusting 69 Mustang 390 GT fastback, the same one as Steve McQueen had driven in one of his all-time favourite old movies, *Bullitt.* A way cool vehicle for anyone with a pulse. I must've watched the awesome chase scene from it on YouTube a hundred times.

We'd tracked this car down to a scrapyard, a broken, rusting shell, and brought it back to restore. We'd even resprayed it the same colour green as the one in the film. Now I couldn't wait to scream past the school bus, the engine rumbling under the hood and doing all the talking for me to those losers on the back seat.

The torch wrench clicked. The polished piston cover reflected the inspection lamplight and sparkled. It looked like a work of art. This was it: I'd finished.

I lowered the hood, stuck my hand into my pocket and pulled out the key. Jules had said not to try the engine till she got back and had a chance to look everything over, but hell, this was another thing I needed to do solo.

I got into the driver's seat and shoved the key into the ignition. The Mustang was the reason Jules and me, although we'd known each other forever, had become best friends. She'd helped me work on it every opportunity she had. But she would understand. Eventually.

Taking a breath, I turned the key over and the engine roared into life, its growl reverberating through the hangar. Damn, it sounded amazing. I let out a whoop. We'd really done it, Jules and me. Dad would be so proud of us. I caught my own reflection in the rear view mirror, a grin filling my face. I pressed the accelerator a couple of times and the engine revved.

With one hand on the wheel, I adjusted the wing mirror and I saw dad's old ultralight stored in the corner of the hangar. I felt a twist of pain. He should be here to share this, sitting in the passenger seat slapping me on the shoulder. I turned the key and the engine burbled to silence. I got out of the Mustang and crossed to the ultralight.

Dad…

Thoughts started tumbling over each other in endless loops and I climbed into the cockpit.

The stars shimmered overhead, framed by a skylight. I reached out my hand to the joystick. I could do it. This once.

I tried to tighten my fingers around the handle, but like always my hand started to tremble and I dropped it back to my lap. Could I ever fly this thing again? Ever since

Dad… My head started to throb and I rubbed my temples with my thumbs. I was all Mom had.

But flying had always been part of our family's life, going way back to my Great Great Grandpa Alex. He'd been one of the early pioneers – flying a homemade aircraft made out of fabric and wood – and surviving somehow. Ever since, each generation in our family included a pilot, but now that tradition had died with Dad.

I breathed in and tasted the tang of old aviation fuel. An image flashed out of my memory – a spring morning – the sun just up and skimming over the cornfields in the ultralight. Dad had let me take the controls.

'You're a natural, Dom.'

After that he'd given me lesson after lesson. I'd never felt so free as when I'd flown this little aircraft. We'd even talked about me getting my pilot's licence – the happiest time of my life. Everything had been an adventure with Dad around.

I imagined his fingers wrapping around the joystick, and breathed in the leather smell of his jacket. I dragged my sleeve across my stinging eyes and clambered out of the cockpit. I followed the moonlit path to the hangar door and hung the jacket back on the peg he'd always left it on.

Outside, the field stretched away, not a murmur of wind stirring the bleached grass of Dad's old airstrip. In the distance the house stood under the oak. An orange bedroom light shone out, a beacon against the blue-grey night.

The hangar door squealed as I shut the ultralight and Mustang away from view.

I made my way through the meadow along the path, my muffled footsteps the only sound in the stillness. The clicking of the cicadas – the constant Oklahoma nighttime soundtrack – had stopped dead. And they never did that.

I swallowed to pop my ears, like I did when I'd been flying, but the suffocating silence remained. The hairs stood up on my neck and my eyes flicked to the sky. Was there a storm coming?

The dome of stars still shone around the curved blade of the moon. Scanning for any patches of inkblot darkness, I saw none.

Trying to relax the clatter of my heart, I started back towards the house. At some point my walk turned into a full-blown sprint. I tore indoors and headed to the electronic barometer in the kitchen.

'Thirty point two-three inches.' Emptiness swept through me. Still high pressure.

I climbed the stairs to the landing, and stepped into the yellow light slicing across from Mom's room. Through the open door I saw her sleeping, still fully dressed. She did that a lot these days.

Slipping my shoes off, I padded to my bedroom and pulled the door closed with a quiet click.

The room's heavy heat swamped me and I crossed to the open window. I stuck my head outside and breathed in the thick, sticky air. Through the branches of the oak, I could see the stars shining fierce and sharp in the silence. I stripped off to my boxers – way too hot for a blanket – and dropped onto the bed. The moon cast spider-web shadows through the tree and into my room.

Like I had done every night for the last year, I pressed my face into the pillow. I wanted to be numb, not to feel anything, just for once.

...

My eyes opened into pitch dark. The window slammed shut and the animal cry I'd heard in my dream morphed into the wind's scream outside.

I reached over and fumbled with the dimpled switch; amber lamplight pushed the night away. I glanced at my watch – 3 am. The bulb wavered, a slow blink between light and dark.

I jumped out of bed and I raced to the window. The view shifted and danced through the swaying branches of the oak, leaves stripped away in flowing patterns. The house shuddered and rain hammered onto the roof. Overhead, scudding storm clouds had swallowed the moon whole.

I could just make out the windsock through the thick veil of rain, streaming straight out and bending its pole right over. The wind howled and the sock broke loose, streaking into the gloom like an orange missile. The rain pelted down and I let out a long whoop.

My door slammed open and Mom burst in. 'At last!'

I rushed to her and we span round in a mad, hugging dance.

'There's going to be some serious red faces for the weathermen, missing this storm,' she said.

I laughed. 'This is just what the farmers needed. What *we* needed—' Booming thunder covered the rest of my words. I ran to the window and saw a colossal cloud boil across the sky.

The window bowed in and out with the gusts and Mom joined me, pressing her face to the glass.

A funnel of darkness rotated down, vapours cabling around it.

She gripped my arm. 'Twister,' she whispered.

'Goddamn, it's massive.'

We watched the spout thicken to the size of a mall. The outer storm wall barrelled straight towards the old hangar and began tearing panels of metal from the roof.

Mom gasped. 'We gotta get down to the shelter, now!' She headed for the door.

I hauled a sweatshirt and pants on, and flew after her, bare feet slipping on the wooden floor. She unlatched the front door. The handle tore from her fingers and the storm bellowed into the house.

Bending our bodies into the gale, we staggered outside.

Stinging rain pelted my face and blurred my vision. Mom grabbed my hand.

'This way,' she shouted over the roar.

Clutching onto each other, we took one heaving step after another, over the yard towards the shutters of the underground storm-shelter. Dirt swept into my mouth and clogged my lungs, making me choke. Cupping my hand and breathing through it, I stared at the coiled vapour revolving around the trunk of the twister, a crazy sculpture come to life. Chunks of earth and trees spiralled around the spout. The destruction echoed through my heart and a single thought filled my head.

Beautiful.

The twister charged towards us. Mom threw the massive rusty bolt of the shutters back. 'We'll be safe in here.'

For one insane moment I thought of running back to get Dad's old camera. A photo of this baby would look so cool on the diner wall. If there was a diner wall left to pin it to.

Mom heaved the door up and grabbed a yellow battery lantern hooked just inside.

She flicked it on and cold fluorescent light flooded the black hole. 'Get in.'

I started to drag my eyes away from the twister, but an intense strobing blue light briefly illuminated the whole spout. I stared harder and spotted a disc of white appear for a second, like a ghostly Cyclops eye in the column. Then it vanished behind a veil of spinning cloud.

Shielding my brow with my hand from the pelting rain, I tried to catch sight of it again.

Mom held the heavy door open. 'Down here – now!'

Like it had been given an electric shock, the twister convulsed with cobalt blue brilliance, and the white disc appeared again in the middle.

I pointed. 'Look, Mom!'

She stared up at the tornado.

I bent my head close to hers so she could hear me over the shriek of the wind.

'There's something inside the spout.'

Mom pushed her mouth to my ear. 'But nothing could survive in there.'

A noise like a thousand thunderclaps split the sky over our heads.

Ears buzzing, the storm became muted. I watched the tornado begin to evaporate and stream away, revealing an oval in its midst. A flash of lightning lit up the whole world and I stared at the streamlined cigar-shaped object with two propellers spinning fast, a third shattered at its stern. Sails extended from either side of the craft like fins of a giant fish, ripped canvas trailing from them in ribbons.

An airship?

The craft hurtled towards us, the last wisps of cloud streaming away from its fins. Mom's fingers bit into my arm. The ship yawed round into the wind till its rear-facing propellers pointed towards us.

I gawped at Mom. She just opened her palms, eyes wide.

The ground shuddered beneath our feet. One second the twister was there, the next it uncoiled like a ball of string and vanished like it had never been.

I'd never seen a big twister do this before. Not this fast.

A flash of flame and I spotted the cabin beneath the balloon, propane blue fire flickering from the burner on its roof, portholes glowing orange. The airship's engines screamed and it slid backwards.

Mom's hands went to her mouth. 'It's going to crash!'

The airship skimmed over the tattered roof of the old hangar into our field and a steel cross sped from its belly, rope shooting out behind. The metal projectile slammed into the far end of the meadow and the airship lurched to a stop, but the wind shook it, an alligator with prey locked in its jaws. The vessel slid backwards, dragging the metal cross like a plough through the earth, straight towards the yard.

'Mom, that anchor's never going to hold in this. We've got to help them.'

She blinked. 'I'm sorry, Dom, but there's nothing we can do.'

'But they need our help.'

'I can't have you risking your life.'

I looked back to the airship sliding towards us. Something hardened inside me. I couldn't turn my back on those people.

Mom looked up at me, eyes narrowing. 'Dom?'

There was no time for an argument. I grabbed the shelter door and slammed it shut, grabbing a shovel and sticking its shaft through the handles.

The door rattled against the improvised lock.

'Dom, what do you think you're doing!'

'What I have to, Mom. There's no time to argue about this.'

The door thumped, but I ignored her shouts and scanned the area. I needed something to hold the airship's anchor in place. I spotted Bessy, our old tractor. An idea sprang into my mind and I charged towards the vehicle.

I clambered into the cab. The whining of the airship's propellers passed overhead.

Grabbing the key from under the seat, I shoved it into the ignition and turned. With a puff of diesel smoke, Bessy's engine clattered into life. I grabbed the stick-shift lever on the steering column and waited. I had to time this just right.

The metal anchor closed at a lick, sending a shower of earth up behind it. Come on...

It hit the lip of the concrete yard and screeched over the hard surface, sparks shooting from it.

Holding my breath, I revved the engine. One, two, three... I slipped the clutch and Bessy surged forwards. Flooring the accelerator, I spun the wheel hard over. The tractor veered straight towards the charging anchor and I gritted my teeth. It slammed into Bessy's nose, ringing her like a struck anvil. The front of the tractor tipped upwards and I grabbed onto the sides of the cab.

I found myself staring at the belly of the airship and saw a logo on the side: an owl surrounded by leaves and swirling clouds. 'Athena' had been stenciled next to it in large letters.

The world stopped tilting and my mind snapped back. For a moment our three-ton tractor hung suspended in a crazy wheelie. Then, with a slow groan, it swung down and bounced onto its wheels, rattling me like a marble in a can. The tether snapped taut and the airship shuddered to a stop above.

A puff of smoke blew from an exhaust stack on the roof of the cabin. The rope vibrated and a large winch under the cabin's belly started to spin. The airship jerked and began edging down towards us, yard-by-yard.

Adrenaline surged through me – I'd done it. Killing Bessy's engine, I leapt out of the cab. The line groaned and the airship bucked like a wild mustang. But it held.

A rectangle of blue light slid open on the side of the cabin and a tingling sensation passed through my body. A figure dressed in dark oilskins filled the doorway, face shrouded under the darkness of a hood. The man cupped his hands to his mouth, but the wind swept away his words.

Pointing at my ears, I shouted back, 'I can't hear you.'

The figure nodded and disappeared back inside. The wind bawled up again and with a groan, the airship lurched backwards. Bessy's nose screeched around and with tyres shuddering, started skidding across the yard.

Clutching onto the doorway of the airship, the figure reappeared and swung something out. With a clang, a metal hook thudded onto the ground next to me, line coiling on top.

I needed to fix this to something real strong. Bessy wasn't heavy enough.

Turning around I saw the oak's branches thrashing around, but its trunk standing solid as a mountain. Perfect. I grabbed the hook. Feet slipping on the wet concrete in the howling gale, I staggered towards the trunk.

A noise like a gunshot went off behind me. I spun round to see the anchor rope break free from Bessy and stream off into the wind.

Everything seemed to go into slow motion: the airship shooting away; the coils of rope whipping out; the man thrown backwards from the cabin door.

I dragged the hook towards the tree and its line reeled away behind me.

Reaching forward, I gripped the rough bark with my fingertips. Every muscle burning,

I heaved the hook with me around the trunk against the wind.

The flicking serpent-rope started straightening out.

I threw myself forwards, the hook fully extended in my hands, and slipped it over the rope. The line hissed taut with a whip-crack and tightened like a hangman's noose around the trunk.

I heard the whine of the winch and turned to see the airship, a salmon on a line, jumping towards me.

The gale pressing on my back, I sprinted towards the ship, which was dropping fast. Another rope snaked down from the cabin and twitched as the man clambered out. Wrapping the line around him, he shoved off from the cabin and abseiled down.

The hooded figure nodded towards me and I clutched the rope with him. The airship dropped to just twenty yards above us. The man leant onto the rope and we heaved together.

A tearing sound came from above and a large fabric panel shredded away from the side of the airship. Shimmering air roared out of the hole and the craft crashed to the ground, sending us tumbling to the dirt.

My companion jumped to his feet and rushed over to another person, limping from the darkened cabin.

I hauled myself up. 'Are you okay?'

The new figure drew down its hood to reveal a woman with tied-up blond hair, ivory skin, and dazzling green eyes. A small smile curled her mouth. 'I'm fine, young man, but I've made better landings,' she said with a soft French accent.

'We owe you our lives.'

I turned to see the first figure lowering their hood too. Not a he but a she, and what a she. I found myself staring at a girl of about my own age. Her long blonde hair streamed out into the wind and she gave me a heart-busting smile, emerald eyes gazing straight into mine.

I stared back at her.

Holy crap.

Chapter Four
VISITORS

The wind squeezed between the boards of the house with a low moan. Trying to drive the storm-chill away, I fed the fire with logs and it crackled into life throwing an amber glow into the room. The girl walked in scattering beads of water across the wooden floor.

'Here, let's get you out of those wet things before you freeze.' Mom helped the woman slip her oilskins off. She'd simmered down with me at last after I'd let her out of the storm shelter and she saw I wasn't hurt. I suspected my chore list might be growing pretty long for the next few months to pay off this particular guilt trip.

'How long before you'll be on your way?' Mom asked the woman, crossing her arms.

The woman shivered. 'We're not sure how bad the damage is yet.'

I'd never seem Mom like this. She was normally the friendliest person with strangers.

You needed to be if you ran a diner.

'Why don't you get some dry clothes on before you freeze to death?' I said, casting a glare at Mom.

The woman shook her arms free of the waterproof to reveal a high-collared green velvet dress. Whatever I'd expected someone to be wearing who flew airships, this wasn't it. She looked more like an extra who'd just stepped off a stagecoach in a cowboy movie, wearing her finest travelling clothes.

Mom's eyes widened. 'What a gorgeous dress – is it vintage?'

'Oh no, I made it myself.'

'It's beautiful, Mrs?'

The woman's hand fluttered to her mouth. 'I'm so sorry, how rude of me. In all the excitement I forgot to introduce myself. My name is Belladonna Castille, but you must call me Bella. And this is my daughter.'

'I prefer to be called Angelique, rather than Angie,' her daughter said, holding her head high. To me it sounded more like a command than a request.

'It's good to meet you. I'm Dom.' I gestured towards Mom. 'This is my mom, Sue.'

Mom gave a sharp nod. Could she make these people who'd fallen out of the sky feel any more unwelcome?

Angelique's gaze swept back to me and I forced myself not to grin like an idiot.

Goddamn – even her name was beautiful. It's not like I'd never seen a hot girl before, I needed to get a grip.

'Angelique, can you give me a hand?' Bella said.

'Of course, Mama,' the girl said, accentuating the second syllable. She took her mother's arm and gently lowered her to the sofa.

Angelique started to slip her own coat off and I was right there helping her out of it.

She gave me a dazzling smile that amped my pulse. When she peeled her coat away the air caught in my throat. If I'd thought she was hot before, she looked stunning now I could see the midnight-blue dress she was wearing. Her bodice, cut lower than her mother's, revealed a fine silver chain with a pendant around her neck – a lightning strike through a sort of stylised spiral. Obviously a kooky taste in jewellery. I felt an itch of memory. I'd seen a design like that somewhere before.

I fought the magnetic pull drawing my eyes down from the necklace towards her chest.

Her hands locked around my wrists. 'I don't know how we can ever thank you enough,' she said in her gentle French accent.

'It was nothing,' I said, trying to sound relaxed.

'But you saved our lives. We would have crashed if it hadn't been for you.' She kissed me on the cheek. The warmth of her lips spread out across my face. Her eyes lingered on mine, a small smile raising the corners of her mouth.

'I still can't believe you survived that twister. But how come you were flying out in this storm?'

'That's a good question,' Mom said, with the same look she used with me for interrogation about a bad school report.

Bella's eyes narrowed. 'We're involved in an attempt to circumnavigate the globe in our airship.'

'You're adventurers, then,' I said. 'But how come you're not all over the news?'

'Oh, we're trying to avoid publicity until we succeed in our attempt so we don't tip off competing teams,' Angelique replied.

'You've obviously done an awesome job of that,' I replied.

Angelique shrugged. 'We've done our best.'

Mom narrowed her gaze. 'Well, it must have been terrifying to be caught in that twister.'

Bella gave a quick nod and spread her hands wide. 'It just came out of nowhere and overtook us before we could do anything.'

Her tone sounded too measured, like someone performing from a script at one of our school plays; a question mark formed in my head. 'You're lucky to have survived something that big. That twister must have been at least an F4.'

'An F4?' Angelique asked.

'You know, a twister with wind speeds up to 260 miles-per-hour.'

'Oh, of course.' She tugged her ear. 'We've flown through worse.'

'You have?' Mom said.

Bella nodded. '*Athena* can handle a lot.'

'*Athena* – is that the name of your airship?' I asked.

'Yes, but she's more a member of the family, if you know what I mean.'

'You almost make her sound alive.'

'Oh, she is to us,' she said, tipping her head to one side as though she was listening to something, then smiling.

'Is there anyone you'd like us to contact to let know you're okay?' Mom asked.

Bella shook her head. 'No, it's fine. There's no one else left in our family…' She cast Angelique a pained look.

They'd lost someone recently?

Mom's face softened and she sighed. She'd recognised that look of hurt too.

I glanced at the leg Bella had been limping on. 'Did you hurt yourself during the crash?'

'It's only a mild sprain. I just need to rest it for a few days and keep it bandaged.'

Angelique raised her eyebrows at her mother.

Mom tapped her lips. 'If you're sure? We could call out a doctor to look at it.'

'Really, please don't worry,' Bella replied.

'At the very least, I'm going to insist you have a hot bath so you can properly relax.'

I smiled at Mom. This was more like her.

Bella sighed. 'That sounds like heaven. We've been in the air for such a long time, I think I've forgotten what a bath's like.'

'Oh, you poor things! How do you cope?' Mom said.

'Lots of sponge baths and a basin,' Angelique said.

I dropped my gaze, trying to stop my imagination before it had a chance to get going. Noticing the dirt under my fingernails, I shoved my hands into my pockets.

Mom was still talking. 'Whilst you stay as our guests, you're to have as many baths as you like.'

'We wouldn't dream of imposing on you like that,' Bella said. 'Once we've had a chance to clean up, we'll sleep in the gondola.'

'You'll do no such thing. After what you've been through you're going to stay in the house – I insist. You can have our spare room, Bella.' Mom turned to me. 'Dom, I'm sure you won't mind sleeping on the sofa and letting Angelique have your bed.'

'Course not,' I mumbled.

Angelique's mouth curved into a smile. 'That's so kind of you, Dom.' Her eyes lingered on mine, a moment too long to be comfortable.

I nodded, feeling like a frozen rabbit.

Bella stretched her foot and winced. 'We need to get the repairs done.'

'You can stay as long as you like,' Mom replied. 'We have an old hangar you can store *Athena* in while you're working on her.'

A gust of wind shook the house and Bella frowned. 'That's perfect. I just hope the damage isn't too great.'

'Expect you want to be out of here as soon as possible – you know – for your record attempt?' I said.

They both looked at the swirling clouds scudding past outside.

'We have to be on the way as quickly as possible,' Angelique replied.

'If there's anything I can do to help, just ask,' I said.

Angelique reached over and brushed my wrist with her fingertips. 'I will. Thank you.'

My blood fizzed like it had turned into soda. I shrugged. 'S'okay.'

The wind moaned down the chimney and sparks scurried upwards.

'When's this storm going to run out of steam?' Mom said.

Angelique pulled up her long sleeves and looked at her watch. I caught a glimpse of brass circles spinning within the dial under the glass, a single green light pulsing in the middle. 'In about five minutes.'

Bella touched her arm.

'How could you know that?' I asked. 'And what is that fancy gizmo you're wearing anyway?'

Angelique yanked her sleeve back down to cover up the device. 'Oh, it's just a special barometer. I can tell the storm's about to end because the pressure's rising quickly, that's all.'

Again that measured tone, like she was almost telling me the truth, but not quite. It was certainly the freakiest barometer I'd ever seen.

I risked glancing into Angelique's gemstone eyes again. 'So...' My voice squeaked, making me sound about five years old. I coughed and tried again. 'So...' – a couple of octaves lower – 'how long have you been flying airships?' I crossed my arms, trying to look like I chatted to beautiful women who fell out of the sky every day of my life.

Angelique drew herself up, face relaxing into a smile. 'Since I was old enough to walk. You could say it's something of a family business.'

'Oh, your husband flies, does he?' Mom asked.

Bella closed her eyes and nodded.

Angelique patted her arm. 'Did fly.'

I caught the sadness in her tone and my heart tightened. 'Something happened?'

Bella bunched up her skirt in her hands. 'He disappeared a year ago…' She looked at the flames licking over the logs and fell silent.

Not them too – the empty chair at the dinner table... his laughter gone from the house, always left wondering…

Angelique entwined her fingers through her mother's. 'It will be okay, Mama.'

Bella's eyes glistened. 'I hope so.'

Mom glanced at me. 'Dom, why don't you and Angelique put some coffee on?' She nodded towards the door and curled her arm around Bella's shoulders.

'Course.' I slipped into the kitchen, Angelique close behind.

I flicked the coffee machine on and Angelique started looking around our ancient kitchen, eyes bright, brow furrowed. She ran her fingers over the fridge like she was stroking the shining hood of a slick set of wheels.

Steam started venting from the filter and I listened to the pelting rain outside. 'So what happened with your dad?'

Her eyes became unfocused, like she was watching a movie in her mind. 'We just lost contact with him...' Her jaw muscles twitched.

I recognised that look – saw it in the mirror every day.

The warming smell of coffee filled the room and black liquid began to trickle into the pot. 'Just like my dad, but he's dead of course – flew into a twister and never made it out.'

Angelique stared at me. 'Into a twister?'

'Yeah – trying to get video from the inside for the TV show – what an idiot. All they found were pieces of his aircraft afterwards.'

'Oh...' Her shoulders dropped.

'Just shows how lucky you were to come out of that thing alive.' I stared at the table and heard her sigh through her nose.

'*Oui* – I mean, yes...'

The wind screeched up and rain smacked into the windows. The glass rattled and bounced in its frame.

I attempted a smile and dug out some mugs and a tray. 'So much for your five minute forecast.'

With a long moan the squall hissed away and the rain stopped like someone had turned it off at the faucet.

Angelique raised an eyebrow.

Silence descended around the house and silver light crept in through the windows. Outside, a crescent moon hung in a clear, starlit sky, the view crisscrossed by the dark branches of the oak standing motionless over the house.

Slack-jawed, I turned to Angelique. 'But…how?'

'It's a very good barometer.'

'With predictions that great, you should take up weather forecasting for a career.'

Angelique laughed, but her eyes didn't join in. She wandered over to the gurgling coffee pot. 'Let's take this through.'

I grabbed the tray and followed her into the living room.

Bella was dabbing tears away from her face with a lace hanky. From the red rings lining Mom's eyes, it looked like she'd been having a good cry-along too. It didn't take much to set her off these days.

Mom squeezed Bella's shoulders. 'Looks like the storm's finally blown itself out.'

'At least the farmers will be grateful for the rain,' I said, setting down the tray.

'Maybe the weather will get back to normal now. We've had such an awful drought, real bad dust storms too, Bella,' Mom said.

'I'm afraid I think the weather is set to be wrong for some time yet,' Bella replied.

I glanced at Angelique. 'Is that what your special barometer-watch says?'

She drew her sleeve down further. 'Something like that.'

Mom leant back into the sofa. 'Oh, I thought...' She waved her hands, fresh tears filling her eyes.

I hugged Mom and watched our visitors. Bella stared into the fire, chewing her lip.

Angelique shifted in her seat, then got up and paced to the window. A log crackled and dropped with a clunk in the fireplace. Bella flinched, and Angelique's head whipped round.

Huh. Why still so jumpy? They were safe from the storm.

A ghostly murmur sighed close by and the hairs on my neck rose up. I glanced around, but there was nothing there apart from Mom's crockery cabinet full of Dad's TV awards.

'Careful, Dom,' Mom said, taking the pot from me.

'Didn't you hear that?'

'What?' Mom asked.

'Just thought I heard someone.' I shrugged. 'Must've been wind down the chimney.'

Angelique looked at me, eyes questioning.

Great – now they had me jumping at the bogeyman.

Chapter Five
DAMAGE

The sound of the phone ringing and footsteps woke me from my dreamless sofa-sleep. My blanket was wrapped tight around me – must've been tossing and turning.

I focused on one of Mom's quilt designs hanging on the living room wall – a twister created with silver patches of fabric against a dark blue background. She'd sewn it with her quilting group as a present for one of Dad's birthdays.

Mom's voice drifted from the hallway.

'Hi, Roddy... Yeah, we're fine. Bit of damage to Shaun's old hangar, easily mended... But you won't believe what happened...' Her voice faded, footsteps wandered into the kitchen.

My neck muscles clicked and I swung my legs off the couch. I padded through in my boxer shorts, rolling my stiff shoulders and hoping to catch the rest of the conversation.

Mom was hunting through a cupboard with her back to me, phone cradled to her ear. 'We've still got power here. You?'

Roddy's muffled voice crackled from the earpiece.

'Why don't you leave Jules with us whilst you're getting sorted out? I'm sure Dom would be pleased to see her and she can meet our guests.'

Opening the refrigerator, I grabbed a bottle of milk and took a swig. Mom turned round, her eyebrows ratcheting up. 'You making a habit of parading around in front of teenage girls in just your underwear, hun?'

I turned and looked straight into Angelique's wide eyes. She sat at the table wrapped in my dressing gown, a cup of coffee frozen halfway to her lips. Her gaze flicked and up down the length of me, her grin growing bigger.

I stared back at her. 'Sorry – didn't realise you were up yet.' I almost dropped the milk back into the refrigerator, spun round and ducked out of the room.

Their laughter bounced around the kitchen as I pulled on my jeans and a shirt. Taking a big breath, I walked back in, trying to put a bit of swagger into it. Angelique and Mom had their heads bent together in conversation at the table. They looked up, mouths twitching at the corners.

Doing my best to ignore them, I poured myself a coffee.

'Want some more milk with that?' Mom asked.

They both exploded into giggles.

'Ha...ha...ha,' I replied, but couldn't stop smiling.

Mom rested her chin on her hand. 'Sorry, Dom, couldn't resist.' She got up and ruffled my hair. 'See you kids later – gotta open up the diner.'

'A dinner?' Angelique asked.

I stared at her. 'No, diner...you know, place where you eat.'

'Oh, of course.' She chewed a fingernail.

'You really never heard of a diner before?' Mom asked.

'I feel so silly,' Angelique said.

Mom patted her shoulder. 'Well you shouldn't. If you don't know something, you just don't. Anyway, maybe they don't have them in France? That is a French accent you've got, isn't it? Or Canadian maybe?'

I noticed a hint of red tingeing the tips of Angelique's ears.

'*Oui* – I'm French,' she replied.

'Thought so,' Mom said, with an I-told-you-so look at me – even though she hadn't. 'Come over and get some breakfast when you're ready and I'll show you a genuine American institution. Bring your mom – she'll need a break by now.'

'Why, what's she up to?' I asked.

Angelique stirred two sugars into her black coffee. 'She's been working on *Athena*.'

Mom sighed. 'Up since the crack of dawn – insisted on making an early start.'

'That's Mama. And we do need to be on our way for the record attempt as quickly as possible.'

'Driven or not, she needs food in her stomach. Dom, could you go and take her a cup of coffee and see if you can persuade her to grab some breakfast?'

'Sure, Mom.'

She smiled, straightened her uniform and disappeared out through the door.

Angelique put her mug down. 'Dom, while we are alone for a moment…' She traced a circle on the table with her finger.

My mouth went dry. Was this going to be an, 'I want to show you just grateful I am' talk?

'I just wanted to say thanks for letting me have your bed last night. The berths on *Athena* are a bit cramped and that was the best night's sleep I've had in ages.'

Oh... The fantasy popped.

I coughed, hoping my internal dialogue wasn't showing on my face. '*Athena*'s an interesting name for an airship.'

'It's the Greek goddess of wisdom...and war.'

'It's different – I'll give you that.'

Angelique smiled and took a sip of coffee.

'Guessing if you have to sleep in her, you rarely get to land?'

She nodded. 'We like to keep in the air for as long as possible.'

To always be flying. Once I wouldn't have been able to think of anything better than to be that free. But Dad's death had been a wake-up call. Now, whenever I seriously thought about being a pilot, the tug on my heart was quickly replaced by a tightness in my chest. I wasn't sure I'd ever be able to fly again. Besides which, I doubted Mom would let me into the air anytime soon. She was bad enough when I even brought up the subject of driving the Mustang.

I sighed and leant against the fridge. 'Sounds like you have a pretty cool life.'

'*Oui*. You know, it really is. From my bed I sometimes get to see sunrises glinting over the mountain peaks.' Angelique's voice thickened and her eyes took on a faraway look. 'Then there are the storm clouds lit up like paper lanterns with lightning.'

Her words tumbled through my imagination. It sounded like Dad's world of adventure – a world I'd always wanted to be part of. I pushed down a pang of jealousy. 'Those are pretty special views to have from your bedroom. All I have is an oak tree, an overgrown field, and a broken down hangar to gawp at.'

She hunched her shoulders. 'You know, Dom, part of me would trade positions with you in a second.'

'You're kidding?'

'Not at all.'

I pulled a grimace. 'What's so great about being stuck in a boring house? Your world sounds awesome compared to mine.'

She gave a little shake of her head. 'Trust me. What you have here is so special. When you spend your whole life on the move, as exciting as it is, you miss somewhere to call home.'

'Exactly how long have you been flying?'

'A long, long time.' She turned to look out of the window and fell silent. Her hair curved around her perfect profile and dropped in waves over her shoulders. That faraway gaze again.

Her silence began to linger and I cleared my throat. 'Okay, I'd better take this coffee out to Bella.'

Angelique shook her head like a person waking, and stood. 'You'll need help dragging her away from *Athena*.'

...

The morning sun blazed in the sky. Angelique and I walked towards the cabin. We traced our way around the edge of the deflated envelope, Now stripped of its metal framework and left lying on the ground. The airship that had seemed to fill the whole sky the previous night now reminded me of a whale skeleton washed up on a beach.

Far overhead a glint of metal shone at the tip of a single vapour trail, crossing the arc of sky. Dad had taught me how to identify all the planes by the time I was six, and I recognised the profile of a fighter jet.

Following my gaze, Angelique grabbed my arm. 'What's that?'

'Just an F16 – probably on a training flight from the air base.'

Her forehead ridged into lines.

'Don't worry, you're safe – they hopefully won't drop any bombs on us today.'

She tilted her head. 'Thank goodness.'

I gave her a sideways glance. Seriously?

The plane disappeared over the horizon and she let go of my arm. I threw the question mark onto the growing mound with the others.

The heat was already building to suffocating levels, but drawing closer to the cabin, goose bumps prickled my arms, like cold air had been blown over me. Slowly I became aware of the tickle of the grass against my jeans; the smell of the oil from the airship's engines; heard the distant drone of the cars on the freeway. A murmur just on the edge of my hearing, like someone had whispered my name. I paused and turned round. No one was there.

Not again. What the hell had gotten into me? Must be the lack of sleep.

I caught up with Angelique and spotted Bella, looking a lot less glamorous today in one of my dad's old overalls. She stood, the top half of her torso inside a copper-clad engine pod. Its hatch had been jammed open with an ornate walking stick. At the far end of the elliptical pod, the splinters of the broken propeller splayed out, like branches of a tree.

We walked past the cabin and I tuned in to the noises around me. Nothing unusual. I thought about asking Angelique, but cancelled the thought straight away. The last thing I needed was her thinking I was a nut, especially when I was trying to play it cool around her.

I took in the ship's design properly for the first time. The cabin had been constructed like a boat's hull, with laminated strips of polished wood and brass framed portholes running the length of it. A blue diamond stained-glass window filled the rear, like something from the captain's quarters of a pirate ship, and gleaming bolts held everything in place. Through the gold-tinted cockpit window, I could just make out what looked like a sailing ship's wheel.

I patted the polished wood. 'This cabin is really something.'

Angelique seemed to grow taller and she beamed at me. 'It's called a gondola and was hand-built by master craftsmen. The design of the airship is our family's own and has been passed down from generation to generation.'

'It's certainly different compared to any airship I've ever seen on TV.'

She laughed, making my heart spin a little faster. 'That pretty much sums up our family as well – different.'

I smiled back at her. I could get drunk just breathing this girl in.

A loud sigh came from the hatch and Angelique's smile fell away. 'How's it looking, Mama?'

Bella's oil-covered face appeared and she shook her head. 'We can mend the main gas envelope, but it's going to be a lot of work.'

'We can fix it, though?' Angelique asked.

'Yes, but that's not the really bad news. The damage to the engine is much worse than I expected. One of the pistons has broken through the cylinder head. Until that's repaired, we're not going anywhere.'

Angelique covered her mouth with her hands. 'But, Mama, the longer we stay here...' She turned away, her shoulders rising and falling.

'Is this going to badly affect your record attempt then?' I asked.

Bella stared at me, expression blank, before her eyes widened. 'Yes, of course, this will affect the whole endeavour. We carry spares for most things, but not a major problem like this.' She wrapped her arm around Angelique's shoulders.

An idea stirred in my head and I hitched my thumbs into the waist of my jeans. 'There's someone we know – Roddy – he's a pretty slick mechanic. So's his daughter, Jules.'

'And they'd help us?' Bella asked.

'I'd bet good money on it. Engine rebuilds are their thing.'

'Oh, Dom, that's such wonderful news. The sooner we can get the repairs done, the sooner we can be on our way.'

My insides lurched at the thought of their swifter departure, but I tried not to let it show. 'Cool.' I glanced at my watch. 'You can ask him yourself if you like. He'll be here any moment for breakfast in the diner with Jules.'

Angelique turned, smearing tears away with her palms. 'Thank you so much.'

I felt my smile go crooked and had the strongest urge to hug her.

'In the...diner?' Bella asked.

Angelique jumped in before I could. 'A diner, Mama – you know, *un restaurante*.'

'Oh, of course, silly me.' A look slipped between them.

Bella stuck her head back into the hatch. 'Just let me finish my work here and I'll be over.'

My gaze lingered over the broken propeller and the splinters streaming from the spindle where the blades should have been.

'So how did you crack your prop anyway?'

'We hit something in the storm and it shattered – that's why we couldn't hold our position,' Angelique replied.

A groaning sound drifted out of the hatch again. 'The drive shaft seems to be jammed. Can you both pull on the prop to see if you can work it loose?'

'Sure,' I said, taking hold of the remains of the broken blade.

Angelique grabbed it as well, her hand almost brushing mine. I wished she had. Jeez, I had it bad. She looked at me through her eyelashes.

'Okay, pull,' Bella said.

My mind snapped back, and feeling my face flame, I dropped my attention to the prop and heaved. It was stuck solid. Gritting my teeth and leaning back with my full bodyweight, I tried again. Angelique hauled on it with me and with a shuddering screech it turned over.

A massive arrow with red flight feathers buried in the hub rotated into view.

I gasped. 'What the heck is that doing there?'

Bella dropped down out of the hatch. Angelique's mouth opened and closed.

'Looks like some crazy took a pot-shot at you – but what goddamn bow fires an arrow that big?'

Angelique shook her head. 'Don't be silly, it must have been picked up by the twister and thrown into the ship.'

'Look, just to be on the safe side, maybe I should call the police.'

Angelique stared at me. 'Please, we don't want any fuss.'

Bella yanked the arrow free and threw it beneath the gondola. 'There's really no need.'

I scratched my ear. 'You sure?'

Bella grabbed her walking stick and let the hatch fall closed with a clang. She hooped her arm through mine. 'I am... And didn't you mention something about breakfast?' She almost dragged me away from the engine towards the diner, with Angelique close behind.

...

The waffle iron steamed and Mom turned out six perfect waffles. I plated them up and arranged the bacon rashers in our trademark spiral on top, placing a poached egg in the middle, maple syrup in a jug on the side.

'Three Eye of the Storm specials,' I called out, carrying them through to the diner. Angelique and Bella looked up from the big photo of Dad with his storm chasing team, the Sky Hawks. It was a publicity shot of them sheltering behind one of their vehicles and pointing towards a big twister on the horizon. It had all their signatures scrawled across the bottom and more than once we'd caught a fan trying to liberate it.

I put the plates down. 'That's an F5 tornado. Dad reckoned the winds wound up to two hundred and eighty miles-per-hour.'

Angelique's eyes sparkled. 'It's so beautiful.'

A tingle ran up my spine. She really got it.

Bella sat down with Angelique at the table. 'This smells superb.'

I pulled up a chair. 'Tastes even better.'

Angelique poured the syrup over her food and scooped up a forkful of waffle and bacon. She took a mouthful and her face lit up. 'Sue, this is—'

'Fantastic.' I raised my eyebrows at Mom.

She smiled and wiped down the counter. 'Alright, alright.'

I leant over and whispered to them. 'If enough people keep telling her, she might start believing it one day.'

Outside, the rumble of an engine grew louder and Roddy's red pickup swung into our lot. Moments later Jules came charging into the diner.

'Dom, what's all this about an airship—' Her gaze snapped to Angelique sitting across from me in my dressing gown. She froze.

Roddy almost walked straight into her. He grabbed her shoulders and moved her to one side. 'Don't stand there like a human road block, there's a man here who needs his breakfast.'

Mom beamed at him. 'Hi, Roddy. These are our French guests, Bella and Angelique, the ones I told you about on the phone.'

Roddy dragged his hand through his hair and nodded. 'Good to meet you, ladies.'

Angelique turned in her chair, expression sharpening, eyes skimming over Jules, before settling on Roddy. One of her dazzling smiles lit her face.

'So you're the man who can work miracles with engines?' Bella said.

Roddy rubbed his chin. 'I wouldn't go as far as that.'

'Well I would,' Mom said. 'He's being modest, Bella. Roddy can fix anything.'

Angelique coiled her hair around her fingers, leaning towards him. 'We desperately need your help, Roddy.'

'We have a flat-eight engine with a bent prop shaft and broken pistons,' Bella said. 'Is that something you could look at?'

'A flat-eight engine...broken pistons... That would mean a complete rebuild…' Roddy's face took on a dreamy expression. I caught the same look on Jules' face before she frowned at Angelique.

Mom snorted. 'Interpreting, I think that means he'd love to.'

He winked at her. 'Sue knows me way too well. I'll have a look at it whenever you like. Sounds like just your sort of project too, hey, Jules?'

She shrugged. 'Maybe.'

What did she mean, maybe? She'd normally kill for a project like that.

Bella sat up. 'I don't suppose I could persuade you to have a look now?'

Roddy grinned. 'Just take me to her.' The two of them headed out the door.

'I'll have your breakfast waiting for you when you get back,' Mom said.

'Great, I could eat a horse,' Roddy called back over his shoulder.

Angelique stared after him, mouth dropping open.

I leant across. 'Just an expression.'

'Oh, of course.'

'Hang on, I could have sworn I heard they eat horse meat in parts of France?' Jules said.

She scowled. 'Not in my part of France.'

I glanced over at Jules, who flicked her eyes at Angelique and back to me. There was something in that look that didn't seem like the Jules I knew – her expression was way too tight.

'Aren't you going to introduce everyone, Dom?' Mom said, starting to plate up another special.

'Hi,' Jules said, doing a small wave like she was cleaning a window.

'I'm Angelique, pleased to meet you,' she said, eyebrows raised.

'Julia, Roddy's daughter and Dom's best friend.' She rested her hand on my shoulder.

I stopped myself jumping at the physical contact.

'Why don't you join us?' Angelique said, sliding over in her seat.

Jules' fingers tensed a fraction on my shoulder. 'In a bit – just going to look at your engine first with Dad.' She turned and disappeared out the door.

'So she's your best friend, then?' Angelique said.

'Yeah, we hang out together. She's been helping me restore a car.'

'Oh what, like brother and sister?'

'I guess.'

'Ah, okay...' Angelique took a large mouthful of bacon and smiled at me, head tipped to the side.

Surely Angelique couldn't be interested in me? She was so far out of my league it wasn't funny. Through the window I watched Jules disappearing around the corner of the diner, faster than a cat with its tail on fire.

I caught Mom giving me a narrowed-eyed look. I picked up the saltshaker and twirled it through my fingers, trying to ignore the squirming inside me.

Chapter Six
STORM CHASERS

The truck's crane whirred into life and the engine rose from the ground in its harness.

It pitched to one side and as the straps creaked, my stomach lurched.

Bella leant harder on her walking stick.

Roddy caught her expression and winked at me. 'Don't worry, Bella, we've got it covered.' Heaving together we swung it over the flatbed of the truck.

Jules, still managing to avoid any direct eye contact with me since breakfast, pressed a green button on the winch. She hadn't even asked about the Mustang.

The airship engine lowered onto the back and settled with a dull clunk.

Bella let the air out of her lungs in a rush. 'Oh, thank goodness. I can breathe again.'

Angelique, now dressed in another of Dad's old overalls but still somehow managing to look sexy with a tight belt that accentuated the curve of her hips, flicked her hair back. 'I wasn't worried for a moment. Roddy and Dom had it all under control.'

Jules snorted through her nose, engine oil war-paint decorating her face.

I glanced at her, but her eyes skated away.

'Roddy, how long do you think it will take to fix?' Bella asked.

'I'll need to have a good poke around before I can give you a proper estimate.'

Bella nodded.

'Looks like you're going to be stuck here for a while yet,' I said.

Angelique looked up at the empty sky.

Jules crossed her arms. 'Don't worry, we'll get you fixed up good and quick.'

I caught the edge to her voice. What was her problem?

Roddy closed the tailgate of the truck. 'Yep, can't have you missing busting a world record on my account.' He climbed into the cab. 'We'll take this right back to the garage and give you a call later.'

'Do remember to keep this to yourself, Roddy,' Bella said. 'We don't want the press finding out.'

'Sure, no sweat.'

Bella leant through the open window and kissed his stubbly cheek. 'We can't thank you enough for your help.'

Roddy blinked twice.

He started the truck up and Jules moved closer to me. 'Like mother like daughter, huh?' she whispered.

'What?'

Her eyebrows drew together. 'Nothing.' She headed towards the truck and jumped in.

The pickup's engine roared into life. 'See y'all later.' Roddy waved, but Jules looked straight ahead, avoiding any eye contact as they bounced away over our field and turned onto the road.

'Angelique, come and help me move the envelope to the hangar,' Bella said, heading off.

'Of course, Mama.' Angelique lingered a moment.

Over her shoulder I spotted a gleaming white speck on the road heading towards us. The speck grew into the outline of a vehicle that seemed vaguely familiar.

'Are you okay?' Angelique asked.

'Huh?'

'Jules...'

'Oh – she's just being weird with me at the moment.'

Her eyebrows twitched up. 'You mean acting all jealous.'

This was starting to do my head in. 'She's just a friend.'

'You think?' She shrugged. 'But I suppose you're just a man – slow to catch on – although a very fascinating one.'

Fascinating? I tried not to stare at her as though she was cracked. The rumble of the vehicle slowed as a motor home bristling with aerials pulled into our lot. I spotted the logo on its side – same as Dad's – a man riding a twister. A silhouette moved behind the windshield and I noticed a camera mounted on the dashboard. The driver's door swung open and my pulse leapt.

'They really came,' I said.

'Who?' Angelique asked.

'You'll see.' I ran towards the vehicle. A giant of a man, dressed in black denim and cowboy boots, clambered out. His dark sunglasses flashed at me.

I reached him and he wrapped his tree-trunk arms around me. 'Dom, will ya look at the size you've got to.'

The air squeezed out from my lungs. 'Easy there, Harry, I think you're about to crack my ribs.'

Laughing, he relaxed his grip and looked towards Angelique.

'And who's this pretty miss, then?' He glanced at me from the corner of his eyes. 'Not gone and got yourself a gal at last?'

'Harry!' My blush headed down to my toes.

He shrugged. 'Just asking.'

Angelique smirked at me and shoved out a hand to Harry. 'Angelique, and I'm just staying here with my mama for a while.'

'Pleased to meet you, Angelique, and isn't that one fancy accent you've got yourself there.' He gave her a vigorous handshake. 'Harry Jacobs, at your service. Storm chasing nut and old friend of Dom's family.'

Angelique angled her head to the side. 'Storm chasing?'

The warmth faded from my face and I looked at her. 'Haven't you heard of that?'

She shook her head, biting her lip.

'It's the name for people who go after twisters. But Harry here is one of the famous ones. He and his team were on TV with my dad all the time – well at least when we used to have twisters.'

'But why would anyone chase a tornado?' she asked.

Harry snorted. 'Like I said, I'm a nut.'

Angelique tilted her head to the side, lines creasing her brow. '*Non*, I think I understand. Twisters are beautiful.'

He hooked his sunglasses onto his baseball cap, revealing sharp grey eyes. 'Most folks live a lifetime without realising that.'

Angelique's smile grew. 'So true.'

They looked at each other, gazes bright. Same look that Dad used to have talking about twisters.

I hooked my fingers onto my belt. 'So you got my message?'

'Yep, but we'd have come anyway. Your tornado lit up the National Hurricane Centre's weather radars like the Fourth of July.' His eyes swept over the diner. 'Much damage?'

I shook my head. 'Nothing major, but you really missed something special. It was massive.'

Harry looked at me. 'Don't suppose you got any snaps?'

'I wish, especially when the airship—'

A pain stabbed into my side and I glanced down to see Angelique's elbow buried in my ribs. I glared at her and she gave me the slightest shake of her head.

Harry scraped his fingers through his hair. 'An airship?'

Angelique shook her head again, more sharply this time.

What was her game? I'd known Harry all my life. He could keep a secret.

I frowned. 'I meant to say it was bigger than any airship I've ever seen.'

Harry scratched his neck. 'That's a more original comparison than the usual – it was the size of a mountain.' He spread his hands wide, like a fisherman talking about the one that had gotten away.

'Well, you know me, hundred per cent original.'

He laughed and patted my shoulder so hard it jarred my teeth. 'Just like your pa.'

I shrugged and Angelique shot me a smile.

'So, was there anything unusual about this twister by any chance?' Harry asked.

'It came out of nowhere and disappeared just as fast,' I said.

'Nah, that's normal,' he replied, gazing out across the fields. 'Can you show me where it touched down when the others get here?'

'Sure,' I said.

Angelique's face paled. 'What others?'

'The rest of the Sky Hawks – the old team are getting back together and they're already on their way.' He grinned. 'Just when I was starting to think our storm chasing days were over with, we've gone and got ourselves a reunion.'

Angelique winced as though someone had poked her in the stomach.

Harry strode off to the motor home and unhooked a CB radio mic from the cab. 'This is Mother Goose. We've got confirmation of a touch-down last night.' A muffled whoop came back over the radio. 'And it gets better. It happened right next to our old HQ, the Twister Diner.' I heard the burble of a reply.

'It's alright, we've been invited.' He smiled at me.

Harry chattered away on the radio and I turned to Angelique.

'Dom, the fewer people who know about our airship, the better.'

'But the Hawks won't be an issue. I'll talk to them.'

'No, please, do this for me.'

Thoughts spun through my mind. 'Are you in some sort of trouble?'

She shook her head and looked away. 'Of course not.'

Too many things weren't stacking up. 'I wish you'd spit it out and tell me what's really going on.'

'I just can't, okay? Please.'

So what was the real story here?

Angelique twined her hands together.

Seeing her pleading expression, I sighed. I wasn't going to get the truth out of her anytime soon, but I'd try again later. 'I guess.'

The diner door slammed behind me. 'Harry?' Mom's voice called out.

Harry's expression stiffened. 'Sue.' He touched the brim of his baseball hat as she approached.

I stared between them. What was going on here? I thought she'd be pleased to see him.

Mom's face was flushed. 'Passing through?' she asked, voice strained.

'I thought we had an invite. Dom contacted us about your twister.'

Mom just stared at me. 'You did?'

'I forgot to mention it.' It had never occurred to me that she wouldn't be pleased to see the Hawks.

But as I saw Mom and Harry exchange tense looks, I understood why the Hawks had never been back. They weren't wanted. Goddammit, how could I be so slow? They had to be a painful reminder for Mom of Dad's old life. Photos were one thing, but his buddies who shared that world, totally another.

Angelique gave me a questioning look. Everyone was silent for a moment.

Harry coughed. 'Look, if it's a problem we can hitch our wagons and go somewhere else?'

'No, no it's fine,' Mom said. 'You're here now.'

'And you always loved Mom's cooking,' I said.

'Ain't that the truth.' His gaze swept over the diner. 'It's good to see the old place. So, how's business?'

Mom's face crumpled. 'We're hardly getting any trade since the drought hit, and of course without you guys around, your fans deserted us as well.'

A small smile crept back into his face. 'Ah, well that may be about to change, at least for a while.'

'Come again?' Mom asked.

'We've been chasing these traces of twisters for the last couple of days, but yours was the first to actually touch down. All the Hawks are on their way.'

Mom stared at him. 'All of them?'

I caught Angelique's flinch again.

'Yep, they'll be here within the hour, bringing their huge appetites with them.'

Mom actually gave him a small smile. 'I seem to remember you liking my Hurricane Chicken, Harry?'

'Like? Love you mean! Especially with your secret barbeque sauce.'

'I've perfected it now – even spicier.'

Harry licked his lips. 'Now that sounds like my idea of heaven.'

Mom glanced at me. 'Can you help me in the kitchen, Dom? Sounds as though we're going to have a rush on. You know how hungry the Sky Hawks get.' She gave me the tiniest smile.

'But I was going to help on the—' Angelique's face screwed up again and I bit the word 'airship' back. 'Sure.'

Mom nodded to Harry and set off to the diner.

Harry watched her go. 'Is Sue really okay with us being here? When I got your message I assumed you'd spoken to her about it.'

'No – I never even realised there was an issue.'

'Sure we shouldn't just make ourselves scarce?'

'I reckon deep down she's pleased to see you.'

'You think?'

I did actually. I still remembered the diner filled with the Hawks' laughter. Back then the Twister Diner had been the best place on the planet to be.

'Give her time,' I said.

He patted my shoulder. 'Cherie should be here soon in the Battle Wagon Mark Two, and her appetite alone will keep you going for months.

I smiled. 'Is that heap of junk still running?'

Harry snorted. 'Don't let Cherie hear you say that about her baby. Anyway, it's better than ever. We've welded additional one-inch steel plate to it. I tell you it could survive anything a twister could throw at it now.'

'Battle Wagon?' Angelique asked.

'Oh, just a little old armoured car we picked up on the cheap from the marines,' Harry replied. 'We study twisters, trying to learn as much as possible. If we do our job right, we might just help save a few more folks' lives. Of course, we've got all our vehicles fixed up with cameras, so we can sell the footage to the documentary channels. All helps to pay the bills.'

She nodded, but gave me a quick glance as if to say, 'What the hell is he talking about?'

'The plan is for the Sky Hawks to use the Battle Wagon to shoot some vid right inside the spout of an F5 class twister.'

'An F5 – that's really strong then?' Angelique asked.

'That's the biggest, meanest mother of them all – can get up to over three hundred miles-per-hour winds,' Harry replied. 'And when we do, there'll be a bidding war between the TV companies for the footage. It will be our one-way ticket to wealth city and we'll be able to fund some serious research.' His grey eyes looked into mine.

'Though it's not going to be the same without your pa's aerial footage.'

Remembering the video Dad used to shoot from a camera mounted beneath his bi-plane, my stomach knotted. I'd sat with him in his study while he edited the footage and he'd told me how he'd danced with death to get it. His stories had often left my mouth hanging open. I so wanted to do half the things he had with his life. I wish I could be just like him, follow in his footsteps.

'I need to freshen up,' Harry said. 'Catch you guys later.' He headed towards the diner.

I hung back for a moment. 'You better warn Bella to get the gondola out of sight. Use our old tractor. You'll find the keys under the seat. I'll tell Mom and the others not to say anything.'

'Thank you.' Angelique took a half step towards me.

I got ready for the hug, but it never came. Instead she stopped, turned and darted towards the field. I sagged inside. Why did I keep kidding myself?

I headed around the back towards the kitchen. By the trashcans I saw the box that Jules had brought the engine valve cover in. Angelique's words swam to the front of my mind: 'You mean acting all jealous.'

Taking a deep breath, I pushed the door open, hoping things weren't going to get weird between Jules and me.

Angelique's life looked more appealing by the minute. Adventure, pure and simple, without worrying about anyone, or anything else. But the question mark about them was also getting bigger. Why so jumpy about people finding out about the airship?

My life seemed to be getting complicated real fast, and in more ways than I wanted to count.

Chapter Seven
LIGHTNING GLASS

I scrubbed the black bits off a griddle with a wire brush, listening to the banter of the storm chasers drifting through the open hatch from the diner. Flames whooshed up from Mom's frying pan, adding to the sticky warmth in the kitchen. The storm had fried the air conditioning unit – god knew when we'd get that fixed.

With all the windows flung wide open, the desert heat crept in and the kitchen felt like a boiler room. My whole body dripped with sweat. Even my insides felt like they were stewing.

Heat, heat, and more heat.

The three hours we'd actually been working seemed more like six. I'd forgotten how I had to bust my ass when we were this busy.

I added the pan to the teetering pile already on the drainer and stretched my fingers with a loud crack. 'Ow, cramp.'

Mom actually managed a small smile in my direction. Tense would have been the understatement of the century to describe how she'd been since the Hawks had arrived.

'Dom, thanks for all your help, I couldn't have coped without you.'

My jaw relaxed. 'Look, Mom, I'm sorry for not saying anything about inviting them.'

She sighed. 'You understand why it's been difficult for me having the Hawks around?'

'Yeah, I do now.'

A roar of laughter came from the diner.

Her expression relaxed. 'Maybe them being here is actually a good thing. I guess I sort of deep down blamed them for his death, you know, like him hanging around with the wrong sort of people.'

I shrugged.

'But the truth is it's time for me to face facts – your dad could be pretty reckless at times. That's the real reason he's not here today.'

A knot tightened inside me. Dad was Dad, living on the edge, that's just how he was.

'It was an F5, Mom. He had to go after it for the show.'

'Did he? He should have been asleep in bed. If he hadn't been woken by that silly dream he would have slept through it all.'

'What dream?' This was the first time Mom had ever mentioned anything about that.

Mom opened then closed her mouth. She breathed out through her nose. 'I can't remember... All I know is he said he was going for some air and the next thing I know is you were waking me up.' She looked away.

I could tell there was something she wasn't telling me.

More laughter came from the diner and Harry wandered into the kitchen with an empty plate.

'Sue, that cherry pie was fantastic,' he said. 'The others were wondering if there was any more?'

She sighed. 'Sure thing, Harry.'

He turned to me. 'Hey, Dom, any chance you could show me that touch-down spot now?'

'Yeah, no problem.' God, I needed some air. I couldn't breathe in here.

Mom watched me with sad eyes as I headed out the door with Harry.

...

Harry squatted on his haunches, staring at the radiating spiral scribed into the ground. 'I never thought I'd see one of these in my lifetime.'

The whiff of burned-out campfire scratched the back of my nose. 'It's just where the twister chewed the dirt up.'

Harry looked over the top of his sunglasses at me. 'Come on, Dom, you can do better than that. Look closer.'

I peered at the pattern. Now I thought about it, it did look way too perfect. 'Guess it's almost like someone carved it with a chisel.'

Harry stood up. 'Exactly. The usual pattern you'd expect to see for a twister touch-down point is more like a big blast mark with a debris channel stretching away from where the spout churned the earth up.'

'So why's this one different?'

He walked to the middle of the pattern. 'There's only been a handful of reports of these sort of markings over the years. And I mean going way back.'

'This is rare then?'

'Rare doesn't even come close.' Harry took off his baseball hat and scratched his head. 'Till now it's just been considered a myth.'

'What, a bit like the Big Foot stories?'

'You betcha. This is major news.' Harry hooked a cell out of his pocket. 'I tell you this for nothing, it's really going to put the Twister Diner on the map.' He started punching numbers on his phone and wandered away across the field.

Wow, maybe this would become a storm chaser sightseeing spot and the answer to all Mom's money problems. I chewed my lip. But what did this all mean? I peered down at the markings. I remembered the strange pulsing light in the tornado. Somehow this had to be linked to the *Athena* coming out of the twister. But how could any airship create markings like this? I needed answers. I looked across to the closed doors of the hangar.

'I'll catch you later, Harry.'

He nodded and I set off at a run across the field.

The sound of bashing metal echoed from the building as I approached. I swung the rusty metal side door open. Luminous shafts from the holes in the roof burned down into the dark interior, giving the hangar a cathedral-like feeling. Bella raised a lump hammer above her and swung it down onto one of the bent runners. An ear-numbing clang vibrated through me.

In the middle, looking like an angel in overalls, Angelique knelt on the canvas under a mosaic of dappled light. Head bent forward, she was busy sewing a rip that extended a good forty yards back along the canopy. Neither of them looked up as I walked in, the sound of my entrance drowned out by Bella's hammering.

I passed the gondola on the far side to where Bella was working on the bent runner. The cabin door was right next to me. I paused. I hadn't been seen. It seemed like too good an opportunity to miss. A quick look couldn't hurt. I might even find a clue in there.

I turned the handle and started to open the door. A long echoey moan burst out from the gondola and I stumbled backwards.

Angelique scrambled to her feet and Bella appeared around the edge of the gondola, staring at me.

'What the hell have you got in there?' I asked.

Bella hobbled over and shoved her walking stick across the entrance. 'Just an alarm system we've got fitted – and just as well it seems.'

'Sorry, I was just curious. Anyway, strangest alarm I've ever heard,' I said, peering through the smoky cabin glass. All I could see was the dull glow of a few lights. 'I've never seen inside an airship, do you mind giving me a guided tour.

Angelique shook her head. 'Sorry, Dom, it's a real mess in there. There are wiring looms all over the floor.'

I really wanted to see inside now. 'Don't worry, I'll be real careful.'

'And I'd never forgive myself if you tripped over and got hurt,' Angelique replied, tone lowering.

Okay, this wasn't getting me anywhere fast. I tried a change in tactic. 'You're probably right. I'd fall over something with my big feet.'

'Another time maybe,' Angelique said.

Yeah, like that was going to happen. Time to test my theory and see how they reacted to the news about the discovery of the strange mark. 'Hey, I haven't told you what I just found with Harry.'

'What?' Bella asked.

I watched their faces closely. 'A strange pattern etched into the ground where the twister touched down. Harry reckons everyone's going to be all over this like a rash.'

Angelique's face paled and she gave me a hard look. 'You haven't said something about *Athena*, have you?'

My jaw muscles tightened. 'Course not. I promised you I wouldn't.'

'Look, it's just important we can trust you,' Bella said.

I glowered at her. 'Trust me? Look who's talking! Something has never smelled right with your story.' I crossed my arms. 'I mean how can any aircraft – let alone an airship – survive a twister?' My voice got louder. 'For god's sakes, my dad lost his life in a plane flying into one, and you come out of one with barely a scratch.'

'We were lucky,' Angelique said.

'No one has that sort of luck.'

'Well, we did,' Angelique replied.

The anger coiled tighter inside me. 'Not buying it.' My finger jabbed towards Angelique.

Faster than I could move, Angelique knocked my hand aside with a fist, and her other flat palm flew forwards. The blow landed in my stomach and sent me sprawling onto the ground.

'Stop!' Bella shouted at Angelique. She crouched by my side. 'Are you okay?'

I stared up at her, clutching my gut. After a couple of deep breaths, I nodded.

Angelique had her hands pressed over her mouth. 'I didn't mean to do that, Dom.'

'Yeah right,' I replied through gritted teeth.

'No, she's telling the truth,' Bella said. 'Angelique studies a form of ancient martial art.

It was her training to protect herself that took over.'

I struggled to a sitting position. 'So this is my fault?'

Angelique waved her hands. 'I just bent your energy back at you, Dom.'

She put a hand out to help me up, but I batted it sideways. Wheezing, I stood up. God, I felt humiliated. I could look after myself with any jock, but she'd just kicked my ass.

'I'm outta here.' I stalked towards the outside door, but Angelique blocked my path.

'It really was an accident,' she said.

'So you keep saying.'

Angelique's fingers brushed my arm with the lightest of touches. 'I'm so sorry.'

I pulled away. She wanted my forgiveness? Seriously? 'Just let me be.'

'Okay...'

I headed towards the door. What had that sound from the cabin really been? Were they keeping something alive in there?

Outside, the basketball sun slid slowly into the horizon. Walking back to the house, I looked across at the people milling around the SUVs and motorhomes packing out our lot.

The Battle Wagon Mark Two, the Storm Hawks main twister pursuit vehicle, painted bright scarlet, stood out among the gleaming silvers and blacks of the other vehicles. The colour was Cherie's idea of a subtle paint job.

In the growing gloom, Harry was leading a procession of people with picks and shovels across the field. What was going on there? Only one way to find out. Setting off towards them, I glanced back at the hangar and saw Angelique watching me from the doorway. I'd had it with their stalling. I wanted answers and I'd get them one way or another.

I strode through the meadow towards Harry and I recognised Cherie by his side.

A doctor at some lab during the day and amateur weather scientist for the Sky Hawks by night, she was dressed in the only clothes I'd ever seen her wear – old combat fatigues. Her hair had been scooped back into her trademark ponytail and a webbing belt was tied tight around her curvy waist, an array of tools dangling from it.

Harry's head torch swept towards us and I held a hand up to shield my eyes.

'Hi, guys,' he called out.

Cherie peered towards us. 'Hey, Dom, good to see ya.'

'You too.' I noticed her oil-stained hands. 'So you managed to get the Battle Wagon all the way out here, then?'

She snorted. 'Yep, only broke down on me once.'

'You really should let Roddy have a look at it, Cherie.'

'I'm not letting him anywhere near my baby. You've got to understand her moods. It's a woman thing. I'll get Jules to look at her instead.'

Jules. I felt like groaning. That was another interesting conversation I had to have. I glanced down at the trowel in Harry's hand. 'So what are you guys up to?'

'Come and see for yourselves.' He set off towards the next field where we'd found the spiral mark. We filed through the gateway and his gaze narrowed on me. 'Can I ask you a bit more about that twister, bud?'

'Sure, fire away.'

'You sure there wasn't anything unusual about it...anything out of the ordinary?'

The image of the airship flashed through my mind. I shrugged and tried to keep my face expressionless. Even though they didn't exactly deserve my trust, it felt wrong to say anything. 'No... Just the biggest tornado I've ever seen.'

'What 'bout any weird lightning?' Cherie asked.

The pulsing light – I couldn't see why it would hurt mentioning that. 'I did see the spout strobe at one point.'

Her face lit up. 'Now that's what I was hoping to hear.'

'Why?' I asked.

She winked. 'Patience.'

We reached the middle of the field and Harry squatted down by the pattern.

'So this is the plasma burn,' Cherie said.

'A what?' I asked, as he flipped open a camcorder and began filming.

'If my theory's on the money, you'll see for yourself in a mo.'

Harry shone camcorder light onto the ground and Cherie unclipped a big hunting knife from her belt. She began poking at the dirt along the line and after three prods, the knife clinked on something solid.

A smile filled her face. 'Jackpot.'

Harry scratched away across one of the lines with his trowel and something sparkled in the torchlight. 'My god, you were right, Cherie.'

I leant forward. 'What is it?'

'Glass,' Cherie said.

'An old buried bottle?'

She shook her head. 'The soil has a high silicate content here, right?'

'What?' Cherie loved to talk in scientific babble. My confusion must have shown on my face.

She smiled. 'Silicate – sand, in other words. Where this channel has been burned, the ground beneath has been melted into glass.'

'Oh...' I locked my hands around my neck. 'But what could possibly do that? A welding torch or something?'

'Nah, something even hotter – a very special sort of lightning.' Cherie beamed at the other Sky Hawks, who'd begun clearing the ground along the rest of the channel. As the line was excavated a thin continuous ribbon of glass became exposed.

Harry took off his baseball cap and wiped his brow. 'Jeez, you usually only find this sort of thing on a beach.'

'How come?' I asked.

'A lightning strike there shoots down through the sand and leaves a fused imprint like the roots of a tree.'

I tapped my fingers on my chin. 'Not wanting to point out the obvious flaw with that, but this is a spiral.'

Cherie snapped a small twig of glass off and stood up. 'I did say special lightning. My hunch – and it's only a hunch, mind – is that this baby was caused by ball lightning. Maybe that's what you saw blazing inside the spout.'

'What the hell is ball lightning?' I asked.

'A rare natural phenomena that scientists don't know much about,' Harry said.

'How can any sort of lightning really leave markings like this?' I asked.

'Have you got a better explanation?' Harry replied.

My gaze flicked back to the hangar.'

I shrugged. 'Of course not.'

Cherie rubbed the glass shard on her sleeve and rotated it through her fingers. It changed from aqua to deep blue. 'Can't wait to start running some tests on this.'

'Tests?'

'We need to be sure this is the real deal before call'n the big guns.'

'Who are they then?'

'Leading scientists in the meteorology field.'

Harry nodded. 'You just wait, once word gets out and this place will be swarming with folks in lab coats.'

Oh, Angelique and Bella were going to love this. 'But nobody outside the Sky Hawks knows about the find yet – you haven't told the TV stations, have you?'

Harry shook his head. 'Nope, not until Cherie has analysed it. We want to be sure of our facts before going public.'

Cherie pocketed the shard. 'I'll run a chemical analysis when I get back. Then we should have a much better idea of what we're dealing with.'

As we started back across the field, a flickering movement just visible round the far side of the hangar caught my eye.

'I'll catch you guys later. Just something I need to do.'

'No problem, see you soon,' Harry said.

I pretended to tie a loose trainer lace, long enough for the others to disappear into the diner, before approaching the hangar.

I peered around the corner. In the shadow of the building, Angelique dressed in her overalls, whirled and spun, golden hair flowing out in waves.

I watched her for a moment Her movements reminded me of the Tai Chi I'd once seen an old man doing in a park in town. But this was faster, dance-like. She moved in a series of spirals and loops, hands carving the air in precise actions, balanced perfectly and shifting her weight from one leg to the other. Roundhouse kicks followed slicing hand blows – an intense fight with an invisible assailant. I'd obviously just been part of her warm up.

Her head whipped round in my direction. Damn, she'd spotted me doing my Peeping Tom impression. I started back towards the house. Last thing I wanted was any conversation with her, but halfway across I heard feet running through the grass towards me.

I turned as Angelique reached me.

'We need to talk,' she said.

Chapter Eight
SANSODO

I crossed my arms and scowled at Angelique. 'What, not here to kick my ass again?'

'Dom, look, how can I make it up to you?'

'The truth would be a pretty good starting place.'

She wrapped her arms around herself. 'I would if I could, but you need to know I'm so sorry about what happened.'

'Yeah, whatever.'

'No really. It's my Sansodo training. I just went into autopilot.' She stared at the floor.

The tightness in my muscles started to let go. 'Is that what you were doing just now?'

'Yes, just my daily training routine.'

'Don't think you need much training. You seemed quick enough earlier.'

She blushed and stepped closer. 'Are you okay?'

I nodded. 'I'll live. You mostly hurt my pride. And my butt.'

Angelique gave me a fleeting smile. 'I'm really sorry about that.'

'I know you are…' And I did. For once what she was saying actually felt like the truth. 'Guess I didn't stand much of chance. Going by your performance you must be a black belt in this Sansodo?'

Angelique smiled, sharp as a knife. 'Oh, I'm way better than that.' She tipped her head to one side. 'Why don't you give it a try? It's sort of like moving meditation – you'll enjoy it.'

'Not my scene.' I noticed the Sky Hawks' head-torches moving around the touch-down point.

Angelique followed my gaze and narrowed her eyes. 'What are they doing over there?'

'Under the burn mark they've found something called lightning glass,' I said.

'Oh?' she said. Her tone was measured again.

'Yeah, Cherie is going to run some tests on a shard.'

'Right...' She couldn't hide the scowl this time.

'You didn't see anything weird when you were inside the twister, did you?'

'Such as?'

'Cherie reckoned the mark might have been caused by ball lightning.'

'We didn't witness anything like that.'

Every fibre of my being told me she was lying. My frustration churned up again like soup boiling over on a stove.

She grabbed my wrist. 'Come on. I could do with a sparring partner.'

I didn't need to be a private eye to figure she was trying to change the topic. 'I can look after myself.'

'Really?' She grinned.

I snorted. 'Well, normally.'

'Come on, let me teach you a few tricks. It will be fun.'

I might as well play along. 'Alright... I guess.'

'Excellent.' She picked up a length of rainwater downpipe that had fallen off the hangar – another job I hadn't gotten around to doing – and handed it to me.

She took up a crouching pose. 'Attack me with that.'

I stared at her. 'Are you serious?'

'Don't worry, you won't hurt me.'

Even though Angelique had her arms lowered, her poise had a sense of purpose, like a cat ready to strike but pretending to be relaxed.

'I'm not sure it's you I'm worried about,' I said.

She smiled. 'As it's your first time, I'll take it easy on you.'

I swung the pipe around my head like a baseball bat, feeling the weight and balance of it. 'You're really sure?'

Angelique beckoned me with the tips of her fingers.

The pipe felt slick in my hand as I drew it back. Angelique looked so fragile – more a ballet dancer than a martial art expert. Swallowing, I swung the pipe in an arc, gritting my teeth for the impact.

Angelique whirled away and the bat sliced through empty air. My balance followed the momentum of the missed strike and I stumbled forward. Completing her spin, Angelique's foot connected with my butt, and helped shove me on my way. The world gyrated and the pipe skittered away across the concrete. I found myself on my back, staring up at the stars.

I gasped and sat up. 'What happened?'

'Sansodo happened.' She grinned down at me. 'I just used the energy of your attack against you.'

'Like you did with me earlier?'

Her grin broadened. 'Exactly.'

'How?' I wiped the dead grass off my jeans and stood.

'Sansodo draws its inspiration from a twister – and you know how powerful those are. It all begins with moving from your centre. Anybody who attacks you is just whirled around you.'

'So now you're a human cyclone.'

She laughed. 'In a manner of speaking.'

I laughed too, but stopped when I saw Jules watching us from outside the diner. Roddy's truck was parked just beyond. I hadn't heard them pull up. Head down, she scurried inside.

Damn. We so needed to talk.

Angelique watched her go, a small smile curling her mouth. 'See you later.' She disappeared back into the hangar, leaving me alone.

I started towards the diner.

But what about the strange noise in the gondola? I felt like slapping myself. Angelique had so neatly sidetracked me with the Sansodo lesson I'd forgotten it for the moment.

My feet felt like stone as I made my way towards whatever reception Jules had in mind for me.

...

I didn't want to see another burger ever again after the hundreds it felt like I'd cooked for all our customers. Taking a quick break I sat with Jules in the corner of the diner as she endlessly twirled spaghetti on her fork, sending little splatters of sauce across her plate.

Around us, the Sky Hawks' conversation filled the diner. But in contrast the conversation between my best friend and me hadn't exactly been flowing. I had tried and failed to find a way to ask what was really going on between us, but my courage kept failing me. Instead I'd filled her in with news about the spiral mark. After that all conversation had petered out. The seconds had dragged out to minutes. I so wasn't used to dealing with this quiet version of Jules.

A shout came from the next table. Harry was trying to wrestle a plate with the last piece of apple pie from Cherie. Roddy leant back and laughed at them. They'd all been swapping stories about the 'Good old days', and there'd been a lot of back slapping on their table and clinking of beer bottles.

Jules punctured our silence with a long breath. 'Dom...' She looked up at me. 'I'm sorry for acting weird.'

My neck muscles loosened a fraction. 'We should be able to talk about this.'

'You'd think, wouldn't you?' She gave me a small smile. 'I don't know what's gotten into me.' She looked out towards the hangar and its closed doors. 'Actually, I do.'

'Come again?'

'Dom, it's obvious Angelique is interested in you.'

I stared at her. 'Me? No way.' Could Jules be right, though? Wow. I tried not to smile, and shook my head.

'You mean you haven't caught the whole Bambi-eye routine she pulls when you're around?'

And Angelique reckons you're jealous... I tried to keep my expression neutral. 'She's just being friendly.'

'Friendly – right. She's winding you round her finger.' Jules sat up, moving a strand of hair from her face.

So was that it? Jules was just looking out for me? The knot in my gut started to relax. 'What are you trying to say?'

'That you're missing the obvious.' She sighed. 'Look, let's put it this way... Are you into her?'

I stared at her, jaw hanging open like she'd just slapped me around the face. We didn't talk about stuff like this. Ever.

'I'll take that as a yes, then,' she said.

That had to be the understatement of the year, but I kept my mouth shut.

The corner of her mouth hooked into a smile. 'To be honest I can understand why. She's drop-dead gorgeous.'

'Is this some sort of trick where if I agree, I'll end up getting a punch in the arm?'

Jules pressed her hands together and fluttered her eyelashes. 'Would I?'

I laughed. 'I'm so not getting suckered in by that. I know you much too well, Julia Eastwood.'

She grinned and raised her eyebrows at me.

I narrowed my gaze. 'So why all the friendly fire, Jules?'

She rotated a woven leather bracelet on her wrist, pink tingeing her cheeks. 'Just feel a bit weirded out about it – go figure.'

'I'm trying to...'

'Guess, well... I just don't want you to get hurt.'

'Ah, okay.' Well, that was a relief.

'Look, I know I've only known Angelique five minutes, but I can already tell she's used to getting what she wants.'

Heat crept into my face and I shrugged.

'But more than that,' Jules continued, 'there's something that just doesn't ring true about either her or Bella. Call it instinct, but I think they're lying to us. I tell you that engine is the weirdest thing I've ever seen, made from some sort of alloy even Dad doesn't recognise.'

I slowly nodded, glad the conversation had shifted direction. 'Yeah I've been wondering about them too.'

Jules stared at me. 'Really?'

'Yeah, I've been thinking it over. I mean, why all the secrecy about *Athena*? And the networks would pay serious cash for an exclusive about them surviving that twister. Who in their right mind would turn down that sort of opportunity?'

'Exactly. Doesn't pass the smell test, does it?'

'And when I saw the arrow that shattered their prop—'

She held her hand up. 'You're kidding me?'

'Nope – claimed it must have been a bit of debris they ran into during the storm. But I have to admit, repeating it now, it does sound pretty lame.'

'Seriously weird.' She hooked her legs under the seat. 'So if the whole round the world record thing is a cover story, what's the real deal here?' Her expression sharpened. 'Maybe they're on the run?'

'You'll be telling me next that they're a couple of international diamond smugglers.'

Jules snorted. 'Yep, obviously an airship makes a brilliant getaway vehicle.'

I laughed, feeling the heat ebb from my face. 'But why else would they be here?'

'Don't suppose you've tried asking them.'

'Of course, but they're not giving anything away. I even tried to get into the gondola and I heard the weirdest sound.'

'What sort of sound?'

'They claimed it was an alarm but sounded more like an animal.'

'Perhaps they've got a ship's cat,' Jules said, smiling.

'But what if it's something that links their airship to those strange marks on the ground?'

'Such as?' Jules said.

'No idea.' I shrugged. 'Look, will you help me find out the truth?'

'Depends on what that involves—'

She was interrupted by the door banging open and one of the Sky Hawks in a check shirt came rushing in. 'Guys, we've got a faint trace, probably nothing but…'

Harry stood up. 'Come on everyone.'

I thought for a moment about telling them what Angelique had said about there being no more twisters. But Jesus, how could she possibly know that, however fancy her barometer watch was.

Roddy raised a beer bottle to them. 'Best of luck, you old pirates.'

Cherie grinned at him. 'Make sure there's some beer on ice for us when we get back.'

He winked at them. 'I'll let Sue know.'

In a rush of bodies all the Hawks headed out the door. I had to fight my desire to chase after them. God, I'd forgotten what it was like when they got a trace. When that call came through, everyone dropped what they were doing there and then. Dad had never let me tag along on a Storm Chase though, said I was too young. With a feeling of envy, I watched the headlights of their convoy carve through the darkness as they sped away.

Mom appeared from the kitchen with a fresh apple pie still steaming from the oven and looked around the nearly empty diner. 'Where did everyone go?'

'They got a trace,' I said.

Her faced paled. 'Oh…' She went over to Roddy, tucking her hair behind her ears, smiling. 'Now here's one hungry-looking man.'

Roddy sat up. 'Have you got any of that fine chilli left, Sue?'

'Not with the Sky Hawks' bottomless stomachs. But I do have some nice juicy rib-eyes,' she said.

'Perfect. I'm going to need all the protein I can get to keep me going on that urgent job we've got on.'

'Dad, you're not going to pull an all-nighter?' Jules said.

'You don't mind, do you? I'm trying to do what I can to shave some time off. Anyway, I'm having a ball with it.'

'I know you are,' Jules replied. She shrugged at me. 'He's even worse than me, and that's saying something.'

Roddy laughed. 'You know me.'

Angelique strolled in, boiler suit rolled up at the sleeves and legs, with her long golden hair tied back. She was followed by Bella, walking upright and without a stick.

Roddy stood and started chatting to them.

Jules leaned towards me. 'Call me paranoid, but I bet they were waiting for the Hawks to go before they showed their faces in here.'

'I reckon you're right. I guess they're worried about being asked tricky questions by them, and we already know they're not keen on those.'

'And have you also noticed Bella's ankle's all better.'

'But she was limping around like she had a peg leg. Nobody is that fast a healer,' I replied.

'What are you saying – she was putting it on? Perhaps she was after a sympathy vote. Playing us all with her damsel in distress role.'

Maybe Jules had a point. Another lie? 'Look, if that's what you really think, will you help me find out the truth?'

Her eyes narrowed. 'Maybe, but it depends... Shush, Angelique's coming over.'

Angelique nodded to Roddy and joined us at our table, dropping into the seat next to Jules.

'I saw the Sky Hawks heading off down the road,' she said.

Jules raised her eyebrows a fraction at me.

Yeah, they'd definitely waited for the coast to be clear before wandering in.

'Where were they going?' Angelique asked, oblivious to our silent conversation.

'They think they might have got a twister trace,' I replied.

Her mouth pursed. She looked at her watch and her expression relaxed. 'They won't find anything.'

Just how could she be that certain? 'They obviously hope they do.' I shrugged. 'So how're the repairs going on the canopy?'

She sighed. 'The damage is much worse than we first thought. Sixteen of the major seams have ripped along the entire length of the airship. The threads will all need to be unpicked, restitched and sealed again with rubber.'

'And how long will that take?' Jules asked.

'We're talking about several miles worth of stitching, so there's about two weeks of work here for Mama and myself,' she said.

'Ah, jeez.' But if Jules was right and Angelique really was into me, I couldn't help feeling a little bit pleased that meant they'd be around a bit longer.

Jules slumped back into her seat and gave Angelique the barest smile. 'Sorry to hear that.'

Yeah, she'd like them gone yesterday. I wished they'd just get along. A plan flashed into my mind.

'Hey, Jules was just wondering if you fancied a slumber party to get to know each other properly.'

Jules glowered at me with a 'How old do you think I am?' look, before fixing a smile on for Angelique. 'Yeah, that's right.'

Angelique arched her eyebrows before giving Jules an equally fixed smile. 'Sounds wonderful.'

'You'll have to use our old camping mattress, Jules, and bunk up with Angelique in my room,' I said.

'Perfect. We can have a real fun time together.'

The ironic edge to her tone almost made me grin.

Jules arched her eyebrows at me. 'If you'd like to get your hair braided, you could always join us.'

'I'll take a rain-check on that if you don't mind.'

Angelique laughed and shook her head.

'Hey, let's go and help Sue with the food, Dom,' Jules said.

'Think she's got it covered.'

'And she could also do with a break.'

Oh, here it came. Didn't think I'd get away with it that easily.

Jules grabbed my hand and almost dragged me into the kitchen. I wasn't surprised when we carried straight on through. Mom inside the walk-in freezer getting a plastic carton didn't notice us pass by.

The screen door swung closed behind us. 'So what was all that about in there?' Jules said.

'You're my Plan A. You play at being best friends with Angelique…see if you can win her confidence. If we get lucky, she might just fess up the truth.'

'And is there a Plan B?'

'Yep, me. Tonight, I'm going to break into the gondola and find out what they're so worried about us finding in there.'

'No way. That's so wrong, Dom.'

'We want answers, don't we?'

'Not like that.'

'Can you think of a better plan?'

She sighed and shook her head.

'There you go then. Look, Jules, if we're wrong and they're all legit, what harm can it do?'

'I'm so not sure, Dom.'

'Well I am. I'm setting my alarm for three. Everybody should be fast asleep by then.

And what they don't know won't hurt them – right?' I crossed my arms.

'You're not going to back off are you?'

'Nope.'

'Maybe you're right. Perhaps this is the only way we'll get to the truth. Okay, you win.'

I smiled and shoved her towards the kitchen. 'Go on, you've got to go and make a new best friend.'

We went through into the diner. Angelique smiled across at us and I felt like such a rat. I might be certain about this, but I couldn't shake the feeling that, however I wanted to parcel it up, this was a betrayal of Angelique and Bella's trust.

But what other option did I have?

Chapter Nine
SUMMONED

Dreams of twisters and airships swirled away. I blinked awake on the sofa and glanced at the luminous hands of the alarm clock.

2.30 am...

Mom's apple pie sat heavily in my stomach. I stretched my legs over the end of the sofa and wiggled my toes, listening to the silence of the house. My brain surfaced and questions crowded into my head: *Athena* appearing from a twister; the strange lightning glass; the broken prop and arrow. They felt like pieces of a jigsaw that wouldn't quite fit together.

The curtains hung limp. Through a crack in the middle I could see moonlight bathing the oak's leaves and branches in silver.

My plan! The alarm hand still pointed to 3 am, so what had woken me?

A vibration tickled at my abdomen. I sat upright, awareness sharpening. The sensation strengthened into an audible noise, like wind moaning through the timbers of a barn. The sound began to rise and fall, weaving around itself in complex modulating patterns that reached inside me – so mournful, so alone. It reminded me of whale song I'd once heard on a nature documentary.

What the hell? Goose bumps spread over my skin.

The sound seemed to be coming from somewhere outside. I leapt off the sofa and fumbled with the desk drawer. My fingers closed around cool metal. I grabbed the flashlight, turned it on and headed to the window.

The beam burned over the motionless grass and I swung it across the field. The motorhomes stood parked in darkness, no sign of anyone or anything. The call came again, louder, resonating through my whole body. Nausea swirled through my stomach and I nearly dropped the flashlight.

The cry itched inside my skull and grew to a roar. Lights began dancing in my vision and with a flash, the points converged and the room disappeared. A new view faded in over the top of a broad violet sky. My mind lurched as I realised I was hovering over vast clouds, tightening into a massive twister. The scene had a dreamlike quality, weaving in and out of focus.

Beneath me, two vague blobs sat within the eye of a building storm like spiders in the middle of a web. I concentrated and the image sharpened, both shapes becoming airships.

The smaller ship was like the green-canvased *Athena*. But the other was massive, with a single prop churning the air with a powerful beat. It was blood red, with a demon painted along its side in bright yellow. Copper-clad gun turrets lining the flanks of the larger ship had their barrels trained on the smaller craft.

A barrage of flaming shells flew from the guns into the rear of the green ship and a huge explosion ripped its stern apart.

No way. My mind seized up like a misfiring engine and I began to gag, guts burning. The image rippled and faded. The whale-like song ebbed to silence and the nausea stopped dead, like someone had flipped a switch.

I found myself back in the house, staring out the window. I grasped the sill to steady myself. Taking deep breaths, I spotted crimson light shimmering through the storm-torn holes in the hangar roof.

Was I dreaming with my eyes open – or going crazy? I stuck my fingernails into my palm.

The red glow remained, growing stronger. Fire? My pulse leapt and I hauled my jeans on and headed for the door.

The stars hung in a clear sky, the moon setting behind a line of trees. Ahead, the glow inside the building had begun to fade.

I sprinted across the field and yanked the hangar door open. Peering into the darkness, I reached across and flicked the wall switch. Nothing. I toggled it several times. Still nothing. I breathed in deeply. No whiff of smoke.

Edging forward into the hangar, my skin prickled. My heart sped up as adrenaline pumped through me – exactly the same heightened feeling I had when I approached *Athena* that first time. I closed on the craft and my legs shook like I'd just stepped off a rollercoaster.

A crackling red luminance crept out through the gondola windows and I shielded my eyes. The light began to dim again and I pressed my face to the tinted cabin glass. I could just make out a faint point of glowing red light. Mouth going dry, I walked round to the side of the cabin and turned the handle. I'd expected it to be locked but it swung open and no alarm screamed out in warning.

Blood pounding in my ears, I stepped inside.

There were wiring cables hanging everywhere from opened hatches. Oh hell, Angelique hadn't been lying about that. But then I saw it in the middle of all the chaos, a metal globe six feet across and set into the floor. As I watched, it split like an eye opening, revealing something within that reminded me of an antique model of our solar system.

But this was different.

Rather than one solar system, the spheres were arranged in layers, stacked like a pile of celestial pancakes mounted on levers and rods, with gears spinning between them.

Crimson light flared from one of the larger planets, marked with a demon logo like I'd seen in the dream of the airship. A smaller green sphere with a lightning pattern on the side lurched and rattled as it descended on its pole, its light flickering.

A ghostly moaning echoed from the open globe and the hairs on the back of my neck rose up: the sound that had been haunting me for the last few days.

I knelt and peered down at a bed of blue glowing coals. My hand flat on the floor, I felt a vibration tingle through my palm in regular thuds, like the beating of a heart. The sensation quickened and a humming grew from within the coals.

Whale song roared into my head. One minute I was staring into the light and the next the red airship filled my mind again. Closing my eyes made the image clearer, like I was watching a film being played back on the inside of my skull.

I hung suspended above clouds billowing across the sky once more. But now below me the massive red airship I'd seen before banked through a billowing column of smoke rising from the ground, gun port barrels pointing downwards. My gaze followed their direction towards a blazing forest fire spreading out in a ring across a snowy landscape. I could just see a crater in the middle, and scattered within it the burning skeleton of an airship draped with green ribbons of fluttering fabric.

The song echoed through my mind again and its sadness cut through me like a knife. My brain locked up with a grief, deeper than anything I'd ever known. I started weeping, salty tears running into my mouth.

A name came into my mind – 'Poseidon' – and I knew it was the destroyed ship. 'The Royal Auxiliary Guard' – the men who'd died onboard.

The whale song became hot and fierce. 'Cronos.' Who?

I screwed my eyes shut. What was happening? I balled my fists, fingernails digging into my palms. I hung onto the stinging pain, focusing my whole attention on it, trying to bring myself back.

My stomach dropped away and air screamed over my ears. I blinked to see the ground hurtling towards me, clawed at the air, kicking and screaming, trying to slow my descent…

Help me!

I plummeted through a plume of smoke and the stench of charred flesh filled my nostrils. Bile rose into my throat. I pulled my legs up into a foetal position.

No!

The ground flashed up, and darkness rushed in like a roaring tide. The image disappeared and the song fell to silence. Opening my eyes, I was in the ship's cabin once more.

I stumbled backwards and something hard pressed into my back. There was a dull clunk, and I turned to see a polished brass lever pointing downwards. Above it, a small plaque was inscribed with flowing writing: 'Deploy Vortex'.

Electrical buzzing came from somewhere beneath my feet. The heartbeat grew louder and the gondola started shaking. I lifted the lever and it flopped straight back down.

Crap!

A loud clang came from outside and through the portholes I saw eight brass spikes shoot out from the gondola, ringing it like a thorny crown. An ear-numbing clap of thunder and a bolt of lightning began to leap from rod to rod. The incandescent spark travelled faster and faster until it became a pulsing blue stream of continuous energy surrounding the cabin.

Cordite filled my nose. Aqua light strobed through the hangar and shadows danced across the walls. The sparks began to arc downwards and blasted chips of concrete from the floor like a welding torch.

This was really happening.

I clutched onto the shaking gondola as a wind howled up. The hangar doors flew open and Angelique and Bella charged in. Before I could shout out a warning, the gale hammered into them, and they both grabbed onto a steel column to stay upright.

'Shut it off!' Bella cried out over the wail.

'How?' I yelled, staring around the cabin.

'Push the red button,' Angelique shouted, her dressing gown flapping in the gale.

My gaze skittered across dozens of brass buttons set into the wooden panels, none of them red. The air began to go opaque around the gondola and a snarling twister formed around the ship. With a screech, the walls of the hangar began to buckle inwards, and a toolbox flew upwards, scattering its contents to join the other flotsam already spinning around the gondola.

Angelique's fingers were pulled free from the pillar by the wind. Bella's arm shot out and grabbed her daughter's hand. Clinging on, Angelique's body rose to the horizontal.

I banged the lever up and down several times. Crap, crap, crap!

The storm howled louder and my stomach twisted. Angelique's hand started to break free.

No!

I fell to my knees and saw a red button hidden beneath the lever. I stared at the word 'Off' and slammed it with my fist. The handle sprung upwards. The raging lightning hissed away and the metal thorns cooled from white to glowing orange. The twister faded and its tendrils of vapour evaporated like steam.

The world stopped shaking.

The hangar became visible again. Angelique dropped to the ground, debris clattering down around her. A screwdriver landed inches from her head.

'Angelique!' I cried out.

She rolled over, clambered to her feet, expression fierce, and tore towards the gondola, with Bella hurtling after her. They pushed past me.

'I'm so sorry,' I said. 'I leant on a lever by accident.'

'We've got more urgent things to worry about than your excuses right now,' Angelique said.

I stared at them. 'What's happening?'

Angelique pulled up her dressing gown sleeve. Her strange watch glowed with a red light. 'Trouble, that's what.' She placed her hand onto the brass globe and stared down into the hole. '*Athena*, show me.'

The rise and fall of her shoulders slowed. The red-lit sphere began to glow brighter and the whale song roared back into my head.

Bella headed to the controls at the helm and pushed a bank of switches down. A crystal chandelier sparkled into light in the middle of the cabin.

Angelique leant forward and gazed into the blue coals. 'We have a confirmed jump – Hades' warship. Oh gods, there's been a battle.'

Red light burst from the sphere like a flashgun and the sound of cogs spinning came from somewhere beneath the floor. The green sphere, light guttering into darkness, struck the coals. Hissing and bubbling, the sphere began to evaporate like an ice cube melting, until nothing was left but a curl of smoke.

'They found the *Poseidon*,' Angelique whispered.

Bella jumped from her chair and grasped Angelique's shoulder.

I stared at Angelique. 'That lightning pattern on that planet is the same design as the one on your pendant, isn't it?'

She didn't look at me, but kept eye contact with the blue coals. 'Yes, but they're not planets, they're ships like this one.'

'They're what?'

Bella's fingers clawed into Angelique's shoulder.

Angelique gave a low moan and slumped to the floor. 'They've killed them.'

Bella nodded, tears streaming down her cheeks.

I stared at them. 'Who's been killed?'

'Friends,' Angelique said, looking up at me, her face hard.

I swallowed. 'Killed because of what I did?'

Her eyes burned. 'No – but by operating the Vortex you may have just given away our position. Now we could be next.'

A real battle – but how could I have seen it? 'I don't understand.'

With a squeal, the globe began shutting, brass eyelids closing over the glass orbs. The blue coals disappeared from view and the itch inside my skull stopped.

Bella leant forward, hands clasped together. 'Dom, we need you to promise you won't say anything about what you've just witnessed.'

'That's not going to happen, I have to—'

Angelique grabbed my shoulders hard. 'You have to say nothing, you understand?' she shouted.

What the hell was going on here? I pulled away and crossed my arms. 'No deal unless you give me some answers. You say people have just died. I many not understand what it all means, but I want the truth.'

...

I sat on one of the velvet-padded seats at the front by the ship's wheel, watching Angelique and Bella examine the instruments.

Angelique turned towards me and questions swarmed through my mind like bees.

'So who's this Hades you're running from?'

Bella clasped her pendant. 'People we have to avoid.'

Through the portholes I could see a spiral mark burned into the floor of the hangar, radiating outwards from the gondola.

'That pattern out there is the same as the one in the field, isn't it?'

Bella and Angelique remained silent. The only sound was the creaking of the metal rods cooling from orange to dull black.

My thoughts raced together. 'So if I've figured this out right – you've got a machine that generates something called a Vortex – that's what carved those markings – and that's what I saw you flying out of in this airship. It wasn't a twister at all. And what was that stuff about the other ship just now' – I made air quotes with my fingers – 'jumping?"

'We have to tell him now, Mama. He's seen too much now he's operated the Vortex drive.'

My toes curled. 'Look, it was an accident.'

'I'm afraid it's too late for regrets now,' Bella said. 'By morning we should know just how big a complication we have to deal with. We'll need to monitor *Athena*'s sensor net to see if there's any sign of pursuit.'

'Let me do it, Mama. I can talk to Dom at the same time. You get some sleep and take over in the morning.'

'Are you sure?'

Angelique nodded.

I stepped towards Bella. 'I really am sorry—'

Bella waved her hand. 'If you are, then listen to Angelique and do what she asks of you.' She turned away, dismissing me with the arch of her neck and walked outside.

I sank into a chair. What had I done? I stared at Angelique. 'Just who are you people?'

'We're Cloud Riders, freedom fighters battling Hades across parallel dimensions.'

She said it so matter-of-factly that at first I just nodded. Then I realised what she'd said. 'You can't be serious?' I breathed through my nose, trying to think.

'I'm perfectly serious.'

A parallel dimension. Freedom fighters? My thoughts whirled. There was so much I wanted to ask, but all I could say was, 'Are you trying to tell me you're not French after all?'

'The only bits of French I know are *oui* and *non*, and a smattering of other words,' Angelique said. 'I was bluffing with the rest, but my accent is natural.'

'So I was right, that wasn't a twister you flew out of?'

She nodded. 'The Vortex is a wormhole-creating device that enables us to travel between dimensions. Originally we developed it as a way to travel between the stars, but during the first test run several centuries ago, our scientists discovered that the machine opened up a portal large enough for a craft to slip through into other worlds. It wasn't long before pioneers set out in specially designed airships and brought back amazing tales of other dimensions.'

I gawped at her. 'So that's what caused the spiral markings when your airship appeared?'

Angelique nodded.

Faint pulses of steam squeezed through the closed crack of the brass globe, accompanied by a soft heartbeat sound from beneath the floor.

I pointed at the device. 'And just what the hell is that thing, anyway – a clock-work radar system?'

'It's an AI computer.'

'AI – as in artificial intelligence?'

'That's right. It's the AI core at the heart of the ship – *Athena*'s soul, if you will.'

Our previous conversation flashed into my mind. 'You almost make her sound alive…' I'd said.

'Oh, she is to us,' Angelique had replied.

'Is this why I keep hearing that weird whale song?'

Angelique's hands shot to her mouth. 'Have you experienced any visions?'

'Yes… Just now I saw the airships you were talking about. Thought I was dreaming at first, but it has to be connected, right?'

Her eyes widened. 'By the god's, you're a Navigator.'

'A what?'

'You can hear *Athena*'s song and see the images she's relaying into your brain.'

'You mean it's your airship's AI talking to me?'

She nodded. 'Dom, this changes everything.'

I sat up straighter, brain thudding. 'Everything? Why?'

'To really explain that you'd better touch the Eye.'

'The Eye?'

'That's the name of the round metal sphere that shields the AI.'

'Those blue coals?'

'They are crystals which contain the quantum computer matrix that communicates with the Psuche gem buried beneath them.'

'A Psuche gem?'

'Think of it as *Athena*'s central processor.'

'And what's going to happen when I touch the Eye this time?'

'I promise you, you'll be fine.'

My mind felt as though it was exploding in a shower of sparks. But how would touching a metal ball prove what she was saying beyond what I had already seen? Only one way to find out. I reached out towards the metal sphere.

Chapter Ten
TRUST

My hand brushed over the warm metal surface of the Eye. A quiver like static surged up my arm. The sensation grew fast like a blazing fire and flooded into my head.

As though my senses had been tuned-up, I became aware of every minute detail of the cabin. The smells hit me first: Angelique's flowery fragrance, the bubbling pot of rubber outside…the unmistakable whiff of Mom's chilli. But that had been cooked hours ago and all the way over in the diner.

Next, sounds filled my ears: the crackle of fire outside, the creaking of the diner's sign in the wind, even the squeak of bats that I knew hunted in the field beyond.

'Are your senses heightened?' Angelique said.

I nodded, realising I could see every line in the grain of the wood, as though I was looking at it through a microscope.

'That's because you're seeing the world as *Athena* does. It's the first step to linking into her. Do you feel sick at all?'

I did a quick mental inventory. 'I feel fine.'

'Good… Now we're going to check on what you saw with a full mind link.'

'A what?'

'Just trust me.'

'Okay, tell me what to do.'

'Touch the Eye more firmly.'

I took a deep breath and placed my whole hand onto the globe.

With a squeal of metal the eyelids opened, revealing the unlit glass globes arranged in their planetary layers. An electrical jolt surged through my veins and whale song echoed through my mind. A warm glow filled my insides – the sort of feeling you get when you meet an old friend you haven't seen for ages.

'Is that *Athena*'s voice?'

'Yes.'

'My god, this is so unreal. I can't get my head around it.'

'I know, but I'm afraid this next bit will hurt a little. I promise it won't last long.'

I gritted my teeth and nodded. 'What's going to happen?'

'*Athena* will start to map your neural pathways in preparation for the full mind link. She only needs to do this once and when that process is complete, you'll be able to really see.'

'I don't like the sound of the hurt bit much.'

'It will be alright. Just breathe deeply and try to ignore the pain.'

The tingling sensation began spreading through me, and I drew in a large lungful of air. Little pops of light fired off like flashguns in my vision and nausea began to build in my gut. 'God, I think I'm going to be sick.'

'It will pass.'

The sparks of light grew stronger and a burning pain filled my head. A spasm shook me. 'Shit!'

Angelique wrapped her arms around me. 'It's alright, it's alright.'

Images started racing through my head, most too fast to register. A few lingered long enough for me to make them out: a rushing point of light that became a huge white lab with men in white coats staring at me; an ice covered volcano, steam venting from its dull, glowing spout; thousands of airships gliding around me engaged in an epic battle, tracer fire arcing through the sky; Angelique smiling and approaching me along a broad granite causeway marked like an airstrip, a green sea crashing far below.

The scenes accelerated, a kaleidoscope of colour and texture. Then they slowed again and came to a gradual stop, like a cartoon flipbook slowing down, and I saw myself, Dom Taylor, rushing into the gondola during the middle of the night. A sense of joy surged through me...but the me, wasn't me… I was *Athena. Athena* was me.

Athena's memories.

Pain pulsed through my mind and a scream built in my throat and squeezed between my gritted teeth.

Angelique held me tighter. 'Just a few more seconds…'

White light filled the cabin and the world around me began to blur. No longer solid, the cabin and hangar walls became glass surfaces. I didn't dare move, convinced that if I did I would fall and keep on falling through what a moment ago had been a solid world. It was like I'd woken and found the real world to be nothing but a dream. But whose dream? Mine? *Athena*'s? None of this made sense.

'Are you okay?'

The lightning storm in my head started to ebb away and the pain receded with it.

I swallowed past the bands constricting my throat. 'Hurt a little – that felt like red-hot needles being driven into my skull!'

Her voice sounded apologetic. 'You'll be fine now the neural link has been established.'

I felt her fingers brush my face and I focused on her for the first time. The breath caught in my chest. Angelique had become a ghost, just a series of etched lines in the air defining the outline of her body, glowing with an inner blue light.

'What's happened to you?'

'Nothing, I'm still here.'

'Here? I don't follow.'

'Just concentrate on the world around you and tell me what you see.'

I forced myself to look away from her eyes, like a drowning man letting go of a life ring. In the world around us the diner began to fade, and beyond it the meadows rippled, as if earthquakes were running through them. The cornfields melted, replaced by vast tree trunks. High above, a leafy canopy blotted out the sky with translucent green foliage.

I stared out at the forest scene, mind whirling. 'My god, where am I? Those are giant redwoods, aren't they?'

'Just keep watching,' Angelique whispered.

The image started to ripple again and the forest floor shifted like it was clay being moulded by giant, invisible hands. The trees vanished and the sky, no longer obscured by leaves, shone again over a plain of vast rolling sand dunes.

I gasped. 'These are other worlds?'

'Dom, what you're seeing are glimpses of other parallel realities, right on top of your own.'

The view shifted again and a huge sprawling city sprung up around us with copper-clad towers. Bright blue and red pendants fluttered at the pinnacles of pointed domes. Hundreds of cable cars crisscrossed the spaces between the structures, like ants crawling along silver lines. In the otherwise empty streets, horse-drawn carriages glided, their drivers' faces hidden under the shadow of broad-brimmed hats. My eyes adjusted and I could just see the outline of the gondola and hangar, superimposed over the whole scene.

'This is astonishing. I can't believe these other worlds are right here.'

Angelique's ghost nodded. 'They always are, but humans are not normally equipped to see them.'

'But linked to *Athena*, we can?'

'Well, Navigators can. Perhaps it's easiest to get your head around it if you think of *Athena* as a sort of parallel reality radio, and you're the tuning knob.'

'This is just crazy – I can't take it in.' An arid sandstone mountain range shimmered into view. To step into any one of these worlds would be the greatest adventure I could imagine. The mountain landscape began to change. An icy snow-covered world appeared around us.

There was something familiar about it; goose bumps spread across my skin.

Then my heart crowded my throat. 'Oh my god, that's the world I saw those ships battling in.'

Angelique stared at me. 'Are you sure?

I took in the snow covered fir trees. The same violet sky. I'd never been so certain of anything my life.

Chapter Eleven
FIRST CONTACT

My heart crowded my throat. 'I'm pretty sure this is the spot where the *Hyperion* shot your ship down. Its wreck must be around here somewhere.'

Angelique let out a sharp breath. 'How do you know that name?'

'I just do. When I saw the vision before, the name just appeared in my head.'

'But ships can't talk to people in words, just visions and song.'

'How else could I know?'

'You didn't overhear us talking about it?'

'No way – it just popped into my mind like somebody whispered it to me.'

'I've never heard of an AI directly communicating with someone before.' She chewed her lip. 'We'll worry about that later – right now this is a more urgent matter. Time to really try out your mind link.'

'How?' I asked.

'I don't want you to think about anything else, just keep focusing on what you saw. *Athena* will tune into the memory.'

I nodded and tried to quieten all other thoughts, just leaving the memory of that chilling battle. I concentrated. Pinpricks of sweat broke out on my forehead. The wintry world wavered in and out of focus. I tried to recall every detail and how it had made me feel.

'You're getting there,' Angelique said.

My clothes stuck to my clammy skin. I felt *Athena* reaching into my mind, her song weaving into my thoughts. The sensation of my own body became blurred and I was aware of the bigger space around me, the curve of the gondola, the metal ribs of the naked airframe above me. It was like she'd become an extension of my limbs; her propellers the tips of my fingers.

Energy pulsed through my skull. A flash of light, and the ghostly outline of the gondola disappeared. The world transformed fully into the landscape I'd glimpsed a moment before.

I almost fell off my chair, which seemed to have been transformed into a rock. Under my hand, although I couldn't see it, I could still feel the warm metal surface of the Eye's metal dome. I gazed around at the snowy fields towards a log cabin where our house should have been. Silent heavy snow drifted down from a white sky, with patches of violet showing through breaks in the cloud. I put my hand out and the flakes fell straight through. I snatched it back, then tried again. Same thing.

A pall of smoke drifted up from a forest to my left. Over the tops of the trees, twisted metal girders pointed upwards, with black specks of crows swarming over them.

Although the perspective from the ground was different, I recognised the broken remains of the green airship at once.

I took rapid breaths – this felt far too real. 'Angelique, are you there? I think I've fallen through into the other world.'

'Don't panic. I'm right here, and you're still sitting next to me. Tell me what you see.'

I took longer breaths and tried to slow my pulse. 'Snow and ice...and the *Poseidon*... Or what's left of her.'

Angelique gripped my hand. 'There were at least a hundred men on that ship. The Royal Auxiliary Guard were like my big brothers at court, always looking out for me.'

'Jeez, I'm so sorry.'

'Can you see any strange patterns in the air?'

I scanned the fractured violet cloud and saw points of luminous blue dust spinning down in columns. 'There's this sort of glowing light.'

'Perfect. That's the negative energy trace of a Vortex jump, a bit like the exhaust trail from a vehicle. Looks like the *Hyperion* has crossed to another reality. At least that confirms they are blind jumping.'

'That's good news?' I asked.

'A bit. Unfortunately, because you operated the Vortex drive they know we're around here somewhere. They haven't picked up our trail and will keep doing random jumps until their battle computers triangulate which parallel world we're in.'

'How long do you think you have until they work it out?'

'About a week. Trans-dimensional navigation involves some very, very complex maths.'

'But you won't have the repairs done by then.'

She sighed. 'I know, and that's the problem. We'll have to speed up repairs somehow.'

The snow started falling faster and swirled over the ridge of the cabin. 'This is incredible, Angelique. Are you're sure it isn't a dream?'

'You tell me.' I felt something soft gently pressing into my cheek, and warmth spread from it.

'What's that?'

'Pull back and see for yourself,' Angelique's disembodied voice said.

'How do I do that?'

'Just don't concentrate so hard.'

'Oh, right.' I blinked and withdrew my hand from the metal surface. The snowy world became a phantom, and I was back in the airship's cabin. In front of me the unlit crystal planets spun on their rods.

Angelique's face, inches away from mine, so close I could see the pores in her skin.

She drew back, lips shining.

'You kissed me?' I asked, staring at her. 'After the trouble I've caused?'

'Of course.'

'But why?'

'Because you belong with me, Dom.'

Did she really mean it? 'What are you saying?'

'Better if I just show you…' She tilted her head to the side and kissed me on the lips.

A quiver ran through my chest: the smell of flowers swept into me, the softness of her lips on mine, the warm taste of her. Oh my god.

A whirring hauled my attention back to the ghostly winter world, shimmering over the view of the cabin. A ruby speck gleamed in the phantom sky. Angelique pulled away from me.

'What's that?' I asked, dazed.

Angelique's expression tensed. 'I should have realised.'

Without thinking about it, I placed my hands back onto the globe. Electricity surged through my brain and the snowy landscape became solid once more. I stared towards the expanding dot in the sky, and the noise of spinning cogs got faster.

'Stop!' Angelique said.

'What?'

Energy poured through my body and *Athena*'s song rushed into my head, hot and defiant. I concentrated on the distant spot and it grew into a red circle, then a hot air balloon. My blood tinged. I felt so alive, like a god that could travel anywhere in this strange new world, and all at the speed of thought.

I could clearly make out the craft now – it had a rudder curving down one side and a man dangled beneath, connected directly to the balloon by a harness.

'There's someone out there,' I said.

'Break contact now!'

'He hasn't seen me and you want to be sure they're looking for you, don't you?' Then like someone had zoomed in on a camera, I could see him close up. 'My god, this is amazing!'

'Dom!' Angelique shouted. I could feel her nails digging into my hand as she shook me.

The man had a small engine with a prop mounted on his back. Just above, a burner pulsed blue flame directly into the balloon. Then I noticed the screen strapped to his arm, a green light glowing on it. His eyes burned like jewels behind the tinted visor of his crested helmet. He seemed to be looking directly at me, with a thin-lipped smile.

Something slapped my face, hard. The landscape disappeared and the hangar became solid around me again. Angelique lowered her hand. Behind her a smaller red sphere in the Eye had lit up and began revolving. Her watch pulsed with a deep ruby light.

'What's happening?' I asked.

'I told you to break contact.' A warbling alarm sounded in the cabin. 'He's got a direct fix on our position! You'd better pray I can stop him.'

The red-lit sphere started to drop on its pole.

'He's coming here? What, through a Vortex?'

'Yes!' She pointed at the descending sphere. 'A Hades' scout, because of you.'

Horror swelled inside me. 'But what are you going to do?'

'Anything I can.'

Angelique turned towards me, her eyes locking onto mine. She unbuttoned her overalls and shimmied out of them. The arcs of her body began to reveal themselves and my heart skipped at least a dozen beats. I tried to look away but my eyes refused to obey. She kicked off the overalls and stepped across the cabin, wearing a revealing basque that I couldn't help notice accentuated every curve.

'What are you doing?' I said, voice wobbling.

'Preparing to fight.' She pulled a camouflaged outfit from of a wooden locker. 'And I stand a better chance surprising him in a chameleon combat suit.' She pressed a tiny black jewel on its collar. Its fabric shimmered to reflect the cabin around it and the cloth merged with the background until the suit had almost disappeared.

Angelique wriggled into the skin-tight outfit and her body became a ghostly outline. By the time she'd got it on and pulled a hood over her head, she was almost invisible.

I swallowed. 'What can I do to help?' I asked.

'Just get to the house and make sure no one comes out. Although they shouldn't – I drugged Julia and your Mom with knock-out drops.'

'You did what?'

She shrugged. 'We didn't need any more witnesses to what was happening.' Angelique pulled out a belt with scabbards dangling from it and fastened it around her waist. The alarm grew shriller. 'The Hades' scout will be here any moment.'

'I can't let you take on that guy by yourself.'

'I'm trained for it and you're not – that's the difference.'

'But what if he's armed?' I asked.

'I'm not going into this empty-handed.' Angelique pulled a handle in the ceiling of the gondola. A rack of vicious-looking swords and daggers slid to the floor. She grabbed several black knives and shoved them into the scabbards built into the suit.

'You're not serious?'

'Deadly serious, Dom.'

I grabbed her arm. 'But you could be killed.'

She shook me off. 'Everyone's dead if I don't try and stop him. If he finds us here, he'll alert the main force and they'll kill everyone in the vicinity – your friends, family, all of them. Then they'll raze this place to the ground.'

'No way I'm standing by and letting you take all the risks.'

Angelique shook me off and glowered at me. 'You've done enough already. Just go to the house and make sure no one comes out till it's all over.' She sped out the door and sprinted across the hangar; the shifting camouflage of her outfit made her look like a flitting shadow.

Outside, the wind whistled up from a sigh to a bellow, and the meadow grass began to swish against the hangar's walls.

Steam pulsed from the Eye and *Athena*'s cry flooded my head. Adrenaline surged through me – the ship's thoughts, her will to fight, becoming my own.

To hell with letting Angelique take all the risks. I stared at the arsenal of swords and unhooked a long thin one with a gleaming silver blade. Blood pounding in my ears, I ran after her.

On the horizon outside, a black cloud boiled outward, an inkblot staining the clear night sky. The centre of the smudge began to tighten into a knot and silent sheet lighting exploded from the building storm.

A thin funnel swirled downwards, an umbilical cord anchoring sky to ground a few miles away along the road. The sword handle went clammy in my hand.

'Angelique,' I shouted.

Only the swishing of the grass answered me. The clouds swept overhead, eating up the blue. I darted towards the diner, weapon held forward, heart slamming into my chest.

Raindrops the size of golf balls splattered onto the ground. The Twister Diner neon lettering glowed pinker in the deepening darkness. In the distance a siren started up, its cry echoing the storm's wail.

A roar shook the diner like an earthquake and the building groaned on its foundations. With a shriek, a crack splintered down one of the laminated windows. I slid past it and hung onto the corner of the building, as the storm pummelled into me.

Peering around the corner of the building into the raging wind, my blood turned to ice.

The twister had already closed the distance to less than a mile. It was hurtling straight towards us, tearing great chunks from the asphalt. A whiplash crack, and the diner's sign broke from its mount and tumbled away, shattering fragments of glass. Then along the road, one by one, power line poles toppled over with golden fireworks.

Blue light began shooting down the twister funnel, casting a glow across the surrounding landscape. A deep humming seemed to come from the ground itself and vibrated through the soles of my feet. Ice gnawed my body and I hauled myself around the building, scanning the field.

There was still no sign of Angelique anywhere.

Her words seared through my mind. 'You've done enough already.'

The twister towered over the diner and began to slow, blue light strobing down the spout in rapid bursts. Hardness filled my gut and I tightened my grip on the sword's handle.

I bent into the wind and staggered through the meadow, the grass blown flat like green waterweed rippling over my sneakers. Dirt swept into my face, blinding me, and I covered my mouth with my arm, breathing through my sleeve to sieve the thickened air.

The twister swerved from the road and crossed the far boundary of our field.

'Angelique!' Only the scream of the wind filled my ears in reply.

The spout twitched and a boom shook the world. The twister began to uncoil and from its core, a single hot-air balloon emerged with a man slung beneath it – the same one I'd seen in the ice world.

I stood transfixed. The wind died away and tornado flotsam started raining back to the ground with muffled thuds. The clouds evaporated like dissolving smoke, and ribbons of blue sky began breaking through. The gale hissed to silence and a distant engine drone became audible.

Angelique called out, 'Get yourself back into the house, now!'

I spun round, but I still couldn't see her.

The pilot's crested helmet turned in my direction, his round goggled eyes lit red. The craft's engine throttled up and the balloon dived towards me, eating up the distance.

The man unhooked something from his leg and aimed it at me. A puff of steam and a dot sped in my direction.

'Watch out!' Angelique shouted.

With a hiss, a red-feathered bolt struck the ground just in front of my feet. I threw myself to the ground and the balloon's shadow sped over me, its propeller slicing the air just above my head. The craft arced away in a climbing turn, steam venting from the crossbow-like weapon.

I needed to draw him away from the house, from Mom, from Jules. I leapt back to my feet and sprinted towards the hangar. Behind me, the engine's whine grew like a wasp coming in for the kill. I clawed the air with my hands, legs pounding like I was going for a touchdown, and leapt through the opening between the hangar doors. The walls clanged and I rolled onto my back to see the barb of the arrow sticking through the corrugated metal. Scrambling to my feet, I yanked the door closed and the balloon droned past.

Something clanked onto the roof and a panel bowed downwards. The metal began creaking as footsteps thumped overhead.

Heart hammering, I backed into a dark corner filled with cobwebs.

The light blinked, and a man's silhouette passed across one of the holes in the roof. With a kick, a thick-booted leg sent a metal sheet crashing to the floor.

A visored head appeared in the gap and peered inside. The blood thundered in my ears. A beam of light blazed out from a torch mounted on his helmet and down onto the gondola.

'I have you now,' the man said in a French accent similar to Angelique's. The light swept across the floor, penetrating the gloomy recesses. I edged into the corner until a corrugated wall pressed into my spine.

A tingle itched through my scalp and into my head. White light flooded my vision and a vibration ran through my body; thoughts – not my own – wove among mine.

Athena's song filled my mind with an undulating wail. I gasped.

A swish of air and sparks flew from the concrete floor and another bolt skidded past.

A single word focused itself from *Athena*'s thoughts. 'Move.'

I clambered behind a barrel and it lurched against me with a clang. The song in my head grew stronger and the world rippled around me.

An image of Angelique perched on the branch of the oak tree shimmered in my head, dreamlike, like someone had cut the camera view from my own eyes to the outside world. She was looking through the tree's leaves towards the hangar at the scout standing on the roof. Her fingers tensed around one of her daggers. His crossbow reloaded itself and vented steam.

The image disappeared and I blinked, back in the hangar once more. The scout's head-torch blazed down over where I'd taken cover. A second bolt struck the barrel and it rocked again.

'Run,' the thought said.

I jumped to my feet and sped towards the doors, the torch beam tracking me like a searchlight. An arrow grazed my scalp and ricocheted off the floor into a hay bale. I touched the stinging wound and sticky blood covered my fingers. Ignoring the pain, I heaved the door open, and sprinted towards the oak tree.

Behind me a prop whirred and I glanced back to see the burner flaming into the pilot's balloon. He took two running steps, buoyed up, like a man walking on the moon, and leapt from the roof into the air.

The grass fizzed to my right. An arrow swept past and I ducked to the left. A stone caught the tip of my boot and I sprawled forward. Rolling over, I saw the scout diving towards me.

He tugged a handle on his chest, like a parachutist pulling a ripcord, and the buckles connecting his harness to the balloon sprung away. Released, he dropped ten feet to the ground and rolled. Above him the craft shot up fifty feet and jerked to a stop at the end of the line.

For a mad moment, the scout reminded me of a child holding a party balloon on a string. Except this was no party.

The engine fell to an idle. The man stood and slid his helmet off.

I found myself staring into two red ruby eyes, set in a square-jawed face.

'Where are they?' he hissed.

I scrabbled backwards, trailing my sword through the grass.

'I said, where are they?' He raised the ornate crossbow and it cocked a fresh bolt with a sigh of steam.

I wiped spit from the corner of my mouth. 'Who?'

'The two fugitives you're hiding somewhere.'

'I don't know what you're talking about.'

'Yes you do – Belladonna and Angelique.'

I tightened my fingers around the sword. 'Never heard of them.'

'Alright, if that's the way you want it.' The man lowered his eye to a sight on the crossbow and aimed it my head. My heart seemed to stop.

'Looking for me?' Angelique's voice called from above us.

The man spun round and his arrow whistled through the leaves of the oak.

My heart tightened. 'Angelique!'

Only silence answered.

'You monster, if you've killed her—' I sprung to my feet and raised my sword, the end of its tip quivering as my hand shook.

The man grinned. In a blur, he spun round. I started to move but he knocked my sword flying with his fist. He was fast, too fast for me, and he continued in a roundhouse kick, a human twister, striking me in the chest with his foot. The air exploded from my lungs and I crashed to the ground.

'You'll have to do better than that, Hades,' Angelique's voice said from somewhere in the tree.

In one fluid movement the man shot another bolt towards the voice. The projectile swished through the branches. I struggled to breathe.

'You need to spend more time at the target ranges,' Angelique called out.

Thank god, he'd missed her.

The pilot scowled as the weapon reloaded itself. 'I tell you what,' he replied. 'I really haven't got time for your childish games. Give yourself up now and I might spare your friend.'

The leaves rustled and the scout let another bolt fly. It arced away. Steam vented from the crossbow and the man's eyes hardened. 'Okay, I'll count to three and then I'll kill him. One...'

I forced the air into my burning lungs. 'Don't do it, Angelique,' I shouted.

'Two...' He wheeled round, aiming the crossbow.

I held his burning gaze, my heart slamming into my ribs.

'Three...'

I clenched my jaw.

'Stop,' Angelique cried.

Grinning, the man turned. She dropped out of the tree, her chameleon suit taking on the pattern of the grass behind her. She walked towards us, slipping her hood back and holding her head high. The scout aimed the crossbow at her chest.

'Now that's better. You do realise this is nothing personal, Princess Angelique, just a matter of politics. Although the price on your head also has its attractions.'

I grabbed a lungful of air. 'Princess?'

'Well, well, well. So you don't know you've been hiding royalty then?'

I looked at Angelique but she just glanced up to the balloon still hovering over the man's head.

'And of course if the princess is here, that means Queen Belladonna won't be far away.'

'Queen? Seriously?' I asked.

The man shook his head, smirking. 'Very remiss of you, Princess Angelique, not introducing yourselves properly to your hosts. Especially as I'm going to have to kill them for harbouring you.'

Angelique stared at the man. 'We prefer to travel incognito.'

He raised an eyebrow. 'Obviously. But after so much effort to avoid detection, it was very lax of you to let me get a lock on your position.'

'We were having an off day.'

'Maybe you needed to spend more time in the classroom on military procedure, and less time toying with suitors at royal balls.' He sneered at her.

She shrugged but kept her gaze on the rope hanging from the balloon to the man's harness. Her eyes flicked towards me and widened a fraction. 'I just hope my mother kills you, Hades, with her bare hands.'

He nodded towards the house. Framed in moonlight, I saw Bella running towards us.

'Don't worry I'll deal with her next.'

This couldn't be happening. I needed to do something. The balloon's burner ticked over above us.

'Don't do it,' Bella shouted to the scout.

I looked at the rope tethering the man to the balloon. I could see that it was connected to a metal lever, mounted just beneath the flickering burner. It looked like it controlled some sort of valve.

In a rush I had an idea. It might just work. I gathered my legs beneath me.

'I wish I could say it's been a pleasure meeting you,' Angelique replied.

'The feeling's mutual, Princess.' His finger tightened on the trigger.

Exploding like I was going for a tackle, I jumped him and knocked his shoulder. The arrow flew wide, and I grabbed the rope.

Angelique, seeing what I was doing, launched herself sideways and rolled away. Too slow to react, I saw the man's elbow loop round and it thudded into my windpipe, sending me sprawling.

A roar came from above us. A huge blue flame blazed into the balloon, which lurched upwards, dragging the man with it.

The scout rose from the ground, legs kicking, and Angelique leapt onto his back. He tried to shake her off, but she clamped one arm around his neck. From his leg quiver he seized a bolt and drove it backwards over his shoulder towards her face.

'Angelique, watch out,' I shouted.

In a blur, Angelique's free hand flashed out and deflected the barb sideways into the man's neck. With a scream, his mouth gaped open, blood spurting from the wound. Body convulsing, his red irises rolled up into his skull.

I watched frozen as Bella reached me.

Angelique locked her arm around his windpipe, choking him, until his breath rattled to silence. A red stain spread through her chameleon suit, mirroring the blood on the scout's flying jacket. She reached up and tugged the rope. The lever sprung back, killing the flame with a whoosh.

The balloon began to descend. Angelique looked down at me. Her eyes shone and her face was flushed and exultant. Against a now clear blue sky, the contrast of her so alive, clinging onto the dead man, sent a shiver through me.

Angelique – princess and warrior.

Nausea surged up my throat and bitterness filled my mouth. I staggered to my feet and hobbled towards her, my skin burning.

The pilot's head slumped and, unable to stop myself, I retched and vomited onto the baked earth.

Chapter Twelve
BURIAL

Angelique cradled me on the ground as Bella watched, face drawn.

My eyes skated over the man hanging suspended from the balloon like a grotesque mannequin. I stank of sweat, and a teeth-grinding headache pounded my skull.

'I guess you had to kill him,' I said, dragging my sleeve across my lips.

She bent her head into mine. 'There was no choice.'

I pulled away from her. 'I know that. But how can you be so relaxed about it?' I gestured towards the body without looking at it. 'That assassin almost killed you.'

'I'm used to it I'm afraid.'

My empty stomach filled with nails.

'You saved my daughter's life,' Bella said.

I nodded, a tremble running through my body.

Angelique massaged the back of my neck with her hand.

I took a long breath and gazed into her green eyes. 'I'd be dead as well if it hadn't have been for you.'

She sighed. 'It's kill or be killed in our lives, Dom. That's the reality.'

Despite the heat of the night, a chill ran through my body. 'How can you ever get used to this?' I nodded towards the dead man.

'To begin with, I was like you,' Angelique said. 'I could never imagine hurting someone, let alone killing them. But then there's that moment when you take your first life – you never forget that – it's burned into your soul, and that changes everything.'

'What happened to you?' I asked.

'A young assassin with a knife who'd slipped into a court banquet when the coup first began…' She frowned. 'From that point it becomes much easier, a necessity of survival.'

Bella glanced towards the scout. 'But how on Earths did a Hades' scout track us down here?'

'It was my fault,' I said. 'I didn't break contact when Angelique told me to.'

'Break contact? I don't understand.'

'He's a Navigator, Mama. I did a full mind link to confirm it.'

Bella stared at me. 'You are?'

I shrugged. 'Seems so.'

She shook her head, eyes wide. 'We're going to need to discuss the implications of all this.'

I became aware of a smell building in the air – something animal, musty – the stench of urine. I glanced up to notice the damp patch staining the crotch of the dead man's trousers. I found myself looking at the corpse's lifeless ruby eyes. It felt like it would never be okay ever again. 'What's happened to his eyes?'

'Hades' troops are forced to use narcotic drops called Plam, an opiate derivative,' Bella said. 'After prolonged use it stains the irises red. It's highly addictive and is one of the many ways Hades is able to command such loyalty from their men.'

I forced myself to look away from his hypnotic death stare. 'It turns them into junkies, in other words?'

Angelique nodded and slipped a long bracelet sporting an array of dials from his arm.

It reminded me of a miniature version of the cockpit display of Dad's old ultralight, but with polished brass cogs spinning in the faces - a little like Angelique's watch.

She tapped a few buttons beneath a screen on the device.

'At last, a bit of good news. From the log on here, it looks like he didn't get a chance to Valve Voice in his position.'

'But surely once they realise he's missing they'll come looking for him?'

'And they won't know his location once I do this.' Angelique pushed a small panel on the bracelet and it slid aside, revealing a glowing yellow crystal beneath.

Unsheathing one of her black knives she popped the gem out and placed it on the ground. With a slam of the weapon's hilt she shattered the jewel; its glass guts spilled over the ground and twinkled like diamond dust in the sunlight.

'That's the homing beacon dealt with,' she said, closing the panel again.

'We're safe now?'

'Not really,' Bella said. 'Hades are going to do some serious number crunching and draw up a list of likely parallel realities. They know that we are around somewhere, so that will reduce the odds of them finding us from one in a million to one in a few thousand. They will send out spies to check each and every one to find out what happened to him.'

'So it's just a matter of time before we get more company?'

'Exactly. If we're lucky it will still take a week for them to triangulate the coordinates of where he jumped to.'

'And if we're not?' I asked.

'If they throw all their resources at it, maybe much sooner,' Angelique said. 'So you'll need to keep an eye open. Tell us straight away if any strangers turn up.'

'This sounds like serious trouble?'

'As long as they don't find us here, and don't think you know anything other than we were passing through, then it should be fine.' She clutched her lightning necklace in her fingers.

'But you can't keep something this big hushed up. People will figure out something's not stacking up eventually. Jules already smells a rat.'

'You're starting to sound like someone who might keep our secret,' Angelique said.

That was the question. How could I not tell the others about this? Hell, this would make Twister Diner really famous, the place where aliens had visited our world.

'You're asking me to lie to my family and friends – people I've known my whole life.' I looked across at the house; the windows were still dark. The knock out drops had obviously worked real well.

'Yes, we're asking a lot,' Bella said. 'But don't think of it as lying, just covering up for us until we can get away.'

Angelique rested her hand on mine in the darkness. 'Take a chance on this, Dom, and trust us.'

My mouth went dryer than Arizona. 'You're asking a lot.'

'I know we are,' Bella said. 'Let's just hope we can figure out how to accelerate the repairs so we can get away.'

'But how?'

'We'll find a way somehow. But first of all we need to deal with our friend here.'

I nodded.

Angelique took hold of one of the man's legs. 'Okay, let's get started.'

Fighting sudden nausea, I grabbed the other boot with Bella and pulled, helping them drag the body to the ground. The corpse's lifeless red eyes fixed on mine. At the edge of my hearing a faint sound filled my ears, like the sigh of a gentle sea on a shore.

Athena's song of sorrow.

I had to fight sudden tears threatening my eyes. Somehow I knew she was singing for me, and the fact I would never be the same again.

...

The sun was now a building smudge of light across the eastern horizon. Bella had left Angelique and me alone to finish burying the man, whilst she monitored *Athena*'s sensors to check if there was any sign of pursuit.

I patted the last of the earth flat with the shovel. Every muscle ached. What adrenaline had been fuelling me had now long gone.

Angelique, back in her overalls, dropped her own spade and lowered her head, pressing her hands together.

'May your soul find salvation in the realm of light, and your atoms return to star-dust.'

Though I never went to church, I found myself mouthing, 'Amen'.

Bella glanced towards the hangar. 'I'll check over that balloon of his later.'

It had taken the three of us to haul it across the field and into the building. The craft now lay deflated and hidden under an old tarp in a dark corner of the hangar.

She hoisted the man's strange crossbow over her shoulder, and I picked up the bracelet she'd removed from his wrist before we'd buried him.

'If you can't get *Athena* fixed in time, is this going to be your Plan B then – escape in the scout ship?' I asked.

'Are you mad?'

'Why? You could be long gone before Hades shows up.'

'But I'd never leave *Athena* behind – I'd rather die first. She's part of my own soul.'

At the edge of my hearing, the hum that had become my constant soundtrack grew louder. I rubbed my ears.

'You can hear her all the time now, can't you?' Angelique said.

'You too?'

She smiled. 'Yes.'

I concentrated and the sound deepened into *Athena*'s song, weaving through the gaps in my thoughts. My mind filled with love and affection, with Angelique at its centre. I suddenly felt like I was eavesdropping on a private conversation.

'She's singing to me,' Angelique said, with a small smile. 'And since the mind link, you'll always hear her whilst you're in range.'

'So I'll never be alone in my own head?' I said.

'Not while she's around. But trust me, she'll eventually feel like your closest friend, someone who's always there for you.'

'A computer who's always there for me.'

'She's so much more than that.'

She obviously meant more than any person to Angelique. Maybe she didn't need anyone else and that's why she'd been so aloof with me to start with. At least until she knew I could hear *Athena*'s song too.

I rubbed my back, aching from digging in the baked earth, and rolled the cut turf over the top of the grave. We both stood in silence for a moment. A man had died. I bit back a lump in my throat.

Athena's song swelled over me and warmth began trickling around my pain. I wrapped my arms around myself and looked to the horizon.

'I'm so sorry you had to go through this, it's the last—'

A clattering engine interrupted her. Over at the diner, dark exhaust smoke drifted up.

There was a familiar drumbeat to the vehicle's sound. The scarlet Battle Wagon swept into view, followed by the Sky Hawks' convoy, and it pulled up with a grinding of rusty brakes. A hatch clanked open and Cherie clambered out.

'It's better they don't see us,' Angelique said.

'Look, it will be more suspicious if you don't show your faces after a twister hit. Like they say, if you're trying to hide something, best to leave it out in plain sight.'

'You mean us?'

'Exactly. Just act along. Trust me, that will look much more natural to the Storm Hawks than you locking yourselves away in the hangar. That will make them curious.'

Angelique slowly nodded. 'You seem to have a natural talent for this, Dom Taylor.'

I shrugged. 'I get it, that's all.'

'I'm glad that you do.'

We set off at a jog towards the others.

Harry climbed out of his motorhome and waved at us. 'We missed the twister here then?' he said as we reached them. 'We saw it on the radar.'

'Yeah, it was massive,' I replied.

'Goddammit,' Cherie said. 'That report we went after turned out to be a dead end.'

I didn't need to look at Angelique to know she was thinking, *I told you so.*

'We were just too far away to get back in time,' Harry said. 'What are the odds of two twisters hitting the same place in a week?'

'Crazy, huh.' I said, hoping they couldn't read my mind.

Mom emerged from the house, dressing gown wrapped around her, stifling yawns with the back of her hand. 'What's going on here?' she asked, reaching us.

'Just talking about your latest twister,' Cherie said.

'Latest twister?'

'The one that hit last night.'

I made sure I didn't catch Angelique's eye. 'You all slept through it.'

She stared at me. 'And you didn't?'

Here I went again, crossing another line. 'No.'

'Oh, Dom. What were you thinking? What if it had hit the house? We should all have been down in the shelter.'

It was the note of disappointment in her voice that cut me up more than anything. Everyone else had fallen silent.

'I didn't think.' The small lie tasted bitter in my mouth.

Mom blinked, mouth turned down. I'd rather she'd be angry with me than that. I couldn't think of anything to say and the silence lingered.

She finally shook her head. 'We'll discuss this later.'

I nodded and scuffed the ground with my foot.

Harry coughed and took off his sunglasses. 'I don't know about anyone else, but right now I need to wash up and eat a huge breakfast.'

'Aren't you forgetting something, Harry,' Cherie said.

'What?'

'The power lines are down so the kitchen won't be working.'

'Hell, hadn't thought 'bout that,' Harry replied.

'What about a breakfast barbeque?' Mom said, at least giving him a smile. 'There's one in a storage unit at the back of the diner.'

'Now that sounds like one fine plan to me,' Harry replied.

'And I can cook a pretty mean steak,' Cherie said.

Harry patted his stomach. 'What are we waiting for? Let's get that beauty lit.'

Mom gave me a final frown and led the others away towards the diner.

'Thank you, Dom,' Angelique said. 'Now we need to talk.'

'Too right we do.' I followed her towards the hangar.

I knew lying to Mom and the others was for their own good, but if so, why did I feel so crap inside. If only Dad were here.

Dad!

The idea slammed home like a lightning strike and I stopped dead as Angelique walked on ahead.

Wasn't it possible that in another reality maybe he hadn't flown into that twister? What if he was still alive in a different world? I broke into a run.

I'd join them. I'd find Dad and bring him back, and everything would be great. Mom would be happy...we'd make the business work, and best of all we'd be a family again.

I ran after Angelique who'd almost reached the hangar.

'There's something I've got to ask you!'

'What?'

'Could my Dad still be alive somewhere?'

Angelique shut her eyes for a moment. Then she looked at me, forehead furrowing. 'Oh, Dom, I know what you're thinking. But that wouldn't be your father, not really. It would be a different version of him and he would have another family, another Dom who loves him as much as you do.'

Something crumbled inside me. I was such an idiot. 'Of course.'

'Look, I know what you're going through,' Angelique said. 'I went through the same with my father. I even had the same idea until Mama pointed out to me what I just did to you.'

'Right...' I looked up. Overhead birds spun and swooped, hunting early morning flies. I watched their graceful aerobatics, trying to push memories of Dad away.

Angelique took my arm. 'Come on, let's go have that talk.' She towed me towards the hangar.

A single bird swooped past us and zipped up into the sky.

Chapter Thirteen
NAVIGATOR

I leant against the Mustang watching the silhouettes of Angelique and Bella through the tinted windows of the gondola. Angelique waved her arms around and Bella shook her head. Moments later the silent movie came to an end with Angelique hugging Bella. The door opened and she strode towards me.

'Were you guys having an argument?' I asked as she reached me.

'More of a debate. Look, Dom, I haven't had a chance to thank you for saving my life.'

So why didn't I feel like a hero, and had a hollowed-out feeling instead? 'A man's dead because of me.'

'You shouldn't think like that. It was me who rushed you into a full mind link. Anyway, the real blame belongs to Emperor Cronos.'

Maybe she was right, but how the hell had I been pulled into all this madness? 'How did this war with Cronos start?'

'It began when our military saw the potential of the Vortex for their own aims. They used it to extend our country's influence. With it, our soldiers could be anywhere instantly and prevent conflicts.'

'So where's the bad in that?' I asked.

'Their ambition didn't stop there. Cronos was a former general who seized control in a military coup, proclaiming himself emperor two years ago. Once he had our planet under his thumb, his ambition turned outwards, even to other dimensions. He developed a massive Vortex engine inside an experimental ship. The field it generated was big enough to move an entire fleet in one go.' She looked at the floor. 'He had to be stopped.'

There was darkness in her words.

'The people looked to us, the remnants of the Royal House of Olympus, to halt his madness,' she continued. 'We sabotaged the drive. But nobody could have predicted the outcome.' She paused, swallowing.

'What happened?'

'His Hades' forces launched a surprise attack on the remnants of our fleet in a last all out-battle on our capital city. Our ships were totally outnumbered, but Father, in the flagship *Zeus*, and Lord Orson in *Apollo*, held off the entire Hades' armada while we escaped. The last time I saw them, *Zeus* was on fire and *Apollo*'s steering was stuck after being rammed by one of the enemy's craft. Both ships had activated their AI cores' self-destruct systems. Cronos' fleet began to pursue us but when they tried to start the drive to jump their fleet in one go, a massive shockwave ripped the core of our planet apart. We'd transported as many as we could to safety, but innocent billions died that day.'

I gasped. I couldn't begin to imagine what that experience would do to me – my planet dying in an instant; everyone and everything I knew destroyed. I tried to push the images away long enough to collect my thoughts. 'But why all the secrecy with us? Why not just tell us this at the start?'

'If our military can turn the Vortex, a device of peace, into a weapon of mass destruction, then so can anybody's. And if they can, they will. We couldn't take that risk. The human species has a talent for war, whatever dimension they're in.'

I remembered the fearful look Angelique had given the fighter flying overhead, and now I knew why. 'I'm so sorry.'

Angelique half turned towards me and leant next to me on the Mustang.

'This is all why I need to ask you something now.' She reached out and brushed the back of my hand with her fingertips.

My skin tingled like I'd been given an electric shock. God, despite the shock of the scout's death, I still wanted her. Perhaps even more now. After everything that had happened I felt a real bond with her.

I tried to keep my voice level. 'Go ahead.'

'Would you still consider joining us – as a Navigator?'

I felt light-headed. 'You're serious?'

'Of course.'

I could see it. Me, at the helm of my own airship, flying through parallel worlds.

She crouched before me. 'Dom, you could make a huge strategic difference to the Cloud Riders.'

'What sort of strategic difference?'

'The Cloud Riders have been a constant thorn in Cronos' side. Although our numbers are relatively small, we struck them where we could inflict maximum impact. We'd started to make real inroads against his forces. But that all changed when Hades developed the Quantum Pacifier. Since then we've lost contact with the other surviving Cloud Riders.'

'The Pacifier?'

'It disrupts our ships' electronic navigation systems. We were working on a device to negate the effect, but it didn't work. Since the Quantum Pacifier's activation we've been isolated from our forces for a whole year.'

'A year ago?' I grabbed her hands. 'That's when our twisters stopped right across the mid-west and the drought began – tell me that's not a coincidence?'

'You're right, Dom. The Pacifier's effects have leaked into parallel realities and, since it was switched on it's disrupted weather systems everywhere. Unless we can find the device and destroy it, your drought will last forever.'

'But all those farmers...'

'Victims of Cronos' ambition.'

I tried to marshal my thoughts. 'Okay, so where does a Navigator fit into all of this? In other words, where do I fit in?'

'I'm the last chance the Cloud Riders have. As a Navigator I can mentally link to *Athena* and act as a tuning fork, filtering out the Pacifier interference that Hades has been jamming her sensors with. Without that we'd be like the rest of our ships – stranded across the dimensions and easy prey for Cronos to pick off.'

'So how long have you been a Navigator?'

'About two weeks.'

I whistled. 'Is that all?'

'It was considered an old-fashioned way of controlling our ships – a dying art that used to be handed down from one generation to another. It was superseded by automated systems over the millennia. It was also considered a rather vulgar talent to have in our culture, and certainly not ladylike. My own ability was kept hushed up. Father didn't approve and wanted to avoid the scandal. But now – the irony – it's people like me who are our only hope.'

'So why do you need me if there are others like you?'

'That's the thing, Dom. The few that did profess to having the ability started to disappear before the outbreak of the war. To my knowledge I'm the only one left on the Cloud Rider's side with the Navigator gift.'

'But how come I've got it, then?'

'It's a marker in your DNA. You were born with it, Dom. But it's really rare – only one in a hundred million have it.'

'Wow, those are some serious odds. But hang on, how come you found me in that case, out of all the people here on Earth?'

She moved closer, the edge of her hip just touching mine.

I swallowed, trying to keep focused on the conversation.

'*Athena* brought us to your world,' Angelique said. 'She must have sensed your Navigator ability across the dimensions.'

'You mean it wasn't your decision to come here?'

'A Navigator normally guides the ship, but when we jumped, *Athena* took over and brought us to your world.'

The thought of *Athena* in a parallel dimension, picking up my scent like a tracker dog, made my head spin. 'And she didn't tell you where you were headed and why?'

Angelique shook her head. 'Communication with an AI doesn't really work that way. One can never know all the thoughts of a core – they run so deep. An old joke among our kind is that AIs think deeper than mountains are tall and make just as much sense to a human mind. *Athena* usually communicates in images and song.'

Her words washed over me and with them images of other worlds. She moved her hand to my face, her eyes green pools, pulling me in.

I so wanted to kiss her. I leant closer, blood roaring in my ears.

'Dom, are you in here?' The hangar door slid open and Jules was there. She froze. Angelique snatched her hand away.

I stared at Jules, my face burning up.

'Sorry, I didn't…' Jules screwed her eyes shut and then gave us a smile. 'Your mom needs you to help with the barbeque.' Her expression tightened. 'She told me about you not waking everyone when the Twister hit.'

I avoided Angelique's eyes. 'There wasn't time.'

She crossed her arms and glared at me.

'I'll give you two a moment,' Angelique said. She shoved off from the Mustang and headed to the gondola.

Jules walked towards me, shaking her head.

'Look—'

She silenced my words with a wave of her hand. 'I don't know what's going on in your head, but just tell me you found out something before the twister hit. I tried to pump Angelique for info last night, but she's more slippery than a greased pig. She side-stepped every question I tried to sneak into the conversation.'

I couldn't tell her. Not this. Not yet. 'Nothing.'

'What do you mean, nothing?'

I picked the first excuse I could think of. 'I forgot to set my alarm clock. Then I woke when the twister hit. There wasn't time to check out the gondola.'

She lowered her head. 'You need to be straight with me, Dom. When I finally woke just now, it was with the worst goddamn headache ever and Angelique was gone.' She raised her eyes to mine. 'Then going by what I just witnessed in here…'

My heart clenched. 'What are you trying to say, Jules?'

'That I'm not so sure you're being straight with me right now.'

A coldness spread through me. 'Don't be dumb.'

Jules held my gaze for a few long seconds. 'So much for finding out the truth, huh?'

I had to get her off the scent. 'Now I've had a chance to chew it over I think we should just let it drop.'

'I don't get you. You were all over this yesterday and now you can't be bothered.

What gives?'

'Nothing gives.'

'I feel like I don't even know you any more, Dom.'

The heat spread to my neck. 'Anybody would think you're jealous, the way you're carrying on.'

'That tells me, doesn't it?' Her eyes blazed. 'You know you can be a real douchebag some days.' She marched off, kicked a wrench across the floor, and disappeared outside.

Angelique appeared at the doorway of the gondola. 'Something you said?'

'More like something I didn't say.'

But why should I tell Jules? It wasn't any of her business and I could deal with this.

Except that I'd always told her everything before. And it didn't feel right, her knowing that I was keeping something from her, even if it was for her own safety.

Angelique walked towards me. 'I know this is difficult, Dom.'

'Do you understand how this makes me feel?'

She nodded.

It was like being pulled in two directions. On one side stood Jules, Mom, my life here where I was needed; and on the other, Angelique and Bella, and the chance to make a real difference. How was I meant to choose between those two options?

'I'd better see if I can cool things down with Jules,' I said.

'I'm sorry, Dom,' Angelique said.

I wondered how true that was as I walked to the door, feeling her green eyes on my back.

Chapter Fourteen
PHANTOMS

The moment I wandered into the diner's kitchen, Mom put her hands on her hips.

'So?' she began.

'Huh?' I replied, avoiding her eyes.

'Dom, you need to do better than that.'

Hell, she'd sussed me. 'Don't know what you mean.'

'Is everything okay?'

Of course, just like Jules, Mom could read me as if my thoughts had been written down and stuck to my forehead. 'Yeah, just not too sharp getting things right at the moment.'

'I can tell. And what did you say to Jules to make her so upset?'

'Oh, you've seen her then?'

'Just stormed into the diner like a mini twister and dragged Roddy away from his breakfast, demanding to be taken straight home even though he needed Bella to look at the engine.'

'How do you know that's my fault?'

She raised an eyebrow.

I sighed. 'You'd make a great detective.'

Mom shook her head. 'Let her simmer down a bit then give her a call. Then you can catch a lift with Roddy when he comes back to get Bella, and then have a good face-to-face talk with Jules.'

'Yeah…' I wound a loose thread of shirt around my finger.

'Hey you, cheer up. It's not the end of the world.'

So why did it feel like it was?

'Could your face get any longer?' She took hold of my shoulders and made me look at her. 'Look, if I can forgive you when I see those puppy dog eyes, so can she.'

'Just hate falling out with Jules.'

'I know, hun.' She patted my hand. 'Nothing you can't make right.'

'I hope so.'

'I know so.' She hung her apron up. 'Hey, do you mind looking after the diner for a bit? Roddy needs Bella to come over and talk about the engine. I'm going to run her down to his garage.'

'Sure, Mom.'

'You're a good son, even if sometimes you don't think as much as you should.' She smiled and heaped a pile of raw bacon onto a plate.

Seemed I was forgiven, but somehow that just made me feel worse.

A point of light drew my gaze to the kitchen window. Through my reflection I saw a low-rider motorbike with swept-back handles appear through the haze along the road, like a lone cowboy emerging from the desert heat on his horse. A red silk scarf flowed out behind the rider. He slowed and swung into our lot.

'Customer, Mom.' The rider wore a long leather coat and a pretty cool helmet – sort of retro with round goggles built into it. He got off and started tinkering with the engine. I realised I hadn't heard the rumble of an engine as he stopped. Perhaps the bike had stalled.

'We'll have to turn him away. I can't cook anything off the menu without power,' Mom said.

I pointed at the plate of bacon. 'He might want some barbeque. Like you always say, any business—'

'Is good business.' She laughed. 'Don't suppose there's any harm in asking. Could you take this bacon out to the barbeque whilst I'm dealing with him?'

'Sure.' Grabbing the plate, I headed out back. Cherie and Harry were sitting together on a bench, sipping coffee.

'How you guys doing?' I asked, putting the plate on the table.

'Better now we've got coffee inside of us,' Harry said.

'And that we've finally got that thing lit,' Cherie said, pointing at the old barbeque and the palls of blue smoke drifting up from it. She grabbed the bacon and headed over to the rest of the Hawks gathered around it.

Harry leant back and yawned. 'God, I could do with some sleep.'

I stifled my own yawn. 'You and me both.'

'Doubt I'll be getting much for a while,' Harry said.

'Why's that?'

'Still been getting traces of other twisters all night, but nothing's been forming. Damnedest thing I've ever seen – they're almost like ghost storms. Instruments say they're there, but we can't see them.'

I tensed. Like Vortex twisters?

A shout came from the front of the diner and a bearded Sky Hawk appeared through the door. 'We've got another trace ten miles away.'

Harry leapt to his feet. 'Like I was saying.'

'What's going on?' I said.

'Could be another one of these phantom twisters – we're going to check it out,' Cherie said, grabbing a bread bun and stuffing it into her mouth.

What if it were another scout ship? Hell, I'd better warn Angelique.

I set off at a run to the hangar as the first of the Sky Hawks' vehicles roared off down the road. I crashed through the door. Angelique and Bella looked up from sewing the envelope.

'The Sky Hawks have got a fix on a twister forming,' I called out.

'It's probably just an echo,' Bella said.

'A what?'

'Hades, will be attempting random blind jumps to see if they can track us down. The Hawks are detecting echoes of those events from parallel worlds.'

'So we're safe then?'

'There's an outside chance a pilot might get lucky and jump here.'

Angelique checked her watch. '*Athena*'s sensors aren't showing anything—' A red light flared onto the watch face. 'Oh gods.' White lights started to pulsate. Her shoulders dropped. 'Okay it's just a partial lock, which means it's close but not in this reality.'

'Could it be another Cloud Rider ship?'

'No, they can't jump without a Navigator,' Angelique said.

'It would still be useful to see if you could get some readings near the event horizon of the twister,' Bella said. 'If nothing else it would confirm whether it's the *Hyperion* is closing in on us.'

'The Sky Hawks are heading off right now,' I said. 'We could catch a lift.'

'Good idea,' Angelique said.

We set off at a run together.

The weather radar had started spinning on Harry's motorhome.

My pulse leapt. This was Dad's world – storm chasing, all the excitement I'd once craved.

We ran towards the lot as Harry turned onto the road. Ahead, the Battle Wagon trundled towards the horizon like a scarlet scarab beetle bellowing diesel smoke.

I waved my arms and Harry's face peered at me from his wing mirror. The brake lights blazed on.

He lowered his window. 'Something up?'

'No, we were just wondering if we could tag along with you?'

Harry tipped his baseball cap up. 'Are you sure? Don't think your mom would be too thrilled at that idea.'

Why not another lie? I was getting past the point of caring anymore. 'She's cool with it.'

'Okay, if you're sure.'

I raised my eyebrows at Angelique. We shot round to the passenger door and opened it.

'Dom!' Mom strode towards us from the diner. 'Please tell me this isn't what it looks like.'

Harry looked between us and sighed. He shook his head at me.

'Please, Mom, this is really important to me.'

'I can't lose you like I lost Shaun,' she replied.

I could see the way she was looking at me, through me, remembering, and I knew it wasn't me she was seeing, but Dad standing in front of her. People said how much I looked like him now.

Harry drummed his fingers on the steering wheel. 'Look, I've got to go.'

'You do that, Harry,' Mom said, folding her arms.

He looked over his sunglasses. 'Sorry, bud.' His engine roared up and the motorhome hurtled off down the road.

Heat burned up inside me. 'Thanks, Mom, thanks a lot.'

'Dom, I only want you to be—'

'Safe, yeah I get it.'

'It doesn't matter,' Angelique said.

'But it does matter.' I glowered at Mom. 'It matters because I'm trapped here.' My frustration boiled out, heating my words. 'I'm not a child anymore, Mom, so can you please stop treating me like one.'

'Oh, Dom.' Her face crumpled, eyes filling.

Guilt and anger squirmed through my stomach like fighting serpents. I knew I was just taking my crap out on her.

Angelique touched my shoulder. I shook her off. 'I know what Dad would do if he was here.' I felt like punching a wall. I turned and marched away.

If I had a way of going after them I would... Of course! I stuck my hand into my pocket and pulled out my car keys. Dad wasn't here but I was. This time no one was going to stop me.

I stalked into the hangar.

Bella looked up as I pulled the doors wide. 'Is something wrong, Dom?'

I didn't answer and climbed into the Mustang. I turned the key and the engine throbbed into life.

Angelique appeared in front of the car, hands spread wide. 'What are you doing?'

'Do you want to check this twister out or not?'

She opened her mouth to say something, but then just nodded and got in. I floored the accelerator. With a squeal of tyres, we shot out of the hangar and bumped across the field. Mom appeared, hands cupped over her mouth as we turned onto the road.

I tried to ignore my insides twisting and didn't look in my mirrors as we roared off down the road.

...

The road stretched ahead, a blur of dark asphalt disappearing into the distance, heat shimmering from it. Despite the fact the ancient AC was on full, sweat trickled down my back. I cranked open my window a fraction to see if that would help.

Angelique glanced at her watch. Points of white light swarmed around the face.

'What is that thing?' I said.

'An early warning device called a Tac. It's linked into *Athena*'s sensor net.' Her face pinched. 'Here we go. I'm getting an echo of the Vortex forming just a few miles ahead.'

I pushed my foot harder on the accelerator and the Mustang growled as it sped forward. No insurance, busting the speed limit wide open, everybody wanting a piece of me – none of it mattered anymore. The engine sung. This car was built for speed. Despite the trouble I'd be in with Mom, this felt great.

I glanced at the rev counter Jules had helped me fit the previous week – a lifetime ago. Its needle crept up towards the redline. The wind whistled past the open windows and for a moment the dash became that of Dad's biplane, the rev-counter the attitude indicator, the speedo, the airspeed display, instruments so familiar that I could picture them with my eyes shut.

'There they are,' Angelique said, pulling my attention back.

At the tail end of a procession of vehicles, the rear end of Harry's motorhome came into view.

The CB radio that Dad had fitted in the Mustang squawked. 'Mother Goose, Scarlet Woman calling – do you receive – over?' Cherie's voice said.

Harry's voice came through. 'Go ahead, Cherie.'

'We're going to try stopping here and see if we can spot this sucker.'

'Roger that – over and out.'

A cascade of brake lights rippled back down along the convoy and the vehicles began parking up the side of the road.

We pulled in behind the Battle Wagon as Cherie clambered out.

A wall of heat hit us as we left the Mustang and ran towards them.

'What the hell, Dom?' Harry said, as he reached us. His eyes travelled to the Mustang.

Angelique stepped between us. 'Sorry, Harry, I persuaded Dom to give me a ride.'

'Don't suppose it would do any good to tell you to turn round and head home.'

I crossed my arms. 'Nope.'

He shook his head. 'You're too like Shaun.'

The way he said it, it didn't exactly sound like a compliment.

'Well, we're here now,' I said.

'Then you might as well have these.' Harry passed me a pair of binoculars.

My neck muscles relaxed. 'Thanks.'

The Sky Hawks gathered around the Battle Wagon. Cherie, perched on top, waved a handheld wind meter above her head.

Harry pulled his shirt away from chest. 'Jeez, just how hot is it?'

'A hundred and eight degrees, hotter than hell,' Cherie said.

We headed over to join them as a warm breeze rippled through the cornfield alongside us. The air tasted dusty and I pulled the shirt away from my soaked back.

Cherie stared up at the sky. 'Pressure's through the floor, so where the heck is it?'

'Looking at the rain radar, we should be sat right in the middle of a huge storm cell,' Harry replied. A murmur of agreement passed through the group.

Angelique leant closer to me. 'They won't see anything, but we should get a data echo with the Tac.'

A faint buzz in the distance began to grow louder.

'What's that?' I asked.

The sound amplified, throbbing, more urgent, coming from a ridge ahead of us.

Like an explosion of buckshot, a flock of starlings skimmed over it and raced past in a rush of wings, their cries filling the air.

'Wow, they're in a hurry,' I said, as we all ducked.

'Seems this one has even got mother nature fooled,' Harry replied.

Angelique raised her eyebrows at me.

The calls of the starlings headed into the distance and the wind died on my neck. With a sigh, the sea of ochre corn stopped swaying.

Harry cupped a hand to his ear. 'Hear that?'

'Can't hear a thing,' I said.

'Exactly,' Cherie replied. 'Could be a sign that a storm's about to break.'

'Shouldn't it be getting more windy then?'

'Normally, but sometimes it gets real still before a big storm lets loose – like the world's holding its breath, y'know?' Harry said.

I nodded and pointed my binoculars up at the sky. Nothing but pure blue filled the eyepieces. Seemed weird that in a parallel world a Vortex twister was forming.

'I'm starting to get a faint trace, but not strong enough to get a data lock,' Angelique whispered.

I scanned the heavens. Silence. A line of sweat tickled down my jaw.

My skin began to itch and goose bumps crept over me. A smell like the ocean flooded my nostrils and I tasted a metallic tang.

'You smell that?' I asked, mouth going dry.

Cherie wrinkled her nose. 'What, Harry's death breath?'

He scowled at her. 'You can talk, sister.'

'No, it's like the smell of the sea,' I said.

Harry looked at me over the top of his sunglasses. 'Or like the smell you get before a lightning storm? Ozone building?'

'I guess…'

Angelique stared at me. 'But I don't smell anything.'

A moan, low and deep, rumbled through my abdomen. 'Jesus, here it comes.'

'What are you talking about?' she said.

'The growl of a twister coming. You gotta hear it now?'

She shook her head.

The roaring sound grew into a wind's howl, but the corn remained frozen. 'God, the twister, it's deafening!' I shouted over the roar.

The group turned and looked at me as though I'd totally lost it.

'I don't understand what's happening to you, but I swear there's nothing there that I can see or hear,' Angelique said.

A movement drew my eyes back to the sky. I shielded my gaze from the blazing sun – nothing but unblemished blue – then the nothing wavered.

The patch of blue darkened and shimmered like a blurred blob coming into focus, and the hairs on my neck stood up. I grabbed my binoculars and examined the shimmering spot. The abstract shape grew denser and formed into a vague long oval shape…

The air rushed out of me. 'The airship's here, Angelique' I whispered.

She looked up to the sky and then at the Tac. 'There's nothing there, Dom, just the data echo.'

How could I see an airship that she and the others couldn't? Surely I was too far away from *Athena* for her to beam things into my brain?

The oval sharpened into a ghostly version of the Hades' ship. The *Hyperion*.

The familiar tingle at the back of my skull began to itch and I gulped air. Then, like a rushing wave, the whale-song roared into my mind. But this was darker, filled with threatening intent. A word formed.

'Kill...'

I began to shake, teeth chattering.

'Dom, you okay?' Cherie asked, looking down at me from the Battle Wagon.

Harry's hand pressed against my forehead. 'Jeez, son, you're burning up.'

The shrieking blotted out my thoughts. I stared at him helplessly. The strength emptied from my limbs and my legs started to fold.

Harry's strong hands locked around my shoulders and supported me. 'I've got you, Dom.'

My own face stared back from the reflection in his sunglasses, features drawn and contorted by pain. Harry's mouth moved, but the howling wind swept his words away. Beyond his head, framed by blue sky, the airship started to dissolve and the dark whale-song ebbed. I became aware of Harry shaking me and of heat creeping back through my body.

The storm died to silence.

'Dom, Dom, speak to me,' Angelique said, holding my hand. Around her and Harry, the Sky Hawks had gathered in a circle, faces anxious.

My tongue was swollen inside my mouth and I swallowed past it, squeezing my words out. 'I'm okay.'

'You had me worried, bud,' Harry said. He turned to Cherie. 'We need to get Dom back home – probably heat stroke.'

'Don't worry, I can take him,' Angelique said.

'You sure?' Harry said.

'No problem – really,' she replied.

'Thanks. I'd like to stay here with the others...just in case our invisible friend decides to make an appearance,' Harry said.

Angelique nodded and guided me towards the Mustang.

Legs quivering, body drenched in cold sweat, I felt the warm wind breathe over my neck.

The world was starting to feel normal again, but inside I still felt the echo of the fear, like the shadow of a nightmare that hangs over you long after waking.

The sky was flawless blue. Angelique helped me into the car. I sagged into the passenger seat, wrapping my arms tight around my chest. She started the Mustang up.

'You okay to drive?' I asked.

Angelique settled herself in the seat and scanned the controls. 'Shouldn't be a problem for a woman who flies airships.' She slipped the car into drive and like she'd been driving Mustangs everyday of her life, swung the car around in a large arc until we were heading back the way we'd come.

My throat started to loosen up. 'What just happened to me?'

'I've no idea, but somehow you were obviously able to see that craft in a parallel world. It's the how I'm confused about. What with that and your ability to hear *Athena* actually speak, makes you a bigger mystery by the moment.'

'It was the *Hyperion*.'

'That's what the Tac told me as well. Okay, I've got an idea that might work.'

'What?'

'I think if you link to the Eye, *Athena* may be able to connect directly to your memory and get a lock. Then we can work out if the *Hyperion* is closing in or not.'

'Okay...' I wrapped my arms tighter around myself and shuddered.

...

By the time we rolled back into the parking lot, I was feeling more like my old self.

'How are you doing?' Angelique asked, as we got out of the car.

'Much better.'

Jules' old Honda moped was parked alongside the low-rider motorcycle and Mom's station wagon. Hell. As though I didn't have enough on my hands dealing with Mom right now.

Angelique grabbed my arm. 'Who does that motorbike belong to?'

'A guy turned up just before we set off after the Sky Hawks. Why?'

Her gaze tightened on me. 'What was he wearing?'

'Long leather coat. Cool retro goggle helmet—'

'I told you to tell me if any strangers turned up.'

'But it was just a guy.'

She pointed at the bike. 'Look at it.'

It looked like a normal bike, except for the copper handlebars and the motor looked as if it was made from polished chrome. 'Seems pretty regular to me.'

'You have combustion engines on this world don't you? What about the fact it hasn't got an exhaust?'

She was right. Where the pipe should have been, there was nothing. 'You mean—'

'A spy. This bike is powered by a small fission plant running a steam turbine.'

'Jesus, that's why it didn't make a sound when it turned up.'

'We've got to find him.'

I stared through the diners' window. It was empty. 'Mom was going to feed him breakfast—' I almost couldn't breathe. 'And Jules is here.'

'Oh gods,' Angelique said. 'Look, the moment he sees me, he'll go into action and if Jules or your Mom are near him...'

'Let me look then. It will be safer.'

'I can't let you take the risk.'

'And Jules is my best friend and doesn't know the danger she's in. I have to do this, Angelique.'

Her mouth twisted, but she nodded. 'I'll check the hangar out, but any problems and you shout for me.'

'You got it.' Heart crowding my throat, I ran towards the diner.

Chapter Fifteen
THE SPY

Inside the diner I spotted a plate with a half eaten bacon sandwich on it. For a moment I thought the place was deserted, but then I heard a clink of plates from the back. I rushed round the counter and through the hatch I saw Jules washing up at the sink.

'Thank god you're okay,' I said.

She stiffened and turned towards me. 'Oh, you're back from your road trip with Angelique then.'

'Jules, you don't understand—'

'What don't I understand? You tell me, Dom. And whilst you're at it maybe you can tell me what your mom doesn't understand too. She's a real mess. What were you thinking?'

'Jules, not now.'

'Why not? Seems like the perfect time to me.' She waved her hands at the empty diner. 'Hardly busy at the moment.'

I grabbed her shoulders. 'Because you, Mom and Bella are in danger.'

Her eyes widened. 'What are you talking about? Anyway, Bella's not here. She went back with dad to the garage.'

'Right, but where's that customer, the guy with the motorbike?'

'Still fixing his bike in the lot, isn't he? Dad offered to help him but he said he'd got it covered.'

'Well he's trouble, real trouble.'

'Let's ring the police then.' Jules pulled her cell out of her pocket.

I grabbed it from her and put it on the side.

'What are you doing?'

'You can't do that,' I said. 'Anyway, where's Mom?'

'She popped over to the house. Look, Dom, you're not making sense. And if this guy's some crazy—'

'I know it doesn't make sense and I know I've been weird around you, but I just need you to trust me this one time. We can't get anyone else involved, but we need to find him right now.'

She gave me a questioning look, but slowly nodded. 'Okay… He was asking about the twisters that had hit. Seemed to know a lot about them as well.' She put her hand to her mouth.

'What?'

'He was asking whether we had any visitors recently. Is this connected with Angelique and Bella?'

'Did you say anything?'

'Of course not, but…'

'Out with it, Jules.'

'I think I may have glanced at the hangar when he asked me about them.'

Crap. Angelique would be over there by now. I rushed to the screen door, Jules right behind me.

I peered out but couldn't see anyone or anything suspicious. But something still felt wrong. Real wrong.

We crept across the field, keeping low and using the taller meadow grass as cover. A small dust devil – a twister in miniature – danced across the baked ground in front of the hangar doors.

Jules let out a stifled shriek and pointed at Mom laying face down in the grass.

We rushed to her. I turned her over and cradled her in my arms.

'Mom, are you okay?'

Her eyes blinked and she winced as she opened them. 'I came out here to make sure that the hangar was closed up in case that stranger went snooping, but he must have snuck up behind me and hit me.' She touched the back of her head and flinched.

'You sure you're okay?'

'I've got a bad headache, but I'll live. I thought that guy might have something to do with our visitors when he started asking too many questions. All very casual, but it was obvious he was looking for them.'

I scanned around us. 'Where's Angelique—?'

Athena's song rushed into me, urgent, her warning killing the question. The view shifted and I was inside the hangar. Angelique lay sprawled on the ground and the spy stood over her.

Dead? I saw her back rising and falling. Breathing. Not dead but unconscious. The man stooped down and bound her hands.

The image shimmered and I was back in the meadow with Jules shaking me. Mom watched, chewing her lip.

'Dom, you okay? You zoned on us out for a minute there.'

I nodded. 'That man also knocked Angelique out.'

'How can you know—' Jules pointed. 'Oh god.'

The spy had appeared at the hanger doorway with Angelique slung over his shoulder like a sack of flour. We ducked down into the tall grass with Mom.

'I've got to stop him,' I said.

'How?' Mom asked.

'Leave that to me.' I gripped Jules arm. 'If something goes wrong, you take Mom in the Mustang and don't stop till you get back to your dad's. You tell Bella everything you've seen.'

Jules swallowed. 'You've got it.'

Mom gripped my arm. 'Dom, there's no way I'm going to let you do this.'

'I have to, Mom, for Angelique's sake.'

She bit her lip, but nodded.

I gave Mom a quick hug and nodded to Jules, her eyes wild with worry.

Keeping low, I tracked the man as he walked back towards his bike with bounding strides, as if Angelique weighed nothing. He was strong. Real strong. If the way the scout had kicked my ass was anything to go by, I wasn't sure I could take this guy in a fair fight. Passing a rock buried into the ground I pried it out with my fingers. I needed to even the odds a little.

The man dropped Angelique onto the bike and tied her hands to the upright chopper seat. He still had his back to me. I cradled the rock in my hand as he slung his leg over and started the bike up with a soft whine. The long grass petered out at the edge of the lot. No cover between us. The bike hissed as he turned the throttle, steam vapour drifting from small round vents. The engine hummed with a quiet note, like someone softly playing a harmonica.

Out of time.

I sprinted the twenty yards towards him, raising the rock above my head. My shadow ran ahead of me and fell across the bike. The spy spotted it and started to turn.

I brought the rock down hard and it glanced off his helmet, but my momentum sent us crashing off the bike together. I locked my arms around him, trying to hold him as we landed.

But the man was already moving, starting to react, reaching for something holstered in his jacket. On top of him, I slammed his hand away and a silver gun skittered across the floor.

Running footsteps. Jules grabbed the weapon and pointed it at the man. 'Okay, bud, let's cool this down.'

The man slackened beneath me, eyes blinking through the goggles. He slowly nodded.

'Think he gets the message,' I said, getting to my feet. 'What happened to running away with Mom?'

'We had a better idea,' Jules said.

'Thank god!' Relief surged through me and I smiled.

Angelique murmured. A ribbon of blood trickled down the side of her head from a gash where she'd been struck. I crossed to her and started to undo the rope tying her to the bike seat.

'You okay?'

Her eyes opened and she nodded. 'He jumped me.'

'And I just returned the favour for you and Mom,' I replied.

'Stop him,' Angelique shouted.

I spun back towards the spy. He had opened a bracelet on his wrist, grabbed something from it; his hand glided towards his mouth.

'Don't move,' Jules said, raising the gun and aiming it straight at his head.

The man looked at her and smiled. I saw the red pill between his teeth. I was too far away to stop him. He clenched his jaw. At once crackling flames swept from his head like a blossoming flower. His smile twisted and his body started to crumble inwards like the air was being sucked out of him. The tongues of fire died away until the only thing left was a pile of glowing ash.

The gun tumbled from Jules' hand, her expression horrified.

Angelique winced as she got off the bike. 'A molecular suicide pill – it destroys the bonds between the atoms. Every spy is issued with one in case they get captured.'

Jules dropped to her knees and wrapped her arms around herself.

Guilt rushed through me. 'I'm so sorry, Jules.'

Angelique picked up the gun. It had a very thin barrel. 'Needle gun,' she said, turning it over in her hand. 'Can punch straight through sheet metal at a hundred yards. The preferred choice of Hades' spies.' She stuck the weapon in her belt.

'Will someone tell me what the hell is going on?' Jules said, tears splashing down her face.

I cradled my arm around her and felt her shaking. I squeezed her shoulder and she blinked at me.

A slight breeze began to blow the ash pile away.

'God, I can't believe that's all that's left of him,' Jules said.

'His choice,' Angelique said, as calmly as if this happened everyday.

Jules stared at her and I felt a surge of annoyance towards Angelique. Whatever her life story, how could she be so insensitive about another dead man?

Angelique grabbed the bike. 'We need to hide this before someone sees it.'

'You can stick it behind some hay bales stacked against the hangar,' Mom said.

We all turned to see her shuffling towards us, one hand cradling the back of her head.

Angelique gripped her lightning pendant and peered at her. 'You saw what happened?'

'Of course I did. I had a hunch that when you turned up here with your mother, it would only be a matter of time before trouble followed.'

Jules stared between all of us. 'Will someone please tell me…' Her words trailed away as her gaze tightened on Angelique's pendant. 'I thought there was something familiar about the design of that.'

I shrugged at her. 'Me too, but this isn't the time—'

Angelique waved me quiet and peered at Jules. 'You have? Where?'

Mom's mouth pinched and she looked away.

Jules drummed her finger on her lips. 'Dom, remember that time when we were small and Dad brought me over… You and I played hide and seek.'

'Yeah, but I don't see how that's relevant.'

'You will. I hid in your parent's room. Climbed into that old chest your Mom keeps the duvets in and there was a small wooden box hidden at the bottom. I had a peek inside…'

'Oh…' Mom said. A flush crept up her neck.

'You mean Mom's secret box. I know about that, but it's just filled with photos of Great Great Great Grandpa Alex. Don't know why you tried to hide them, Mom, and not put them in the album with the other family photos. They're kinda cool.'

Mom looked away. 'I had my reasons.'

Reasons? But why would she hide old photos? A memory surged into my mind and suddenly I knew exactly what Jules was getting at.

'There's a photo with Grandpa Alex wearing a medal with a lighting design similar to Angelique's, isn't there?' I said.

Jules beamed at me. 'You've nailed it.'

Mom gazed at me and pressed her hands over her mouth, as sudden tears rolled down her cheeks. 'Oh, Dom, I'm so sorry.' She held her arms out to me.

Without even thinking I stepped forwards and hugged her. She was probably in shock. 'Please don't cry, Mom, we'll make this alright somehow.'

'You don't understand, this is all my fault.'

'What do you mean?'

'You need to know the truth, Dom. You all do.'

Angelique narrowed her gaze on Mom. 'It sounds like Mama and I aren't the only ones with secrets around here. But first things first. I need Dom to do the mind link with the Eye. That spy may have got a distress signal away and if so, we need to find out if anyone heard it.'

Jules stared at her. 'Mind link? Eye? What?'

Mom just nodded, like she knew exactly what Angelique was talking about. But how could that be possible?

Jules looked at the ashes and took a shuddering breath.

I squeezed her shoulder and she gave me a broken look.

'I so didn't want to drag you into this craziness,' I said.

'It's a bit late for that,' she replied.

Angelique took hold of the bike and started pushing it towards the hangar.

Mom smeared her tears away. 'I'll see you over there, Dom. I just need to fetch something from the house.'

'Okay, Mom. But you sure you're okay?'

'Just wishing I'd told you the truth a long time ago.' She put her head down and hurried towards the house.

I watched her go. The truth? What was the big deal here? That Grandpa had a medal with a similar design to Angelique's pendant. So? A lightning logo wasn't exactly unique. But I felt something was staring me in the face and I wasn't quite connecting the dots.

'I need some answers, Dom.' Jules said. 'You owe me that much.'

'I know I do,' I replied. Jules was involved now, whatever I'd wanted.

I headed with Jules towards the oak tree. The meadow grass brushed over her long, jean-wrapped legs. At some point she had gotten taller, leaner, more athletic. How come I was only noticing that now? She had kept a real cool head when things had gone wrong as well. Should've known that really.

We sat under the leafy shade of the oak and my gaze flicked to the corner of the field and the darkness filled me again.

Jules caught my expression. 'Okay, Dom, just talk to me until you're empty. You should've have trusted me with this.'

A sudden lump filled my throat. 'Oh god, Jules, it's all been so crazy.'

'Just start at the beginning.' She patted my shoulder. 'I'm here for you, okay?'

I nodded, the lump in my throat growing into a boulder.

Chapter Sixteen
THE NET CLOSES

I'd sat with Jules under the tree telling her about the dark memories swirling around my mind: the arrow burying into the man's throat, the rattle of the death breath, his rolling red eyes... And now how another man had crumbled to dust in front of us, smiling as he'd died. All I'd wanted to do was escape the thoughts crowding my head, curl into a ball, and sleep.

But she'd kept me talking and the more I'd talked, the easier it had become. The weight I'd been carrying about lying to everyone, even if I thought it had been for their own good, had lifted off me bit by bit as I shared with her. But the mood had lightened as I'd told her about the parallel worlds. I could see my own sense of wonder about it all reflected in her eyes.

Jules leant back against the trunk after I'd finally fallen silent. 'And you're seriously considering joining them?'

'They need my Navigator ability, Jules. If I can help swing things against Hades, then surely I have to go – right?'

She let out a long sigh. 'Maybe. But you really need to think hard about this. What happened with that scout, that spy, is the war that Angelique and Bella are caught up in. Death is always hanging over them. Is that something you could cope with? Really?'

It was good question. A very good question. Whether to stay or go looped through my head for the thousandth time.

'What would you do in my situation?' I asked.

'Oh, no way. This has to be your choice. I'm not having you hold this against me for the rest of your life.'

'But every time I try to think about what to do my thoughts get all stirred up like a hornets' nest. I don't want to leave Mom alone, but…' I shrugged and gazed at the sky. Already, the whole experience of glimpsing the other worlds seemed like a dream. 'It would be so much easier if I stayed.'

'Then if that's what your instinct is telling you then maybe you should.'

I thought of the way Angelique had killed the scout. Did I really want to be like her? Beyond caring if another person died for the cause, even if she was trying to stop a ruthless enemy.

Jules twirled a piece of dry grass between her fingers. 'Look, I just want to say this. If you do want to go, I wouldn't stop you.'

'Okay…' But Mom needed my help. My internal question looped back to the start.

Mom appeared from the house, carrying her jewellery box. She spotted us under the tree and headed in our direction.

'I'm sorry, Jules, for not telling you the truth before.'

She held up her hand. 'Dom, seriously, you keep underestimating me. You're my best friend. I needed to know what you've been going through.'

I gave her a small smile. 'Thanks, I don't deserve you.'

She nudged my shoulder. 'Maybe you don't.'

Roddy's pickup approached and pulled up into our lot. Bella got out and headed towards the hangar, whilst Roddy strolled into the diner. I could guess at Bella's horror when she heard the news about the close call with the spy.

Mom reached us. 'Jules, can I have a quick word with Dom alone?'

'Of course. I'll see how Dad's got on with the engine and then see you over in the hangar.' For a moment she looked like she wanted to say something else, but she turned away and jogged towards the diner.

I felt a tug in my chest to follow her, but instead stayed to talk to Mom.

'Are you okay?' I asked.

She shook her head. 'Not really.'

'I'm sorry about heading off after the Hawks but it was something I had to do.'

Mom pulled me into her. 'I was worried sick something would happen to you.' She let out a stifled sob and tears started to wet the side of my face.

I cradled the back of her head. God, I hated this. I loved Mom and it was so hard seeing her in this mess, especially knowing I was the cause.

She pulled away and dragged her palm across her eyes. 'You're becoming more your dad's son every day.'

I nodded, but kept quiet, not trusting myself to say anything right at the moment.

'Just as irresponsible.'

I heard the Twister Diner sign creaking in the wind.

'It scares me when I think you might get hurt, and I've just been trying to protect you – do you understand?'

'I know, Mom.' I risked a glance into her eyes.

'So when you find out the truth I'm going to ask you to forgive me.'

'Forgive you? Surely it's the other way around?' It sounded like she'd something she badly needed to get off her chest with me.

Mom placed her hand on the side of my face. 'It really isn't. All I'm saying is don't act on impulse in future. You're better than that.'

'I'll do my best, Mom.'

'Good, we understand each other then.'

There was a familiar squeal of brakes and I pulled away to see the Battle Wagon, followed by the rest of the Sky Hawks' vehicles, rolling up into the lot. Roddy and Jules walked out of the diner to meet them.

I gave Mom a small smile, trying to lighten the mood. 'Customers.'

She shrugged. 'It'll have to be more barbeque, I'm afraid.'

'I don't think they'll mind, especially if you smother some steaks in your peppercorn sauce.'

'Oh, Cherie used to love that. Harry was always after my secret recipe.' She sighed. 'You know I'm actually beginning to enjoy having them around, even if them being here seems to make my son lose his head.'

I gave her a long look. Sounded like I'd been forgiven, but I also had a hunch that it had a lot do with what she'd been keeping from me.

Mom smoothed her apron down. 'I'll deal with the Hawks and then join you to tell you everything.'

'Good. And, Mom…'

'I know you do.' She kissed me on the cheek.

I set off at a sprint towards the hangar. What was happening with the *Hyperion*? Would it be arriving in our skies any moment?

When I entered the gondola, Bella was holding a device to Angelique's head that spread a faint golden glow across it. When Bella removed her hand I realised the wound on the side of Angelique's head had vanished.

'But how?' I asked staring at them.

Bella showed me the amber stone she was holding. An orange glow faded within it. 'I was a healer at our major hospital and I'm trained in using Chi stones. They can directly manipulate human cells and speed up the body's natural healing process.'

'Is that how you sorted out your ankle so quickly?' I asked.

'I had to insist she did it,' Angelique said.

'Like most doctors I'm afraid I'm not very good at looking after myself,' Bella replied.

Angelique raised her eyebrows at me. 'So how does my head look, Dom?' She presented her perfect profile to me for inspection.

'Fine. But you were lucky that spy didn't kill you on sight.'

'He was probably going to try to extract information by torturing me – not that that would have got him very far. We're trained to withstand a lot of pain.' She shrugged.

This all seemed trivial to her, unlike for Jules and myself. Irritation tightened inside me.

'Let's get down to work and see if we've been detected,' she said.

...

Angelique and I squatted before the open Eye, with Jules and Bella watching. Jets of steam hissed from the open dome and a red glowing sphere bathed the cabin in light.

I rubbed my scalp where Bella had used the Chi stone. The skin still tingled there but the injury had vanished, just like Angelique's.

Jules interlocked her hands around the back of her head, staring at the glass planets. 'So let me get this right, Dom, *Athena* talks to you telepathically?'

'I know it sounds out there, but yes, she does,' I replied.

'Okay, the thing I don't get is how come you have this ability at all?'

Bella shook her head. 'That doesn't make any sense to me either. In all the history of my people we've never found the Navigator gene in humans of any other world.'

Angelique tilted her head to one side, eyeing me like I was something in a museum display cabinet. 'Whatever the explanation is, right now we need to use that gift.' She placed her hand on the Eye. 'Come on, Dom, let's see if *Athena* can get a lock on the *Hyperion* via your memory.'

I nodded and placed my hand next to hers. At once the whale song that had been humming in the back of my mind sharpened into individual notes. I felt her voice as a physical sensation, almost like water running through my head. The red-lit glass sphere spun faster on its brass rod and the air swirled as the cabin around me became shadowy.

A blurred picture started to form in my mind, a grainy abstract image of lights and darks. I could just make out the shape – a long dark oval set against a wavering backdrop of stars. A vast twister had begun to form around it.

I scrunched my eyes and the cabin became solid again.

'What did you see?' Bella asked.

'The *Hyperion*, I think.'

'You really saw something?' Jules asked, eyes wide.

Angelique put her finger to her lips.

Jules scowled at her.

A whirring came from beneath the floor and the glass sphere started to lower to the next level.

'Jump commencement confirmed,' Bella said.

Angelique twisted her lightning necklace between her fingers. 'Oh no, they must have picked up the spy's broadcast.' She pointed to a clear glass sphere, right at the bottom of the Eye. 'That's *Athena*'s position in trans-dimensional space. With each successive jump the *Hyperion* is getting closer, and when the red sphere reaches the bottom level...'

'We're out of time?' I asked.

She gave a sharp nod.

'How long have we got left?'

'Around forty-eight hours,' Bella said.

'But the repairs, you won't have finished the canopy by then will you?' Jules said.

Angelique shook her head. 'Not with just Mama and myself working on it.'

'You can obviously count me in,' I said.

Jules sat upright. 'And I'll help in any way I can.'

Angelique gave us both a smile, a real smile that reached her eyes. 'We might just have a chance then.'

'And I will help with anything else – it's the least I can do,' Mom said.

We turned to see her standing in the doorway, cradling her jewellery box.

Bella gazed at Mom, eyes full of questions. 'Angelique tells me that your great grandfather had a medal with a similar design to Angelique's?'

Mom settled into one of the cockpit seats. 'Not just similar, it's exactly the same.' She laid the box on her lap.

My mind scrambled, trying to make sense of what Mom had just said. 'How can that even be possible?' I asked. 'He found it somewhere?'

Bella sat next to Mom. 'You had better tell us everything, Sue.'

'Oh, I intend to. Dom needs to hear this, you all do.'

Jules shot me a 'what the hell' look.

Mom began to undo the catch on the jewellery box. Whatever she was about to tell us had everything to do with the contents of that box. I held my breath as she opened it.

Chapter Seventeen
ANCESTOR

Mom took out a bound bundle of old brown photos that had faded around the edges. She gazed out through the hangar doors towards the horizon for a moment, eyes tight. She looked afraid, real afraid. But why?

She looked back at me and her gaze felt like falling into a parallel world, one I'd never seen before. In that moment everyone and everything else fell away and there was just the two of us.

'The first thing you need to understand, Dom, is that I promised your dad I wouldn't tell you anything until you were eighteen, old enough to make your own decisions,' she said.

'Dad knew something about this too?'

She nodded. 'Have you ever wondered why Shaun was so obsessed with every twister that appeared? About why our family has always chosen to live right in the middle of tornado alley?'

My mind clung to the world and the people in my life I knew. 'Because he wanted to make a difference by helping to improve forecasts for them?'

She gave me a fleeting smile. 'That's part of it, but there's an even bigger reason, a secret that's been handed down from generation to generation in the family… From the moment Grandpa Alex arrived in this world.'

The air caught in my throat. I heard Jules gasp and became aware of the other people with us. A tingle spread up my spine. 'You're saying he was actually a…' I took a deep breath. 'Are you saying he was a Cloud Rider?'

'I am.'

Excitement flooded through me. Angelique and Bella stared at her.

It all fitted, and like morning mist burning off our fields, everything began to slot into place in my head. 'That's why I've got the Navigator DNA marker.'

Jules clapped her hands together. 'Oh, Dom, of course.'

Mom ran her fingers over the wooden leaf design covering her box. 'He told us one day a ship would sense that gene and come here to track his descendant down. That's why Dad kept a look out for every twister.'

Angelique blinked. '*Athena* came for you, Dom, and I never knew.'

Athena's song swelled in my mind, filled with joy. She'd come for me – for me – across countless dimensions. I felt light-headed just thinking about it.

Bella stared at Mom. 'So you knew we were Cloud Riders when we arrived?'

'Yes.' Mom spoke so quietly it was almost a whisper.

'So why all the attitude at first towards them, Mom?' I asked.

'Because I thought they'd realise you were a Navigator, Dom. But when they just seemed intent on passing through, I relaxed.'

'That doesn't make sense. Why would you be worried about that? I may be missing something, but from where I stand this has to be one of the coolest things I've ever heard. I have a gift, a honest to god gift, that makes me pretty unique.'

Jules crossed to Mom and wrapped an arm around her. 'Isn't it obvious, Dom?'

'Not to me.'

Mom clenched the photos so hard that her knuckles stood out. 'When Shaun lost his life, I was worried you would take over his role and that one day... ' She hung her head. 'I was worried about you leaving.'

Leaving... So she'd guessed what I'd been thinking. Of course she did. She was Mom. I kept quiet and stared at the floor.

'Tell me if Bella and Angelique offered you a berth on *Athena* right now, you wouldn't be off with them like a shot?'

I met her gaze, opened my mouth to tell her why she was wrong, that I couldn't leave her to fend for herself – but nothing came. Why the hesitation?

Was Mom right to think that I was basically an adventure junkie who would leave her behind as soon as I got a ticket out of here?

Guilt squirmed through me as Angelique and Bella exchanged a silent look. Jules fiddled with her fingernails, face drawn. Why wasn't she rushing to my defence? Because she knew the truth, just like I did?

Mom lifted her head and her eyes had filled with tears again. 'It's not just that, Dom, and goodness knows I can understand why you'd want to leave. Things have been so hard here since we lost your dad. But you see the thing you don't know is that your Great Great Grandpa tasked his descendants to complete his life's work.'

'Just who is this Cloud Rider?' Bella said, almost to herself. Her gaze fixed on the photos in Mom's hand. 'Are those photos of this Alex?'

Mom nodded.

'I'd like to see them,' she said.

Mom's fingers trembled as she handed them to her. We peered over Bella's shoulder as she examined them.

The photo on top was of a distant shot of Grandpa Alex in front of our house, which was only half constructed. Dad had told me he'd built it with his bare hands. Bella started flicking through the rest.

There was a shot of an old fashioned plane. It looked more like a kite than an aeroplane, with fabric panels, wooden poles and hundreds of wires holding it all together.

'He was one of the early pioneers in flight,' Mom said to Bella.

'No wonder if he was a Cloud Rider,' Angelique said. 'Flying would have been his whole life.'

Bella reached the last photo. A close-up of Alex standing in front of his plane, flying goggles pushed up to the top his head, wide smile framed by a grey beard. I peered at the medal pinned to his pocket with the lightning design that had snagged Jules' memory, and mine.

I noticed Angelique's and Bella's expressions had frozen.

'By the gods, it can't be,' Angelique said.

'What?' I asked.

'Not what, but who,' Bella replied. 'As I live and breathe sky air, that's the lost King.'

My mind tumbled. 'Are you trying to tell me my Grandpa Alex Taylor was Cloud Riders' royalty?'

'His full title and real name was actually King Alexander Galson,' Bella said.

Jules gawped at her. 'You're saying Dom and Angelique are related?'

Bella shook her head. 'King Alexander was the last of his bloodline in our world, but I suppose they are distant relatives.'

Angelique's gaze had fixed on me, her expression unreadable. Even though she hadn't said anything, I could feel that things had changed between us and she was seeing me in a new light.

In my head I tried to get hold of the new universe I now occupied. 'But why did Grandpa Alex come here to our Earth in the first place, and what's this about him being your lost King?' I asked.

'King Alexander, according to Cloud Riders' history, was searching for this mythical ship called *Titan*,' Bella said.

'What sort of mythical ship?' Jules asked.

'According to the folklore among our ships' programmers, it was the first AI to be born and the ancestor of all ships alive today. Like human DNA, AIs share common data strands in their code that can be traced back to a single ancestor.'

'This ship, *Titan*?' Jules asked.

'Just so,' Bella replied. 'Of course his original AI code has evolved with countless new sub-routines, but basically *Titan*'s code strings can be found in any of our ships' AIs, if you dig deep enough. You will even find them on Hades' vessels.'

'Okay, I can see that's kinda interesting in a geeky way, but why was it important enough to make Alex go search for it?' I asked.

'Alexander was quite a secretive man and also something of an amateur scientist. He had one of the royal stable blocks converted into a laboratory.'

'But I'm still not seeing the "why"' Jules said.

'According to my father, King Alexander believed the answer to achieving sustainable peace lay in finding *Titan*,' Angelique said.

'But how would finding a ship help with that?' I asked.

Angelique frowned. 'I wish I knew.'

'I might be able to answer at least part of that,' Mom said. 'Alex said that any descendant who shared his bloodline was likely to have the Navigator gene. But more importantly that they might be a Ship Whisperer too.'

'A what?' Bella asked.

'Alex was trying to develop the ability to telepathically talk to his ship,' Mom said.

'All Navigators can communicate with their ships like that,' Angelique said.

'No, I mean *talk* to them.'

Angelique stared at her. 'You mean like Dom is able to hear *Athena* speak to him with words sometimes?'

'You can?' Mom said.

I nodded. 'Thought I was hearing things at first.'

'So it's all come true,' Mom said. 'Shaun hoped that one day he'd develop the ability, but it turns out that you've been given this gift. You are the Ship Whisperer, Dom.'

'But why me?'

Angelique peered at me. 'I've never heard of anyone with this ability before among my people.'

'That's because Alex had been experimenting on himself, altering his own DNA so he could form a deeper link with ship AIs,' Mom said.

Any fog lingering in my head blew away and everything I thought I knew shifted. I was descended from a Cloud Rider and my parents had known all about it. Till now, Mom had been a woman who'd run a diner, but now I was starting to discover she was so much more – and so was I.

'And that's why Dom can hear *Athena*, and Angelique can't?' Jules asked. I caught the sideways look she shot Angelique like she was aiming to score points.

'It would seem to be so,' Mom said.

But I could see thoughts flickering behind Angelique's eyes. I could tell she wasn't seeing me as a rival, but as somebody with a gift that might prove useful to her.

'Okay, this is all seriously blowing my mind, but why did Alex end up on this world?'

Jules asked.

'I think I can answer part of that,' Bella said. 'He had been searching for *Titan* for some time. As a king he didn't want to attract too much attention, so was travelling undercover in a small clipper ship called *Storm Wind*. The last known contact with him was just before a Vortex jump. Alexander entered the wormhole and never emerged on the other side. We believe his craft was probably attacked by the Shade during the jump.'

'The Shade?' I asked.

'Creatures who feed on energy, and live in the dimensions between realities,' Angelique said. 'His ship was most likely damaged during a run-in with them. He must have been marooned here, otherwise he would have attempted to get back home.'

'That's right,' Mom said. 'He crash landed close to this very spot and ended up marrying Dom's Great Great Great Grandma.'

She turned the box over on its side and pressed one of the lacquered fern leafs. Something clicked.

'What are you doing?' I asked.

'This is a puzzle box and if I do this…' Mom slid the second leaf on the base to reveal a rectangular hole. She tipped the box and a velvet bag slid into her hand. She handed it to me. 'Dad would want you to have this on your eighteenth birthday, but I think now's more appropriate.'

I opened the bag and took out the lightning medal I'd seen in the photo.

'It's *exactly* the same as yours, Angelique.' And it was. The same identical stab of lightning through a spiral. No, not a spiral, a twister! Why hadn't I realised that before?

Angelique nodded and leaned in closer to inspect the medal. 'I thought so.'

'What?' I asked.

She smiled. 'Your mother's box isn't the only thing with a secret compartment. If I do this…' Her fingers probed the sides. The medal sprang open to reveal a crystal inside.

Mom blinked. 'I never knew that was there.'

'You weren't meant to,' Angelique replied. 'Only another Cloud Rider would realise what this was.'

I peered closer. There was a faint glow coming from inside the gem. 'Is that what I think it is?'

Bella nodded. 'It's a Psuche gem – I expect it's the AI core from *Storm Wind*.'

'But why has it been put in the medal?' Jules asked.

'Sometimes if a ship itself is badly damaged, a Navigator uses a pendant like this to hold a stone until it can be transferred to a new vessel,' Angelique said. 'By keeping the Psuche gem close to them when it's not powered by a ship, it helps to maintain the link with the Navigator.'

I realised *Athena*'s constant ship-song hum had become quieter for a moment. A tingling sensation spread through my mind.

'Hold me,' a man's voice said.

I looked around me. 'Who said that?'

Angelique raised her eyebrows at me. 'Who said what?'

Mom and Jules shook their heads.

'I could have sworn—'

'Hold me in your hand,' the man's voice said. Then ship-song, so faint that I'd almost missed it, grew in my mind. But its tone was deeper than *Athena*'s. *Storm Wind*'s voice?

I stared at the pendant. 'I think this Psuche gem just spoke to me.'

'It did what?' Angelique gripped her pendant. 'You mean in the same way that you heard the name *Hyperion* through your whisperer ability?'

'I guess so.'

'What did he say?'

'He wants me to hold it.'

Her gaze widened. 'Here, you better take him and let's see what happens.'

Heart racing, I reached out. My fingers touched the warm surface of the crystal and the familiar surge of energy rushed through me. A man's face filled my mind. He was lying in bed, eyes heavily lined. Old, real old.

'This is a message recorded by me, Alex Taylor, or perhaps I should say my true birth name, Alexander Galson…'

Someone shook me. I opened my eyes into Angelique's.

'Dom?'

'I'm getting this sort of recorded message broadcast by the gem and it's playing back inside my head. It's from Alex.'

'Holy crap!' Jules said.

Mom clasped her hands together. 'Oh, how I wish Shaun was here to share this.'

So did I. More than anything. I closed my eyes again and concentrated.

'I have left this message in the hope that one day someone is able to make use of the information contained in this Psuche gem from my ship, Storm Wind. If you are hearing me speak to you, it means that you too have the gift.' Alex's voice began to fade.

'Dom, I don't know if this means anything, but the gem is dimming,' Jules said.

'It running out of power.' Bella replied. 'That gem must be over a hundred years old.

I'm surprised the radioactive charge lasted that long.'

I dropped it onto the bunk like it was hot coal. 'Radioactive?'

'Don't worry, the unique crystalline structure of Psuche gems keeps it contained. You could wave a geiger counter over this and it wouldn't register anything,' Angelique said.

I picked it up again and at once the voice continued in my head, but it was now so quiet I could barely hear it:

'I was searching for the ship Titan *and I finally discovered its whereabouts. Unfortunately my ship was attacked by a gigantic flock of shadow crows. I have never seen the foul creatures gathered in such numbers and at least a thousand attacked my ship. Storm Wind's systems were badly damaged, including the Valve Voice set, and I was unable to send a distress call. I crash landed on Earth DZL2351. Cut off from my own people I had no other choice but to accept my fate.'*

'It was the Shade attack that crippled his ship – a thousand of them,' I whispered.

'Good gods,' Angelique replied.

'Stranded here, I was unable to fulfil my quest, but before I die I will bequeath the details of where I believe Titan to be hidden. I leave this Psuche gem in the hope that one day, my descendant will develop the gift and hear this message to complete what I was unable to do – to find Titan and halt the ignorance that threatens to tear my own Earth apart.'

By gift he had to mean this Ship Whisper ability. But how could that help anything?

'Take a ship and you will find Titan hidden in…'

My heart gripped as I waited for the location. The silence stretched on.

'Dom, the light in the gem's gone out,' Jules said.

I opened my eyes to see the darkened crystal.

'Damnit, Alex was about to tell me the whereabouts of *Titan*.'

I shook the pendant like it was a dead flashlight, hoping it might spark back into life.

Nothing happened.

Angelique sucked air through her teeth. 'Perhaps there's still a way to find out the answer.'

'How?' I asked.

'I think I may have a solution, but I will need to consider the logistics of the operation first.'

That had a risky ring to it. But whatever Angelique's plan turned out to be, if it got it working again, it would be cool with me.

'First things first,' Bella said. 'The priority is to repair the airship's gas envelope.'

'Sewing, right?' Jules asked.

Bella nodded.

'Now that's something we can all help you with,' Mom said.

I gazed into the *Hyperion*'s red globe glowing in the Eye and pictured the craft it represented. Within forty-eight hours it would arrive here, and then what? If *Athena* wasn't on her way by then, I didn't want to think about the consequences. And now the other thing I had to work out was whether I'd be onboard her or not? Big Questions, the answers to which would change the rest of my life.

I caught Mom watching me and knew she was thinking the same. I pushed the thought away. My head was already crammed with enough stuff to keep me awake for a whole year, let alone dealing with my own personal guilt trip.

I stood. 'Let's get those repairs going before we run out of time.'

Chapter Eighteen
REPAIRS

The growing darkness wrapped around the hangar. I wiped a bead of sweat from the end of my nose. My fingers ached from gripping the needle for hours. As the afternoon had worn on, the dance of needles had grown faster, the dipping of heads lower, everyone concentrating on getting the job done as quickly as possible.

We'd watched three more jumps in the Eye as the Hades' ship drew closer to our dimension. Each jump had turned like a key in my chest and wound me tighter. I didn't need to be a mind reader to see that everyone else could also feel the shadow of the enemy ship too. There'd be no stopping for sleep tonight.

Smoke hung inside the hangar, drifting up from the rubber solution Angelique was using to paint and seal the seams. Bella carried a lantern, a ball of light in the foundry gloom, and moved over the canvas to inspect our handiwork.

The warmth of *Storm Wind*'s Psuche gem ebbed through the metal of the Cloud Rider medal. Mom had found me a length of leather cord and it now hung around my neck under my shirt. No way I was letting it out of my sight.

I swallowed a large mouthful of coke and felt the caffeine knock back the fatigue aching throughout my body.

Bella walked across to me and gazed at my stitching. 'You're doing a good job, Dom.'

'Mom is a great sewing teacher,' I replied.

Mom gave me a smile as she knotted the end of her thread.

'You've all been real assets,' Bella said. 'Out of the sixteen damaged panels we're down to the last seven.'

Some of the tension I'd been carrying let go. 'So we're on track?'

'It's looking that way, but you all seem exhausted,' Bella said. 'Everyone should have a brief break and get something to eat before we push on through the night.'

Jules and I exchanged looks. Her pale face looked as tired as I felt.

'Come on,' Jules said, grabbing my hand and pulling me to my feet.

'Tell the others I'll be over in a moment to check the barbecue,' Mom said.

'And I'll finish painting this seam and join you over there,' Angelique said.

'I got the impression you were trying to keep a low profile?' I replied.

A smile flickered across Angelique's face. 'I think we're past that point don't you? In less than two days it's all going to become a moot point.'

I nodded, but avoided her eyes. Angelique, if her careless attitude towards life was anything to go by, was starting to leave a bitter taste in my mouth. Did I want to end up like her?

Outside, framed against the sunset afterglow over the cornfields, I could see the Hawks chatting with Roddy, and drinking beer by the diner. In the middle of the gathering, Harry, Cherie and Roddy clustered around the smoker, flapping hands, blowing hard and nursing the fire at its base. Harry tipped his head back for an extra big blow and a swarm of sparks swirled over their heads like fireflies.

My gaze skated over the corner of the field where we'd buried the scout and I shuddered. Jules was right. That was the reality of Angelique and Bella's life.

Jules stopped. 'You alright?'

'Just thinking.'

She looked at me. 'You've been put in an impossible situation, haven't you?'

I shoved my hands into my pockets and shrugged.

'But it must have been amazing, glimpsing those other worlds?'

That was the one hook that still snared me. 'I wish you could have been there, Jules, seen what I've seen. Knowing they're right here on top of us is mind-blowing and all I want to do is explore them.'

'And I wish I could explore them with you, one day.'

'Really? But I thought you were wedded to Oklahoma for life.'

'Yeah, and I've always wanted to be a mechanic, carry on the family business. And Dad's still in a mess over Mom dying, needs me around a while longer.'

A sadness filled me, remembering how Jules had taken over her mom's role. Roddy had been like a zombie for the first six months, but Jules had stuck at it, doing everything she could: cooking meals, doing the housework, giving him the space to slowly come back to life.

'You've been a hero to your dad, Jules. But what about my mom? What will she do if I go?'

Jules gave me a sad smile. 'At first she might not want you to bail on her, but deep down, she'll understand if that's what you felt you really had to do.'

'You think?'

'I know. But I'm not saying you have to go, either. You still have to work out what you want, Dom.'

'Yeah, I know.' No one else could make this decision for me. Not even Jules.

'Good. We get each other, then?'

I nodded and breathed the world in, feeling my head clearing a little bit. The smell of night dew drifting in through the crack in the door mingled with her scent. Jules had always been there for me, through every twist and turn of my life. The one person I could lean on. She really was amazing.

I gazed at her. 'You're so my best friend,' I said. And I meant it. If anything, Jules being so kind made it even harder to think about going.

'And you're mine.' Her smiled deepened into her dimpled one.

God, that smile. 'Glad we have that all sorted.'

'Come on.' She pulled me towards the barbecue.

...

The impromptu party was in full swing. The radio from Harry's motorhome blared out a stream of rock anthems.

It was the way that the Hawks loved to wind down after a chase, successful or not.

Jules spat out the mouthful of steak she'd been chewing seemingly forever and pushed her plate aside.

'Still not hungry?' I said.

She shrugged. 'Just keep getting flash backs to what happened to that spy.'

My gaze snagged again on the scout's grave. 'Yeah, I know what you mean.'

Angelique, dancing with one of the younger Hawks, his hands on her waist, whirled past. She'd made quite an impression on the group, but when anyone started to ask where she was from she had quickly turned the subject back to the talk of twisters. However, she'd also been giving Jules and me furtive glances as we sat talking together for most of the evening. What was that all about?

The music faded away and Angelique kissed her dancing partner on the cheek. She looked my way and wandered over, winding her fingers through her hair.

'Oh, think you're up,' Jules said. 'I'm off for another coke. Fancy one?'

'No, I'm good.'

'Have fun.' She raised her eyebrows at me and wandered over to join Roddy, Mom and Cherie, all sat on a table piled high with cans.

'So when are you going to ask me to dance?' Angelique asked.

I so wasn't in the mood. 'I think I'll pass.'

'But it's you I've been waiting to dance with.'

I noticed the man she'd been with chatting to the others and watching her. 'Sure you're not short of offers.' I heard an edge creeping into my voice.

Angelique crouched in front of me. 'Have I upset you, Dom?'

I nodded towards the corner of the field.

'Oh, I see.' She shrugged.

'And today was just another day at the office, huh?'

'Dom, it's not like that. As awful as it is, it's war and in wars people get killed.'

'It might be alright for you, but I can't see me being able to do what you did today,

anytime soon.'

She sighed. 'Okay, look. Dancing is exactly what you need.' She took my hand and pulled me to my feet. I reluctantly followed her to the middle of the yard.

The last song faded into one with a softer beat.

Angelique took my hands and placed them on her hips. Wrapping her arms around me, she began to sway me in time to the music. 'So, you've been talking to Julia about whether you should come with us?' she whispered.

'Yeah...'

'And I guess she's been persuading you to stay?'

'No, not at all. Just told me I had to make up my own mind.'

'Oh good...'

This all felt unreal. I tried to focus my thoughts. 'Shouldn't we be getting back to the repairs?'

'Just a moment longer, please.'

The warmth of her body touching mine started to release the tightness inside me. Her face was so close that I could see the flecks in her green irises glowing in the lantern light. She leaned her head into my shoulder, exposing the curve of her neck, her hair caressing my face. My pulse began to match the drumming of her heart against my chest.

The seconds slipped into minutes. With a start I realised the last notes of the ballad had begun fading. An electric guitar heralded a new song and the world rushed back in.

Angelique's hands slid off my back and she stepped away. My body felt like part of it was missing. What had just happened between us?

She smiled at me. 'Look, Dom, I'm sorry about earlier. I was being insensitive. You must be traumatised by what happened?'

'I'm not sure I'll ever be able to sleep again without seeing those scout's dead eyes in my head.'

'It will fade over time.' She sighed. 'And what you said about me – I hate to admit it but maybe you're right. It's just hard not to be like that when so many people I've cared about have been killed.' For the first time that day her eyes softened. 'I'm sorry, Dom.' She squeezed my shoulder.

I saw Mom watching us, eyes thoughtful. I looked around at the place that had been my home for as long as I could remember. The place where I'd taken my first steps; the fields over which I'd had my first flight with my dad...

My gaze skimmed back to the hidden grave and my stomach flipped.

Was anything really worth that price?

It wasn't. It couldn't be, not for me. Unlike Angelique, I wasn't trained for this, certainly couldn't ever see myself as emotionally switched off as she was. I closed my eyes, but faces filled my mind: Mom, the Hawks, Roddy, but most of all, Jules. I saw her dimpled smile.

A stone filled my gut.

'Dom?' Angelique repeated, giving me an encouraging smile.

I just couldn't. I couldn't leave Mom alone. She needed me. And how could I leave Jules? Someone had to protect them in case Hades made an appearance again.

'You okay?' Angelique asked, peering into my face.

My thoughts fell together, like leaves settling after a storm. At last I knew what I wanted to do, what was right for me. There were bigger, more important things in life than being a Cloud Rider, even it was in a noble cause and offered the chance of adventure.

She sighed. 'You're thinking about not coming, aren't you?'

'I need to be here for Mom, for Jules – it's home, you know?'

She tried to smile but her mouth curled down. 'We better get back to work.' She hurried away back towards the hangar.

Jules wandered over. 'Everything okay?'

'I just told Angelique I'm going to stay.'

Jules suddenly looked on the edge of tears, but a smile lit her face. 'You're sure, Dom?'

I looked at her and I'd never been surer of anything in my life. 'Yeah, I really am, Jules.' I nudged her. 'Come on, let's go and help get *Athena* flying again.'

She beamed at me, eyes shining. 'You've got it.'

We set off back towards the hangar. Overhead, the brightest stars had begun to appear, faint pinpricks of light against the darkening blue. This was my home, my world, and where I belonged.

Chapter Nineteen
FLYING LESSON

The night had crept towards dawn and I felt a certain satisfaction examining my seam, sporting its neat line of stitches. However, in the same time it had taken me to repair one rip, Mom, Jules, Angelique and Bella had finished three each. But with our combined efforts, a whole third of the gas envelope had now been repaired. At Angelique's suggestion, the others had taken a break and gone back to the house to catch up on some sleep. In a few hours they'd be back so that we could do the same.

The first birds started chorusing out over the clicking of the cicadas. Angelique emerged from the cabin where she's been checking *Hyperion*'s progress and looked towards the gap in the hangar doors where the dark sky was fading to slate grey.

'I think it's time for a break,' she said.

I tied off a stitch and stretched my fingers, which had cramped around the needle.

'Shouldn't we keep going till the others come back?'

'Actually there's no real need now as we've made such good progress. We'll be long gone before Hades get here.'

'That's fantastic news.' I stifled a yawn. 'I could do with some more coke, but we're all out of cans.'

'I had something more exhilarating in mind to wake myself up.'

'Such as?'

'Whilst everybody is still asleep, I'm going to take the scout balloon for a little test flight.'

'You're what? That sounds dangerous.'

'Not for me, I'm an experienced pilot. And anyway, I've been stuck on the ground for too long – I need to breathe some sky air.'

I looked at the ultralight parked up at the other end of the hangar and remembered how flying with Dad had been the best feeling – complete freedom. 'I guess I know what you mean.'

'Then you'll help me prepare the balloon?'

'If you're sure?'

'I am.' Angelique crossed to the tarp and pulled it back, revealing the blood-red folds of the balloon's fabric.

...

The scout balloon hovered in the grey twilight before dawn like a ruby jellyfish, its burner casting a blue pool against the muted landscape. Angelique emerged from the hangar, strapping the wrist control onto her arm. Shadows danced across the hangar's wall in time to the movement of the flame, its roar drowning out the background chatter of the cicadas. I glanced towards the motorhomes and house, but so far nobody seemed to have been disturbed by the sound.

Angelique stepped forward, tumbling blonde hair lit up by the burner like frozen flames in the cold light. She clipped her harness onto the suspended engine pack.

'I'm really looking forward to trying her out. I haven't flown a small ship like this for years.' She pulled up the zipper of her leather flying suit.

'You're sure this is a good idea?'

'It makes sense to give it a test flight to check everything's okay, in case we need it one day.'

'But what if there's a problem?'

'There won't be.'

I chewed my lip. 'I've got a real bad feeling about this.'

'If you're going to insist on worrying so much, you can double-check my harness is secure.' Angelique pulled on her long gloves.

'You got it.'

It took several minutes to check over every buckle and karabiner – twice. The whole time, the burner shot a steady blue jet into the balloon, and by the end my t-shirt was soaked with sweat.

Adjusting her thick suit, beads of moisture ran down Angelique's forehead.

'How the hell can you stand this heat, wearing all that?' I asked.

'Trust me, you have to. As soon as you get to any real altitude, even with the burner at full blast, it's freezing up there.'

I remembered how Dad had always got me to dress up warm when flying with him. 'Of course.'

'And there's something rather special about this particular outfit,' Angelique said.

'Such as?'

'Oh, you'll see for yourself in a moment.'

I gave the harness an extra tug across her shoulders. 'I think you're good to go.'

She smiled. 'Could you be any more thorough?'

I shrugged, but a smile spread across my face.

Angelique nodded towards a shining brass telescope on the ground. 'You can use my spyglass to track me.'

'Just how high are you planning on going, exactly?' I asked, passing her the visored helmet, which was made from incredibly light silver metal.

She scooped her hair back and slid the helmet on. 'No idea.' Her eyes, visible through the round semi-opaque amber goggles, gleamed at me. 'Okay, stand clear.'

I stepped away.

Angelique pressed a button on the wristband. The engine spluttered and with a roar the propeller span into a blur. She slid a switch forward on the bracelet and the prop screamed faster, whipping the grass up and making her stagger forward a few feet. She moved the control back and the prop slowed to a steady whine.

'Everything okay?' I shouted over the growl of the engine.

Angelique gave me a thumbs-up and reached for the lever connected to the burner above her head. She yanked it down and a huge gout of blue flame blazed up into the balloon. The canopy swelled and the vessel rose into the sky.

She became a shrinking dot fast and I craned my neck to track her. The throaty roar of the burner and the burble of the engine fell quiet. For a moment all I could hear was birdsong and then, far above, the whine of the prop started up again.

Pilot and balloon sped forward across the sky and zoomed towards me in a banking dive. Another jet of flame billowed from the burner and over the howl of the engine I heard Angelique whoop. My heart soared with her.

I wrapped my arms around my sides, watching her fly like a swooping hawk.

Angelique kept on climbing in a turning circle and levelled out a good couple of thousand yards above my head. The faint drone of the engine died again.

I picked up Angelique's telescope from the ground and located her through it. She seemed to be fiddling with her harness. I frowned, trying to bring her into focus. What was she up to? The buckles flicked away like snakes, and she dropped from the balloon. My stomach tightened and the telescope slipped from my fingers.

No!

She plummeted, arms pulled tight into her sides like a diver aiming to hit a pool. I couldn't breathe, my eyes locked onto her, and she hurtled towards the ground, my stomach travelling with her.

No, no, no...

Angelique spread her arms wide and her body took on the silhouette of a winged bird.

She swooped out of the dive, hissing through the air like a bullet.

'What the hell?' I said.

She banked and swept back towards me. She passed directly overhead and the wings became clearer – taut triangles of leather between her arms, torso and legs. Angelique sped to the end of the field and turned back towards me, still descending fast, too fast, still going to crash.

She pulled at a handle draped over her shoulder as my heart slammed in my chest. Fabric billowed from her back like a blossoming flower and exploded into a small round parachute. She jerked upright and dropped to less than ten feet over the ground, legs windmilling.

Angelique landed at a run, skidding to a stop right in front of me, then heaved off her helmet, gave me a massive grin, and did a little curtsey.

Having forgotten to breathe, I managed to take in a massive gulp of air. 'I thought you were about to die!'

'I just wanted to show off, but don't tell Mama – she hates it when I do that.'

I glowered at her. 'So do I. Next time, warn me.'

Angelique put her hands on her heart. 'I will, promise.' Her eyes curved into crescents. 'But you have to admit that the low-level air-chute braking is pretty – what's that expression I heard Cherie use? – oh yes, rad.'

I sighed. 'Or just plain crazy.'

She laughed. 'My instructors were always telling me off for leaving it so late... You're really meant to deploy at least five hundred feet up. But where's the joy in that?'

I tried to force my face into a frown, but ended up snorting through my nose. 'You know, you're full of surprises.'

Angelique laughed. 'By the gods, I hope so.' She ran her fingers through her hair, eyes the brightest thing in the field. In that moment, I'd never seen anyone look so alive... and so beautiful.

My mind buzzed like a fly in a web.

I gestured towards the balloon to distract her. It had become a tiny red blob in the sky. 'Okay, Miss Genius, how about getting that down, huh?'

Angelique slapped her forehead with her palm. 'I knew there was something I'd forgotten.' Her mouth bent into a grin. 'Oh, hang on…'

The balloon had started growing bigger.

'Hey, it's descending by itself,' I said.

'That's because I activated a slow release valve and if I judged the wind right...'

The balloon twitched, drifting along the field back towards us.

Her grin grew wider. 'And it looks like it should land right here at our feet.'

'How the hell do you manage to judge something like that?' I asked.

'Practise, practise, and more practise.'

I whistled. 'I bet.'

Angelique began gathering up her chute. 'Speaking of which, are you ready for your first lesson?'

My pulse quickened. 'No way.'

Angelique curled a strand of blonde hair around her fingers. 'Come on, Dom. Harry was telling me how you loved to fly with your papa.'

'But since he died, I just go into a cold sweat even at the idea of it.'

'Oh, I see... but you know what the best way to get past a phobia is, don't you?'

I stared at her. 'I can't.'

'Of course you can. What would your papa say if he were here?'

God, she knew how to push my buttons. 'He'd tell me to go for it.'

'There you are then.'

Could I do it? Really? 'But I can't fly that thing solo.'

She giggled. 'Even I'm not that mean. What do you say to a tandem flight?'

'I'm so not sure, Angelique.'

'Oh come on, it will be fun flying together.'

A swallow wheeled through the sky. So free. I slowly nodded. 'But only if you promise you're not going to do your dive-bombing routine?'

She drew herself up. 'I give you the promise of a princess.'

I smiled. 'I guess that'll have to do, then.'

...

I peered down past my dangling legs at the patchwork of fields surrounding the house and diner, the silence broken only by the gentle ticking of the burner. It seemed like I'd left my fear down on the ground. The moment we'd taken to the air, I felt like I'd come home. Up here the sky seemed boundless, the horizon so wide that it curved away on either side of us. From this altitude I could see the rim of the sun over the eastern horizon. The last time I'd seen our place like this was flying with Dad.

I breathed in the leather smell of his flying jacket, remembering how his biplane had skimmed over the diner and Mom had waved at us. Then we'd climbed and dived straight down, me whooping the whole way. The ground had rushed towards us and I'd closed my eyes, before feeling the yank on my guts as he'd pulled up...the biggest rush of my life. Of course Mom had scolded him for days over that little stunt, but I didn't care – it had been the best moment of my life. Until now.

'It's great, isn't it?' Angelique's voice said through the headphones clamped onto my ears. She rested her chin on my shoulder.

I shook my thoughts away. I'd almost forgotten I was strapped to her for the tandem ride. The warmth of her body pressed into mine.

I tried to remember how to speak. 'Yeah.'

'I just wanted you to experience this with the engine off. I always think the silence makes it feels like real flying. The only thing better is a free-fall drop.'

'No way, you promised!' I tried to turn round, but ended up yanking on my harness instead. The balloon rippled above us.

'I did, didn't I?' She giggled. 'Relax, I was only joking. The fly-dive suit can only support one anyway.'

'Good. Don't think I'm quite ready for anything that full-on yet.'

'How about flying the balloon?'

'Really?' I replied, remembering this time not to jerk round to look at her.

'I couldn't be more serious. I want you to know what flying a craft of this sort feels like. This is your world, Dom, carving up the sky as a Cloud Rider.' She gestured towards the house, diner, and hangar, which had become tiny toy buildings in the world beneath us. 'Not being weighted down there with lead feet.'

I pictured Jules asleep in the house below. 'That world means a lot to me.'

'I know it does, but you need to know what you're missing. So, how about taking over?'

So that was it. This was a sales pitch after all. But one I realised deep down I still wanted to hear. 'I guess.'

Angelique brought her arm forward, placing the wrist control in front of my face. 'Let's begin by restarting the engine. Just press the round button.'

I pushed it and the prop clunked over behind us. It spluttered into a roar and the balloon shuddered.

'Now, move the lever a fraction.'

I slid it forward and the prop whined up. A gentle push in my back and we surged forward, sending a tingle running up my spine. 'This is fantastic.'

'Okay, now take hold of the steering lines above our heads.'

Reaching up, I grabbed the two swaying wooden handles.

'I want you to do a gentle turn to the right.'

I pulled the right handle and we whipped around in a tight bank, the ground spinning fast beneath us. Tugging the other handle snapped us back.

'Whoa, Dom, I said gentle turn. Don't over-control.'

'Sorry...'

'Try again and don't pull so hard.'

This time I tried exerting a slight pressure and we did a gradual bank to the right.

'Much nicer. I may get to keep the contents of my stomach down after all.'

A laugh burst from somewhere inside me and the tiredness filling my limbs evaporated with a surge of adrenaline that swept away my lingering fear of flying. 'This is incredible, Angelique.'

'I told you. Now you know the basics, how about you show me what you can really do?'

I grinned inside my helmet. Angelique might think she was a good pilot, but I reckoned I could show her a trick or two Dad had taught me. It was all coming back so quickly.

'You asked for it.' Heart hammering, hands clammy inside Dad's old flight gloves, I pushed the lever and the prop screamed up behind us. The engine thumped into my back and the balloon hurtled forward like a thrown discus.

Angelique laughed. 'Oh my goodness.'

The world burned into gold beneath us and the sun continued to climb. Long tree shadows stretched across the landscape like giant's fingers. Along the freeway, cars crawled like glistening metal ants towards their destinations, their drivers stuck on the ground not knowing what they were missing up here. The chilled air tasted sharp and clean on my tongue. Here I could really breathe. Angelique was right, this was where I belonged.

I pulled the balloon over into a hard forty-five degree turn that slid my gut sideways, before levelling off.

'You're obviously a natural,' Angelique called out. 'Want to try something more challenging?'

Fresh adrenaline swept through my body like an electric tazer shock. 'Let's go for it.'

'See the lever above us on the burner?'

I glanced up at the polished silver lever and nodded.

'That controls our height – try it.'

Reaching up, I closed my gloved fingers around the control and gave it a gentle tug.

Flames burst into the balloon and we surged upwards.

Angelique pointed to a dial on her wrist control, spinning clockwise. 'That's the altimeter. We're at about four thousand feet. Without the helmet's emergency oxygen supply our ceiling is ten – any higher than that and we're in danger of blacking out.'

'Got it.' I noticed a second smaller lever to the side of the main one above us. 'What does that do?'

'Opens a cloth flap at the top of the balloon to lower us.'

'Can I give it a try?'

'Be my guest.'

I pulled it down and through the interior of the balloon saw a patch of sky appearing at the top. The canopy creaked and began to ripple.

'Okay, don't leave it open too long otherwise we'll drop like a stone.'

I let go of the handle.

It didn't move.

I stared at it, blood chilling.

We started dropping faster and my stomach felt as though it was rising into my chest. I yanked the handle harder. Blood roared in my ears louder than the wind whistling past, as the hole flapped wildly at the top of the balloon. Below us I saw a speck of a person appear from the house.

Angelique slammed the handle and it still didn't budge. 'Gods – it's jammed solid!'

As we sped up, the landscape below sharpened into the one bounded by our fields. I stared at the altimeter on

Angelique's wrist, spinning backwards. The needle dropped past two thousand feet. My heart rose to my mouth.

The speck on the ground became Jules in a dressing gown.

We were going to die. There had to be something we could do. I looked up past the burner back to a ring of retracted electrodes, like the one's that had surrounded *Athena* when I'd powered up the drive. The Vortex!

'Angelique, let's jump. It will buy us time to try and fix the balloon.'

'That might just work.' She opened a panel on the bracelet, revealing a lit blue bar divided into eight segments, and punched a ruby button just beneath. The copper electrodes sprang out to their full length and began crackling with blue sparks.

The altimeter sped past a thousand feet and I saw Jules staring up at us. Her hands flew to her mouth.

Ten seconds...

The air shimmered and vapour started building around us. I breathed in hard, my guts pulling into a ball, already feeling the impossible slam of the ground into my body.

Seven seconds...

I could hear Jules shouting from below.

The vapour thickened into a spiralling cloud tube, greying the world around us.

Five seconds...

The Vortex rods pulsed with plasma, and concentric circles of light started speeding downwards.

Three seconds...

The pulses sped up, accelerating to a continuous corridor of steaming energy. The smell of cordite flooded my nose and static crackled over my skin. I raised my knees into a foetal position, bracing for the impact.

Two seconds…

The ground rushed towards us, wavered, and an inky black hole appeared directly beneath us.

Someone was screaming. Me.

Athena's voice filled my head, her warmth flooding my thoughts.

We plummeted into the hole and the darkness clamped around us.

The ship's voice hissed into silence.

Chapter Twenty
WORMHOLE

The seconds stretched forward and when no bone-shattering crash smashed my body, the scream faded on my lips.

My eyes began to adjust to the twilight world we'd dropped into. In silence, scudding cloud walls skimmed past like frozen smoke, and I became aware of the sound of my panting breath reverberating in my helmet.

We were shooting down a tube like a bullet towards a distant point of darkness. Tendrils of vapour connected the balloon to the shining misty walls, and clouds curled and twisted around us like the writhing walls of a monstrous gullet.

My mouth filled with a metallic taste. Lungs burning with fire, I began to see spots in front of my eyes. Angelique's hands tugged at something on my back. Cool air flooded my helmet with a hiss.

'Are you okay?' her voice said through my headphones.

I coughed past the tightness banding my throat. 'I was choking.'

'I've just turned on your helmet's oxygen supply. The only air out there is what came with us when we jumped.

Just enough to keep the balloon buoyant, but not enough to breathe.'

'Where the hell are we?'

'In the wormhole, thank the gods, otherwise we'd have been smashed all over the ground by now.'

I fought the fear crawling through my body. 'So has this balloon got an AI like *Athena*'s to jump?'

'No, this bracelet is too small for an AI, but it is equipped to compute direct jumps, which is what the pilot did when he got the lock on you.' She began tugging on thc release valve. 'We've got to get this closed, otherwise we'll just crash into the ground when we appear on the other side in a couple of minutes.'

'Let me have a go.' I reached up to the handle and yanked it, but it was still stuck solid.

'Dom, I'm so sorry. I wanted to win you over. I wanted to take you to somewhere we could charge up *Storm Wind*'s psyche gem.'

'Where?'

'Sneak onboard a Hades' ship and use its fission reactor.'

'You're telling me this was of one of your schemes?'

'Not the part of making an uncontrolled jump. That wasn't my plan.'

She'd duped me. But that didn't matter now if we couldn't sort this out. I pulled harder on the lever, but it didn't budge. I pushed my rising fear aside and examined the lever mechanism. I had to think my way out of this.

I noticed that a ratchet had fallen, locking the handle into position. A secondary spring that should have pulled it back was dangling free. Hope pulsed through me. Trying to stop my hands shaking, I pushed the pin with my thumb.

It released and the handle sprang downwards. At once the hole at the top of the balloon began to close and the envelope started to fill with hot air.

Angelique gasped. 'You've done it!'

I unclenched my aching jaw and started to focus on my surroundings. Something was moving in the opposite direction beyond the spinning cloud wall. I looked harder and the shape resolved itself into a number of dark smudges, swooping and diving together like a flock of birds. There was something predatory in the way that they circled, like crows hunting for carrion. Prickles scattered across my skin.

'There are creatures out there,' I said.

The flock turned towards us.

'That's the Shade I told you about before,' Angelique replied.

Hearing the fear in her tone, and realising I'd never heard her afraid before, even when she'd tackled the scout, my prickles deepened to goose bumps.

'Creatures of darkness that live in the empty space between realities,' she said.

'What, you mean like ghosts?'

'More like demons. They feed on people's life force, some say souls.'

'You're kidding me?'

'I wish I were.'

One of the crow-like shapes swooped close to the Vortex wall. I stared out at the strange creature. It seemed to be carved from darkness, with no solid body and wings as such, just suggestions of both, formed from shifting shadows.

It turned onto its side and lazily raked the cloud wall with dark, glistening talons. Black streamers trailed from the claw marks and dissolved into the spinning mist, like smoke trails from a jet.

Its eyeless head swivelled towards us and a chill gripped me.

'Are we in danger then?' I whispered.

'Don't worry, this is just a small flock, so they won't be able to break through the wormhole walls.'

The shadow-crows circled around us one final time and then flapped away into the darkness.

My muscles relaxed a fraction, but my pulse still thudded.

'Here we go,' Angelique said.

I glanced down and tensed again. At the bottom of the twister a circle of pure white was rushing up to meet us. The balloon was swelling and the harness started pulling on my shoulders.

'Come on…come on, inflate,' Angelique's voice whispered through my headphones.

Stars started to blink through the walls of spinning vapour, and I got fleeting glimpses of snow-capped mountains.

'We're punching through – altimeter's working again – two hundred feet,' Angelique called out.

The balloon swelled faster.

'One-hundred...'

The harness bit harder and we began to slow.

'Fifty...'

The opening of the tunnel rushed towards us. Something smashed into my body with an explosion of cold, driving the breath from my chest. I choked in freezing air, and an ice blanket wrapped me tight. I couldn't breathe.

'Angelique,' I shouted into my helmet's mic.

Something began hauling me upwards and the icy fist released its grip on my body. I scraped my hand across the visor and white powder tumbled away. A sky filled with brilliant stars appeared.

'Hang on,' Angelique said, breathless.

Her fingers locked onto the burner lever and we began to shoot back up into a night sky filled with unfamiliar constellations.

I gasped. 'We're alive.'

Her snort echoed through my helmet. 'Evidently.'

'But we hit the ground?'

'Look for yourself.'

I glanced downwards and saw a round crater blasted into deep snow.

'The drift broke our fall,' Angelique said.

If I hadn't have been strapped to her front, I would have hugged her. 'Hell, we were nearly pavement pizza,' I said, shaking the impacted powder from the sleeves of my flying jacket.

'We weren't, thanks to you.'

'That was too close.' I stretched my legs, aching from the impact but otherwise okay.

I took in the glittering landscape around us. The layout of the fields looked similar to those in my world in most other respects, but this one had a single log cabin instead of our house. There was no sign of a diner and hangar, but the world was still familiar. Although it wasn't home, I knew this was a variation of it. The same one I'd seen through my link with Athena. We'd crossed over into a parallel world. A tingle swept up my spine.

Two figures, a woman and a boy about my age, rushed out from the cabin, their silhouettes pointing up towards us, stark against the snow.

A realisation hit me like lightning. 'Oh my god...is that Mom and—'

'Yes, that's you,' Angelique said. 'Well, at least in a manner of speaking – someone almost like you – but that Dom won't be the same because of his different life experiences.'

And was the other Dom's dad down there? Just to see him alive, even if it wasn't really him… I stared at the dwindling specks, still waving to us. 'Can't we go speak to them? Would be kind of cool talking to myself.'

'Best not drag them into this—' Angelique exhaled sharply. 'By the fires of Hades, look east.'

Over a ridge of snow-capped mountains, which didn't exist in my Oklahoma, a line of flying craft appeared. There were two red balloons like our own and the massive bulk of the *Hyperion* between them. In the vision I hadn't quite realised the scale of the craft. I could see now that this huge vessel was at least twice the size of a football stadium, hundreds of glowing portals running its entire length.

'The *Hyperion* must have jumped back here when the scout didn't radio in,' Angelique said.

The smaller balloons started to pull ahead of the slower ship.

'We haven't got the correct squawk codes so they already know we're not legitimate.' Angelique banked us hard away. 'The *Hyperion*'s destroyer class so we don't stand a chance against them. That craft is also Duke Ambra's flagship. He's a heartless butcher who's personally had innocent thousands executed, and if we fall into his hands...'

My imagination graphically filled in her missing words. 'How come we've jumped to this world of all places?'

'It was locked into the auto-return navigation coordinates of the bracelet. There wasn't time to recalibrate it.' She pushed the slide control on the wristband and opened up the throttle. We began to speed away, the snow-dappled forest skimming fast beneath us.

'Let's just power up the Vortex and escape,' I said.

She tapped on a blue bar edging upwards on the wristband display; over half its segments remained unlit. 'It will take thirty minutes until we're fully charged and can jump again. At least we don't have to recompute the jump manually which would take days; the coordinates are already stored in the bracelet's memory.'

Behind us the *Hyperion* was dropping away, but the smaller crafts were still closing.

'How come they're gaining?' I asked.

'It's because we're riding tandem and it's making our balloon sluggish.'

'So how the hell are we going to lose them?'

'We hide.'

'Where?'

She reached up and opened the valve. 'On the ground.'

My muscles contracted as we began descending fast towards a wooded valley, the glitter of frozen lumps of ice visible in a river snaking through the middle. However, it was the jagged rocks and dark woods that really caught my attention. What sort of creatures were going to be down there waiting for us? Wolves, bears – worse?

Our craft dropped closer. Looked like we were about to find out.

...

The droning of the scout ships searching for us echoed along the valley like a buzz saw. Angelique covered the burner pack with small branches, whilst I threw armfuls of snow over the deflated canopy.

'I still don't see why we had to deflate it,' I said, kicking powder over the balloon.

'Just safer this way. They're much less likely to spot it from the air.'

'So how long now for the Vortex to recharge?'

'Twenty minutes, but we'll have to be airborne again before we try to jump.'

I stamped my feet and whacked my hands against my side to fight off the icy numbness. 'Why?'

'It's really risky making a jump on the ground. All you need is a slight variation in height in the landscape and we could end up materialising right inside a hill on the other side. That's why we use airships to jump in the air.'

I gazed at our handiwork. The balloon was completely invisible under the mound of snow. Breathing in the frozen air made my lungs sting. I noticed frost had started forming on Angelique's eyelashes.

'Hell, it's cold – couldn't we just keep the burner ticking over?'

'Too risky… We could always use each other's body heat.' She raised her eyebrows at me.

My irritation spiked. We were in mortal danger because of her and she was actually flirting with me.

Her expression became alert and she put her finger to her lips. A distant drone – deeper than the smaller ships – drifted along the valley. The bass sound grew and began reverberating through my gut, sending small clumps of snow dropping from the trees in a shower of white.

Through the cracks in the branches, I saw the large airship lumbering into view across the valley. It began to descend and from its belly spotlights blazed out and played over the ground.

'What's it doing?'

Angelique groaned. 'Looking for a place to land. There'll be at least three hundred Shock marines on board. They'll come after us on foot.'

'Just when I thought this day couldn't get any worse.' I glanced at the four remaining blank segments of the Vortex charge indicator on the wrist-pad. Angelique buried it under the snow. 'Will that hurry up—'

She clamped her hand over my mouth.

The voices of men drifted from the hillside above us.

'Where did they come from?' I whispered.

'Must have already been on the ground. By the gods, I'm such a fool. They were probably looking for their lost scout.'

Pinpricks of orange appeared in a line between the trunks of the trees.

'They'll be right on top of us any moment now,' I said. 'We're going to have to make a run for it.'

'Okay, let's start digging the balloon out.' I headed back towards it.

Angelique grabbed my arm. 'There isn't time.'

I stared at her. 'Are you saying we just have to abandon our only way out of here?'

'We've got no choice. We'll slip away and double back for it later.'

She pulled my hand and, keeping low, we crept further down into the steep valley, our breath billowing.

I didn't want to think about what would happen if they caught us...

Through the darkness I could just make out some of the men carrying the lanterns. They wore red trench coats fastened with ivory buttons, with big fur hoods hiding their heads.

A loud bark echoed through the forest.

My palms went slick inside my leather gloves. 'Dammit, they've got dogs.'

'And they'll pick up our scent any moment. Come on.'

We increased our pace and clambered down the steep hillside, half slipping and sending small flurries of powder tumbling ahead of us.

I glanced back at our footprints in the deep snow. 'They won't need dogs to track us through this – all they'll have to do is follow the path we've left for them.'

A yell broke through the silence. 'The balloon,' shouted a man's deep voice.

The lanterns converged towards each other.

Angelique gave me a grim look that twisted my gut.

'Does that mean we're stuck here?' I said.

She grabbed my arms. 'Dom, never give up. We'll find a way.'

But my legs felt full of stone. In this world there was no gentle *Athena* song to ease my fear.

A branch cracked from behind us like a gunshot, and fresh fear surged through me.

Angelique pulled me forward and the slope steepened. We slid down it on our backs, grabbing onto tree trunks to slow our descent. The dog barked again and the men's shouts grew louder. The lanterns started bobbing down the slope behind us.

'Hell's fire, the dog's already picked up our trail,' Angelique said.

My heart pounded and my mouth went dry. Just beneath us a trickling sound whispered in the night. We clambered over a drift and saw a fast-moving stream ahead, dropping through the forest. Angelique slid towards it and leapt over in one graceful jump.

An idea flashed into my head. 'Hey, get back here.' I slid down the bank into the shallow water.

She skidded to a stop and turned. 'Why?'

The dog's barking grew nearer, and the line of lanterns snaked down the trail behind us.

'I saw this film once.'

Angelique stared at me. 'Look we haven't got time to discuss—'

'You don't understand. It was about prisoners of war escaping from a camp. They were being chased by guards with dogs, but managed to shake them off.'

She jumped down next to me and stared at me. 'How?'

'By running along the stream. Dogs can't follow a scent over water.'

She gave a sharp nod. 'That has the sound of genius to it, Dom.'

'Come on.' Leading the way, I began to scramble along the stream, each foot sending an explosion of spray flying. The freezing water tingled inside my sneakers, turning my already cold toes into icy stumps.

There was a shout and we turned to see the soldiers silhouetted by the lantern light, milling around the point where we'd entered the stream.

I groaned through my teeth. 'Dammit, of course, our footprints just stop at the embankment.'

Our pursuers split into two groups, each heading off in different directions along the stream. A big white wolf-like dog strained at the lead held by one of the men, splashing down the slope in our direction.

Angelique rushed to a tree growing from the embankment and toppled over into the crook of another. 'Okay, so we'll climb and hide in the branches. If you leap onto that first trunk and clamber up, you won't leave any footprints.'

'But if they spot us, we'll be trapped.'

'Let me worry about that.' She shoved me towards the tree.

I climbed the sloping bough, gripping it hard between my knees, leg muscles shaking. Reaching the other tree the first had fallen into, I hooked my leg over a branch and hauled myself up into the thick canopy of the tall pine. The baying dog was almost on top of us.

Angelique looked up at me, eyes hardening.

'Get a move on,' I hissed.

She shook her head. 'Keep completely quiet.'

'What do you mean?'

'Increasing our survival odds. Stay here.'

'No way, I'm coming with you.' I started to descend.

'Dom, please, no. It has to be this way. Whatever happens you have to stay hidden, just remember that.' She gave me a dazzling smile, teeth biting into her lower lip. 'It's all up to you now, Dom.'

Before I could respond she turned and sprinted into the forest.

Shouts filled the night. The knot of men splashed around the bend in the stream and stopped directly under my hiding place.

Blood roaring in my ears, I held my breath.

'Where the hell is he?' a tall man said, pulling back his hood to reveal a face with a broad nose and the same burning red eyes as the scout. I could see the glint of a sword at his hip.

The man with the dog shook his head. 'Only the gods know, but he's not going anywhere now we've found the balloon.'

I clung to the trunk and saw the dog pulling towards the tree I was hiding in.

'What is it, boy? Picked up a scent?'

The dog's tail began to thrash as it sniffed the base of the sloping tree. Sweat dribbled under my bomber jacket. The man holding its lead glanced up into the branches. I stayed completely still, trying to stop the shivering in my body.

Angelique's head appeared around the side of the tree trunk, clearly in view of the soldiers as she looked back at them. What was she thinking?

The tall man drew his sword. 'That's Princess Angelique, as I live and breathe. Duke Ambra will pay us our weight in gold when we drag her in.'

The dog's head turned towards her. 'Go get her boy, and make us all rich.' Its handler untied the lead and the beast streaked away, barking.

No! I realised at once what Angelique was doing, deliberately drawing them away from me. She stumbled in the deep snow and sprawled forward. My heart clenched. I fought the desire to rush to help her.

Please, Angelique, run…

She grabbed hold of a branch and hauled herself back to her feet.

Come on!

The dog was closing like a speeding dart over the snow.

Everything slowed in my numb brain – Angelique started to turn as the creature gathered itself in one fluid moment and leapt.

It smashed into her and time sped up again.

Angelique tumbled into a drift with the beast on top, snapping and biting at her back.

The soldiers whooped and slapped each other's shoulders.

'I can almost smell that gold bounty,' shouted one as they ran towards her.

The dog clamped onto Angelique's arm and shook her, its growl growing frenzied.

I closed my eyes and pressed my hands to my ears, trying to shut out her cries that seemed to echo from every dark corner of the wood.

Chapter Twenty-One
ALONE

The men's laughter mingled with Angelique's cries as they dragged her away.

The cold bit deeper into my thoughts and body. I trembled.

They were going to kill her.

I stretched my stiff limbs and, with teeth chattering, began to clamber down the tree.

The silence hung thick and heavy in the snowy wood. I dropped onto the ground and looked towards the vast airship, a towering red craft that had landed next to the river a few miles away in the middle of the valley. I began following the footprints of the soldiers, weaving between the trees, and headed towards it through the snow.

Angelique's words rose up inside me: *It's all up to you now, Dom.*

A shudder shook my body, half-cold, half-fear. I stamped my feet, which tingled with pinpricks of pain, my sneakers soaked and useless in the snow. Sticking my hands under my armpits to try and heat them, I raised the furry collar of the bomber jacket around my neck and shuffled into the woods, following the churned trail.

The trees' claws reached up into the darkness around me. Somewhere close an owl hooted.

I was alone – a stranger in an alien world.

The minutes stretched onwards and the cold seeped deeper under my skin, dulling my senses. I kept walking, willing my limbs forward, the desire for sleep lapping around my brain like fog.

It's all up to you now, Dom.

The forest was filled with stark shadows, the only sound the crump of my footsteps through the snow and the huff of my breath.

I kept my eyes fixed on the vast ship, now less than a mile away, the focus point for hundreds of converging lanterns. Every so often great gouts of steam blasted out like geysers from vents dotted along its sides.

It's all up to you...

I bit my lip hard and felt the sting of warm blood briefly thaw it.

I concentrated on my target, drawing up all the energy I'd left in my body. The distance closed until the mile was reduced to a few hundred yards. I halted at the edge of the wood.

Closer to the *Hyperion*, the sheer scale of the craft became clear. It towered above me like an alien mother ship from a movie, the smaller pinpricks of light revealing themselves to be portholes. I imagined the countless lives contained behind each and every glowing window. The odds stacked against me seemed impossible.

The sound of barked orders drifted over the tundra and a column of soldiers assembled into regimented squares on a ramp leading up into the ship. The crack of a whip snapped the air from somewhere behind me. I ducked back into the shadows.

A beautiful white horse appeared from the gloomy wood like a ghost. Behind it a sled, bathed with the orange glow of a single lantern, carried two soldiers. They cantered towards my hiding place and as they passed, the horse's hooves sent flurries of snow flying over me.

One of the men, his face wrapped in a scarf, turned to his companion who held the reins. 'Get a move on. Duke Ambra will have us flogged if we don't get back in time for her execution.'

My stomach hollowed out on his last word. The sled carried on towards the man-made mountain. On its back I noticed the deflated red fabric of the scout balloon bunched up in a heap, the burner pack and our flight helmets were piled on top.

It's all up to you...

Heat surged through my body. Before I had time to change my mind, I sprinted from the shadows of the pine-woods, across the open snowy ground and towards the sled. The snow muffled my steps and, breathing hard, I tried to ignore the tightness clutching at my throat.

Zigzagging around the frozen tundra, following the scar of the sled's runners, I closed the distance. The horse's harness, chinking in time with its trot, grew louder. The soldiers were like two huddled gargoyles silhouetted against the glowing red oval of the airship.

When I was less than ten feet away I leapt and grabbed the back of the sled. Taking my weight on my arms, my feet dragged behind me, ploughing trails through the snow. I gritted my teeth, biceps screaming, and hauled myself over the edge, quickly pulling the canvas on top of me.

Breath rasping, I peered through a gap. The soldiers still had their eyes on the *Hyperion*. I was in the clear for now.

The driver leaned towards his companion. 'It's going to be quite a show, and best of all, Ambra will be in a great mood after this.'

The other man nodded. 'It'll make a change. He's been foul since his nephew went missing with that scout balloon.'

'Apparently she's already confessed to killing him.'

The driver let out a long sigh. 'I almost feel sorry for Princess Angelique. He's really going to make her suffer. They've been saying on the Valve Voice he's going to put her to death in the flame room.'

The thought sent a chill through my body.

'Gods, what a sadist. She's still a kid, really.'

'A kid who was caught red-handed with one of our ships. A kid who, as a member of the royal household, has been given mental training to endure torture. Duke Ambra knows there's no point interrogating her to find out the whereabouts of the Queen, so he's going to have her executed as an example. '

'I know, I know, but even so...'

The two men fell silent. My stomach knotted. I raised the heavy cloth and saw we were passing under the airship's belly. A group of men directed a steam jet to melt the huge icicles that hung off it.

There was a clink and the control wristband that Angelique had hidden in the snow with the balloon, rolled towards me. I grabbed it and stared at the eight segments, now all lit up.

If I could find her, maybe there was still a chance...

'What have you got there?' a voice shouted.

Body going rigid, I whipped my head under the canvas and held my breath.

'Whoa,' the driver said.

The horse snorted and the sled slid to a stop. Footsteps clumped through the snow towards us and my pulse thudded to each one. I cupped my hands over my mouth, trying to keep the telltale steam of my breath shut under the fabric.

'It's the recovered scout ship,' the driver said.

I moved the canvas a fraction and peered out through the gap.

A soldier with three stripes on his arm stood directly in front of the sled. 'Okay. Carry on.' The soldier waved the sled past.

The driver nodded and flicked the reins.

I watched through my small window onto the outside world, feeling sick, as we swung towards the massive ramp at the rear of the *Hyperion*. The sled lurched and its runners squealed over the wooden planks. We slipped between two columns of soldiers marching up into the belly of the ship.

Once inside, warmth washed over me. The interior was a sort of crazy metal fabric-draped cathedral. Massive red struts curved overhead to meet in the middle, and walkways crisscrossed the towering space above. Around me the walls rippled and shifted with canvas gas balls, each held fast behind screens of webbing. It felt like I was in the belly of a whale.

A shower of sparks drifted down from a man suspended in a harness high overhead. He was welding an immense brass pipe that ran the entire length of the chamber and disappeared out through the rear of the ship.

The driver glanced up. 'They're still trying to fix the drive shaft then?'

His companion nodded. 'Never been the same since *Apollo* destroyed our prop during that battle. You have to give them credit, they gave us a hell of a fight.'

'They really did, considering we used the secret weapon on them.' The driver pulled the reins to one side and we turned into one of the arched alcoves.

The soldiers jumped down. 'Come on, we'll unload the balloon later.' the driver said. 'It'll be more than our lives are worth to miss the ceremony.'

'I need to warm up with some Plam first.'

The driver tied the horse to an iron ring. 'Right then, let's get ourselves defrosted.'

They hurried off out of the alcove.

I waited until their footsteps had faded away before poking my head out between the folds of the canopy. From my shadowed hiding place I could see the main chamber, and soldiers disappearing through a round door at the far end, shaking caked snow off their boots. Through the open ramp, large flakes swirled down, reducing the view to a blizzard.

Clambering out of the sled, heart thundering so loudly I was sure somebody would hear, I took cover behind a large beam to one side of the stall. The horse snorted and looked round at me.

I patted her. 'Quiet,' I whispered.

She snorted again and turned her snout towards a hay bale, just out of reach.

'Okay, I get the message.' I crept past and dragged the bale closer. With a soft whinny she dropped her head and began munching the food.

A klaxon warbled somewhere deep within the bowels of the airship. The few remaining soldiers in the loading bay darted past, and the man who'd been welding the driveshaft abseiled down a line to the ground. He landed neatly, shook off his harness and dropped his visor to the floor. He slipped off the overalls to reveal a crimson uniform underneath and a spanner emblem emblazoned above the demon logo on his arm. An engineer?

He walked over to a guy who looked younger than me, maybe sixteen. He was examining dials across a bank of cylinders, with a spider web of blue painted pipes radiating from them.

'How's it looking?' the engineer asked.

The boy spun around and snapped the engineer a salute. 'Good, sir. The buoyancy helium bladder reserves are at seventy per cent, propane lifters at fifty. We have enough gas to fly for another month before we need to refuel at Hells Cauldron.'

'Excellent news. Duke Ambra will be pleased. You can tell him yourself after the execution.'

The young man beamed. 'Yes, sir.'

'Come on, or we'll be late, and that would never do, would it?'

'No, sir.'

The engineer slapped the young man on the shoulder and they strode out through the round door.

The distant drumming of footsteps reverberated through the walls; the marching of worker ants heading somewhere with purpose. The round door at the far end stood open.

I crept out of the alcove and scanned the loading bay. It was empty and I let out my breath. The enormity of what had happened pressed down on me. All alone and against an army – I didn't stand a chance.

'Dom, Angelique, can you hear me?' a faint voice said.

I froze.

'Are you guys there?'

Jules' voice came from the direction of the sled. I charged back to it and hunted through the back.

'Just let me know if you're receiving this and that you're okay?' she said.

The voice was coming from one of the flight helmets. I grabbed it, unhooked the headset with the mic attached and slotted it over my ear. 'Jules are you there?'

'Oh, thank god. You two scared me to death. Are you okay?'

I clung to her voice like a lifeline thrown to me from my world and into this alien one. My words came out in a rush. 'No, I mean I'm okay but we're in a parallel Earth. Hades have caught Angelique and they're going to kill her.'

'Oh god, no.'

'I don't know what to do, Jules.' I couldn't mask the tremble in my voice. 'I've sneaked onto the *Hyperion* where they've taken her.'

'Okay, okay. We'll think this through together, Dom.'

But I could hear her fear for me in her tone.

I had to be straight with her. 'I may not make it out of this alive, Jules.'

'Don't think like that. You've got to concentrate on rescuing Angelique and getting home. And that's all you should focus on.'

I thought of the crystal around my neck. 'But there's one other thing. It turns out the reason Angelique brought us here was to recharge the Psuche gem – not that she told me that till we arrived here.'

'She said she had a plan to recharge it, but this?' I heard Jules sigh. 'Okay, what's happened obviously wasn't part of her plan.'

'Obviously.'

'Let's step through this. You say you're onboard, presumably hiding somewhere?'

'I'm in a stable at the moment, but when someone spots me I'm history.'

'So you need a disguise, a way of blending in, don't you?'

My breathing slowed. Talking to Jules was helping to order the chaos of my thoughts.

My gaze swept over the engineer's discarded overalls. 'Think I've found something I can use.'

'That's more like it.'

I slipped the overalls on over my jeans and bomber jacket. 'How come I can hear you anyway?' I took a tool belt with spanners hanging from a peg nearby and fastened it around my waist.

'It was *Athena*'s idea.'

'Sorry, she spoke to you?'

'Not the fancy way she does with you. Instead she just kept flashing lots of lights on this box in the cockpit till I took notice of it. It's got Valve Voice written on it.'

'That's how the Cloud Riders keep contact with each other across realities.'

'Whatever it is, it's pretty amazing that I can talk to you in another world.'

'Thank god you are. I was on the verge of losing it, Jules.'

'Not on my watch, mister.'

Even if hers was false confidence, a story to keep the nightmares at bay, it was exactly what I needed.

I pulled the welding mask onto my head. Fumbling on the side of the helmet, my fingers clamped around a small handle. I turned it. The screen flicked down and my view of the world muted green. I prayed it would be enough to disguise the unclouded colour of my eyes.

'Okay, I'm ready. So now the tricky part of freeing Angelique and then trying to recharge the Psuche gem.'

'Hang on, that might not be the best plan.'

'Why?'

'No one knows you're there right?' Jules said.

'So far.'

'In that case you still have the element of surprise on your side. But I'm pretty sure the moment you try to rescue Angelique, the heat will be quickly on.'

'You're suggesting recharging the gem first?'

'I would if it was me. After all, you don't want to have a return trip to try this again. Then when you've found

Angelique all you have to do is concentrate on getting yourselves back home.'

'But how do I recharge the crystal? Something tells me it's not going to be as easy as plugging a cellphone into a wall socket.'

'Didn't Angelique say anything about her plan?'

'Only something about *Hyperion* being fission powered and using that.' I fingered the lightning medal beneath my shirt.

'Fission – a nuclear reactor in other words,' Jules said.

'Doesn't a reactor usually mean radioactivity?'

'Yes!'

'Okay, I won't have a clue what to do when I find it and I don't much fancy being turned into a human glowworm either.'

'I'll see what I can do to make sure that doesn't happen.'

Behind the false brightness, I could hear the tension ratcheting tighter in Jules' voice.

But she made it sound so easy. Then again, she wasn't the one standing inside an enemy destroyer with hundreds of soldiers onboard. But she was making sense.

I tried to push aside the fear churning in my gut. This didn't seem much of plan but it was all I had. 'Okay, I better get to it.'

'You can do this, Dom, I know you can.'

You mean you *hope* I can. I didn't voice the thought. Seemed that everything relied on me pulling this off. The problem was I really wasn't sure I was the right guy for the job.

Cold sweat running down my back, I ran along the loading bay and through the large door at the end.

Chapter Twenty-Two
THE REACTOR

I found myself at a junction with three corridors leading away from it, when the klaxon's shrill cry echoing along each suddenly died. Couldn't be a good sign.

I scanned the walls for something, anything, to indicate which direction the flame or reactor rooms might be. A cluster of four blue pipes ran along the ceiling of the right-hand corridor, thick red cables headed down the left.

'Jules, I can see what I think are gas pipes leading away one direction and electricity wires the other. I overheard the guards mention something about a flame room and burning Angelique to death in it.'

'Oh Jesus. So you think if you follow the gas pipes they'll lead you straight to her?'

'Hopefully.'

'And maybe the cables might lead you to the reactor?'

'Has to be worth a shot.' I turned down the left hand corridor, just hoping I was making the right decision by making Angelique's rescue my second priority.

I came to another four-way junction, cables from three of them all merging together and heading down the one leading straight ahead. This had to be the way to the reactor.

Sure enough I was only another hundred yards on, when I saw a red skull surrounded by lightning bolts on a door.

'I think I just found it.'

'That's fantastic.'

My gaze fell on a brass panel with numbered rotating drums on the door. I had a bad feeling about it. Sure enough, when I tried the handle, it wouldn't turn.

'I spoke too soon. There's some sort of numbered keypad that I'm guessing opens this door.'

I heard Jules groan over the headset. 'Of course there were going to be security systems for something like this – I should've thought.'

'You and me both. Okay, let me just try some random number sequences and see if that gets us anywhere.'

I spun the look at my watch to know that time was ticking away.

At least three minutes passed and frustration churned through me. 'Jules, I don't—'

A warmth grew against my chest and I glanced down to see a faint light glowing through the gaps in Alex's medal. *Storm Wind*'s Psuche gem? A wavering image appeared in my mind.

'What did you say, Dom?' Jules asked.

'Hang on a second…'

'Numbers.' A male voice whispered in my mind.

I closed my eyes, trying to concentrate, and the image sharpened. I could see the keypad with its drums rotated to nine, four, six, two, six, three. It couldn't be, could it?

I opened my eyes and entered the sequence as I'd seen them in my head. Something clicked in the door mechanism. I tried the handle and it turned.

'Jackpot, I've cracked it,' I said.

'How the hell did you manage that?'

'Not sure, but I think maybe something to do with my Ship Whisperer ability and *Storm Wind*.'

'I thought his crystal was dead?'

'No, I think just low on juice. I saw him glow just now and the image of the correct combination appeared in my mind.'

'However you cracked it is cool with me, but you need to get a move on. Just be careful.'

'You can take that as read.'

Apprehension coiling in my guts, I pulled the door open and entered a bright white room. I relaxed a fraction when I saw there was no one inside. Seemed like Hades thought the number pad was enough to keep this place secure.

Down the far side was a large flickering monitor. Displayed on it was a black and white view of a round chamber. That room had a lattice floor, beneath which water lapped over a wide silver cylinder with pipes connecting it to the walls. A dome crowned the cylinder, with a metal hoop on top. I spotted the same skull logo as on the door on the dome.

'Jules, I think I've found the reactor.'

'Okay. Tell me what you see.'

'There's a big round cylinder underwater that looks like a plumber's dream.'

'That'll be the reactor core. The nuclear rods inside heat up water and that's what runs the ship's power turbines.'

'How do you know all this stuff, Jules?'

'Being a geek mechanic and wasting way too much time on Wikipedia rather than Facebook.'

Despite my tension, I smiled. 'Right now I'm really grateful you're a social outcast.'

I heard her snort.

For the first time I took in the rest of the room I was standing in. The wall to my left was filled with radial dials, needles all pointing into green zones, and from behind the ceiling panels, I could hear a loud hum. I could almost taste the power being generated in the next room.

'So any ideas how I recharge the crystal?' I asked.

'Angelique said something about the Psuche gem absorbing radioactivity. I'm guessing we'll have to expose it to the core.'

'Sounds dangerous,' I replied.

'Have you've got any better ideas?'

'No, I'm fresh out. So dangerous it is.'

'But there must be a safe way for the engineers to access the core for maintenance. If you look around there should be some control for raising the rods.'

I peered into the reactor chamber. Two large brass mechanical claws, constructed from bars and cogs, hung from the ceiling. In my room, two brass gauntlets, smaller versions of the claws, had been mounted on rods that looked like metal strings for an upside down puppet.

'I think I can see how,' I said. 'There's something a bit like one of those grabber-claw games where you try and hook up candy.'

'You'll be playing for slightly higher stakes than that here,' Jules said.

'Tell me about it.' I crossed to the controls. I slipped my hands inside the gloves. The metal felt cold on my skin. I flexed my fingers and with a whir of cogs, the giant versions inside the chamber mimicked my movements.

'Okay, it's working,' I said. 'There's a metal lid with a loop on top of the metal tube in the chamber that I think I can get hold of with the claws.'

'The reactor rods will probably be connected to the lid, so lift them out nice and easy,' Jules said.

'I wasn't planning on juggling them.' I flexed my left hand and rotated the gauntlet, moving the rods connecting it to the floor. One of the giant hands swung across towards the reactor. A bead of sweat ran down my forehead.

I extended the claw into the water and towards the hoop. Nice and easy, Dom… I pinched my hand and the claw clamped onto the hoop. Holding my breath, I raised the claw slowly and the massive metal lid rose with it, like it weighed nothing, and broke through the surface. I blew out my breath as I saw six dull rods hanging beneath it, steaming in the air.

'Think I've done it, but the exposed rods aren't glowing or anything.'

'That only happens in the movies. But right now, glowing or not, that chamber will be flooding with radioactivity.'

'Just as long as I'm safe in here.'

'The reactor will be heavily shielded like a nuclear power plant in our world. I doubt even Hades would want to kill its own technicians intentionally.'

'Thank their gods for that,' I said. I carefully withdrew my hands from the gauntlets and took Grandpa Alex's medal out from beneath my shirt. 'So any ideas about what I do with *Storm Wind*'s Psuche gem?'

'You need to get it inside the chamber somehow and we'll see what happens when it's exposed directly to the radiation.'

I scanned the room and spotted an industrial oven-like round hatch. It had the word 'Maintenance' written above it and a green light bulb. It also looked like the only way into the chamber from here.

I took hold of the handle, praying I wouldn't get fried like a burger. Heart thumping so hard I was surprised it didn't burst out of my chest, I heaved the hatch open. I blew out a sigh of relief when I spotted a second door with another skull logo, behind it.

My gaze flicked to the monitor, and in the background of the view of the reactor was a door with a second identical logo. It had to be the other side of the second hatch.

'Think I've got it figured out,' I said. 'There's something like an airlock. I think I can place the gem inside it and then move it into the chamber with the mechanical claw.'

'I think I can picture that,' Jules said. 'Okay, nice one.'

I unhooked the Psuche gem from Alex's medal, placed it in the hatch and pushed the door closed. The green light started to blink.

I slipped my hands back inside the gauntlets.

Here goes nothing...

I swung the right claw towards the hatch in the chamber, grabbed the handle and pulled. The door on the monitor screen swung open. The Psuche crystal came into view inside the airlock. I'd been right.

The green light flicked to red. I guessed that meant that radiation had begun filling the airlock. I cast a worried glance at my hatch, but it looked shut tight enough.

'Okay, I've got the crystal into the chamber but nothing obvious is happening,' I said.

'Try moving the gem as close as possible towards the rods,' Jules replied.

I imagined her listening to me back in the gondola like a radio play – one with me cast in the lead role – one where I got to live or die in real life.

'I'm on it,' I said.

Storm Wind's Psuche gem looked tiny held in the giant claw. I tried to slow my breathing and imagined I was gripping one of Mom's fragile glass Christmas baubles – and I'd broken way too many of those over the years. The claws whirred closed onto the crystal. I breathed out through my nose when I didn't shatter it.

A sudden blast came from the klaxon in the corridor outside and I jumped. Bad timing, very bad. My hand flinched and the mechanical claw flicked open in response to my unconscious movement.

The gem tumbled towards the lattice floor and that frozen second became an eternity in my mind. Time accelerated as desperation surged through me. I made a grab like I was catching a baseball and seized the gem with the tips of the claw. My blood roared in my ears. That had been way too close. I swung *Storm Wind*'s crystal towards the rods, daring to breathe again.

For a minute I thought my hands were shaking, but both the claws in the chamber had begun to vibrate. I had to be feeling feedback through the control gauntlets. A burst of sparks flew from the control rods and into the gem that had started to glow.

'I think it's working, Jules. There's a regular firework display going on inside the chamber.'

'Brilliant. Whatever you're doing, keep doing it.'

I held the gem steady as an alarm warbled in the room. I glanced at the instrument wall to see the dial needles twitching and rotating backwards. Was the power being drained? Inside the chamber the steam from the rods had turned into smoke, and fire flickered around the crystal.

The vibration in the gauntlets around my hands grew stronger, and the claws started to buck. Something told me they wouldn't last much longer.

A high pitch whine filled my ears and a huge blaze of light suddenly filled the room. The crystal became an incandescent sun and the screen whited out. The moments ticked past and the view gradually faded back in. I half expected to see the crystal blasted into fragments, but instead it was still held in one of the claws, now shining like a beacon.

'It's worked!' I said.

Jules whooped over the Valve Voice. 'Get it out of there.'

'You've got it.' I swung the claw back to the hatch, but the gauntlets started to shake and I heard a grinding sound of metal on metal from the chamber. I breathed through my nose, trying to compensate for the building vibration and manoeuvred the claw into the hatch.

'You can do this, Dom,' Jules whispered, like she was thinking to herself out loud as she listened to the radio play.

I let go of the gem and heard a clang on the other side of the hatch. I shoved the outer hatch closed as a screech came from the chamber. On the monitor I saw cogs spin free from the claws and fly apart. The control gauntlets went limp on my hands. I'd really busted them up. I also doubted Hades would be able to use them again, anytime soon.

The red light blinked on and fans powered up somewhere inside the airlock.

'What's going on?' Jules asked.

'Think I've made a bit of a mess of their reactor, but we're good.' The red light turned green and the fans whirred down. I hoped that meant the radiation had been scrubbed out of the air in the chamber. There was only one way to be certain though. I swung the hatch open, took a deep breath, reached in and grabbed the jewel. It felt warm in my hand.

I breathed out. 'Got it.'

'No burning sensation?' Jules didn't need to add – *from radioactivity?*

'No, all fine—'

My skin itched. Oh hell, had I spoken too soon? I half expected to see blisters erupting over my skin, but instead a familiar surge of energy shot up my arm.

Storm Wind's voice flooded into my mind. *'Angelique, save her.'*

My relief at not being burned alive rushed away. The klaxon outside blasted a second time. The final call to her execution?

'I've got to get to Angelique now. I think time's just run out for her.'

'Get a move on, Dom!'

The dials dropped faster and the first warbling alarm in the room had been joined by others. Whatever was going on in the reactor couldn't be good.

What I'd just done had been dangerous enough, but what was waiting for me next could mean instant death at the end of a crossbow bolt.

Ignoring the spike of fear inside, I shoved the crystal into my pocket and ran from the room. Please, god, I wouldn't be too late to rescue Angelique.

Chapter Twenty-Three
THE FLAME ROOM

I sprinted along the curved passageway and came to a steep metal staircase. Grabbing the handrails, I leapt up it two steps at a time and caught the buzz of voices building from somewhere ahead. Reaching the top I pushed open a door and stepped out onto a narrow walkway high above a vaulted chamber.

Below me the soldiers had begun forming into regimented squares to encircle a raised dais in the middle. A tall man with white hair and a long cape, stood talking to another man decorated with numerous medals. He gestured upwards to a round room in front of me, six burner tubes sticking out of its roof and connected by blue pipes to the red fabric of the main envelope.

It had to be the flame room.

On the gantry, two soldiers stood in front of a thick metal door set into the outside of the structure. They looked at me with ruby eyes. One guard I possibly had a chance against, but two? My throat contracted and I gripped onto the handrail, but the taller guard just nodded at me and looked down into the chamber. I forced my fingers to relax.

'Okay, Jules, I've got company. I'm going to have to hide the headset in case they spot it. Look, if I don't make it I just want to say—'

'Don't talk like that, you'll both be fine,' Jules replied. 'And good luck.'

I just hoped she was right. 'I'm going to need it. Over and out.' I pocketed the earpiece, and legs trembling, my head a wall of noise, I took the long walk along the gantry towards them. The shorter guard looked straight at me and I made myself breathe. I noticed a bright red scratch mark across his cheek.

Here went nothing.

I tried to lower my voice to a gruff tone with a hint of French. 'There's a problem with one of the gas jets. They've sent me to look at it.'

The taller guard's eyes widened a fraction. 'You'd better get a move on. Duke Ambra will be incandescent if the execution is delayed.'

'Tell me about it. Oh, and he personally asked to see you both.'

The shorter guard's gaze narrowed on me. 'He did? About what?'

'Some urgent matter about tracking down a second fugitive who's been detected.'

The taller guard gestured towards the gathered soldiers below us. 'Why us? The Duke's not exactly short of manpower.'

I needed to come up with a plausible reason, and quickly. 'Apparently he's been keeping an eye on you both.'

'Been keeping an eye on us? Not sure I like the sound of that,' the shorter guard said. He eyed his companion. 'You haven't been fiddling your Plam ration again have you?'

The other man shook his head.

'No, nothing like that,' I said. 'Apparently he's been considering you for a long overdue promotion. Your sergeant put in a good word.'

'That hell hound did? Really?' the taller guard said.

They actually seemed to be buying it. 'Really.'

'But we can't leave the flame room unguarded.'

I gestured with my chin towards the flame room. 'Don't worry, I can handle her if she tries anything.'

The shorter man pointed to the scratch mark on his face. 'That's what I thought.'

The other guard rubbed the back of his neck and gazed at his companion. 'Okay, I'd better go and see what this is all about. But you stay here with the engineer and watch his back.'

I kept my groan inside. At least one guard would be better than two.'

'Will do, but make sure you do get back here,' the shorter guard replied. 'I don't want to have to clean the flame room of her ashes all by myself.

I balled my fists.

The tall guard grinned and headed away along the walkway.

The remaining guard hooked his thumb back at the oval door. 'I suppose you need to go in there then, if it's a problem with the gas jets?'

'Yes.'

'Just be careful. She's more dangerous than she looks.'

'Thanks for the warning.'

The man nodded and turned to the doorway. He spun a circular lever and six bolts slid out from around the door. It swung open and the smell of cinders wafted up my nose.

'Coming back for some more!' Angelique's voice shouted from inside.

Relief surged through me.

'Shut up, vixen, and no more funny business,' the guard replied.

'Why don't you come here so I can take your eye out this time and add it to your other memento?'

He snarled and stepped aside to let me pass.

Angelique stood in the middle of the chamber, hands lashed behind her to a metal pillar. A large bruise coloured one cheek and a trickle of blood streamed from her nose. Her flying suit had been ripped, exposing the arc of one pale shoulder. Dog teeth marks punctured the leather of the other sleeve.

Angelique glowered at me as I entered the flame room. 'Oh, just what I wanted – more visitors.'

'Just don't get too close,' the soldier said to me.

I pretended to examine a series of pipes set into the blackened brick walls. When I glanced back, the soldier had turned away.

I crossed to Angelique. 'Are you okay?' I whispered.

Her eyes widened. 'Dom?'

I put my finger to my lips and pulled the welding mask from my head.

Angelique blinked, then her face crumpled. 'Oh, thank the gods. I knew you wouldn't let me down,' she whispered.

'Wish I could've been so certain.' I started to untie her hands. 'We haven't got much time.'

She gestured with her chin towards the guard standing with his back to us. 'What about that stunted ape?'

The rope fell free and dropped to the ground. I unhooked a wrench from my belt and handed it to her. 'Looks to me like you've a score to settle.'

Angelique gave me a fierce smile and clutched the tool. She put her hands behind her back again. 'Can you get him back in here and keep him distracted for a moment?'

'Sure.' I turned to the doorway. 'Hey, could you give me a hand in here?'

The man turned, his red eyes skimming past me to Angelique. 'That vixen giving you trouble?'

She glowered at him.

I unhooked an adjustable wrench from my tool belt. 'No, just one of the bolts on the jet feeds is stuck. I need your help to move it.'

He stepped in through the door. 'We can't have that. Needs to be nice and hot to melt the ice princess.' He stood right in front of her and ran a finger over her naked shoulder.

Staying perfectly still, Angelique scowled at the man, emerald eyes locked onto his.

A grin twisted his mouth. 'What a waste. We could have had such fun together.'

Angelique spat into his face.

His hand blurred and struck her across her cheek, slamming her head sideways.

Rage burned through me and I drove my fist into his back.

He spun round, starting to draw his sword. 'Well, what have we got here?'

I squared up to him and unhitched a hammer from my tool belt. 'Someone who's going to teach you a lesson you won't ever forget.'

He swished the tip of the sword a couple of times. 'Whoever you really are, it's time to die.'

He lunged forward.

Fear accelerating my reactions, I ducked to the side, but I hadn't spotted the small pipe in the floor. It caught my foot and sent me sprawling.

The guard grinned down at me and raised his sword. My body tensed, anticipating the slice of the blade into my chest.

But then I spotted Angelique creeping up behind him, like a cat hunting with focus and purpose. She slammed her spanner across his neck. With a groan, his eyes rolled and he toppled to the floor.

She stepped over the guard, clutching her spanner. 'That's for calling me a vixen.' Then her foot lashed into his side and his body spasmed. 'And that's for ruining my flying suit.' She turned to me. 'What happened to our plan?'

I rubbed the back of my neck. 'I was just trying to keep him distracted. And when he hit you I sort of went mental.'

She smiled. 'I think I may have been underestimating you all this time, Dom Taylor.

What you lack in experience you make up for with sheer bravery.' She looked towards the open door and grimaced. 'Someone's bound to spot me the moment I step out onto that walkway.'

'You need a disguise, too.' I crouched over the unconscious guard, heaved him over and began unfastening the scrolled brass buttons of his jacket.

'Now there's a plan that's got merit.' She slipped her other shoulder from her flying suit and began to wriggle out of it.

I tried to stop my gaze snagging on Angelique's body as she undressed. I pulled the uniform off the man and passed it to her.

Grabbing his hat, she stuffed her long hair up into it.

'Our balloon is in the loading bay,' I said. 'Oh, and I recharged the gem in the reactor chamber with Jules help, via the Valve Voice.'

Her eyes widened. 'You're starting to seriously impress me.' She pulled the peak of the hat far enough down to hide her green eyes with its shadow.

'Let's go.'

Angelique followed me through onto the walkway, pulling the door to behind us. I glanced down to see the cloaked figure raise his hands and the assembled mass of soldiers fell quiet, all eyes towards him.

'It is time for celebration, my comrades,' the man shouted.

'That's Duke Ambra,' Angelique hissed.

'In a moment's time Princess Angelique will be executed.'

We reached the end of the platform. She grabbed my arm and stopped me. 'Hang on, I want to hear what my treacherous countryman has to say – we might find out something useful.'

'With her death, there will be one less obstacle to the throne for Emperor Cronos.'

Angelique's fingers clamped harder onto me. 'So he wants to be king now, as well as emperor.'

'And we're closing on the trail of Queen Belladonna,' Ambra continued. 'I look forward to presenting her head on a silver platter to the Emperor.'

'And the monster's not speaking figuratively, either,' she whispered.

'So let us begin this glorious path to victory by vanquishing the captured member of the Royal House of Olympus, Princess Angelique.' Duke Ambra stepped to a polished bronze lever and pointed upwards. 'And this is how we deal with enemies of Emperor Cronos.' He pushed the lever forward. Several loud clicks came from the room behind us.

I spun round. 'The guard – we've left him in there!'

'It's too late for him,' Angelique said with a shrug.

A great whooshing came from the chamber and through the portal window set into the door boiling blue fire appeared. Six great gouts of flame glowed through the tubes.

Despite the sudden heat radiating from the room, the scream from the flame chamber chilled my blood to ice.

A roar of cheers erupted from the chamber below. I stared at the flame room, feeling sick. Angelique shook her head.

The man's cries stopped and there was only the crackle of flames beyond the door.

Bile rose up my gullet.

'Victory will be ours,' Duke Ambra shouted.

Angelique's hand closed around my fist. I gripped the railing hard. She pulled me along the gantry. 'Snap out of it, Dom.'

I stared at her for a moment and nodded.

The cheers echoed from the chamber as we began to run.

...

Angelique reached the loading bay ahead of me. Through the open hatch the blizzard had thickened and the wind's low moan raised the hairs on the back of my neck. I pressed my shoulder to the heavy round door, pushed it shut, and spun the lever clockwise, pivoting large steel rods into place.

'We need to jam it as well,' Angelique said. She grabbed one of the larger spanners from my tool belt and wedged it into the door mechanism.

Outside, the wind howled and sent a swirl of snow scurrying past the open ramp. An icicle dropped like a shining dagger from the collection hanging off the lip of the door and shattered onto the ground, its crash echoing around the loading bay.

I pointed to the alcove. 'The balloon's over there.'

'Let's get it inflated,' Angelique said.

We began to drag the canopy off the back of the sled. The white horse in its stall whinnied at us.

Angelique froze and stared at it. 'It can't be,' she whispered. Moving to the side of the horse, she let out a small gasp. She began rubbing a dark, heart-shaped mark in the otherwise perfect white coat. 'Amethyst?'

The horse whinnied and nuzzled her fingers.

'No...' She buried her face into the horse's flank.

I touched her shoulder. 'What's wrong?'

'This is Lord Orson's horse.'

'Look, we really need to go.'

She stiffened under my hand. 'If Amethyst's here, that means my father is dead.'

'Huh? I don't follow.'

She clenched her fists. 'I know it was a desperate wish, but I'd held out a hope that somehow they'd escaped that last battle. Not now.'

'Amethyst was onboard one of those ships?'

She nodded. 'On Lord Orson's ship, *Apollo*.'

'But surely her being here means that maybe they survived as well?'

Angelique started pulling at the buckles fastening the horse to the sled's harness.

'You don't understand. Even if they did, you've seen what Ambra's like – he would have had them executed on sight. And I know Lord Orson would never have given Amethyst up. The only explanation is that Ambra must have pulled her from the wreckage.' She ducked round to the other side of the horse and started undoing the remaining buckle.

'What are you doing?'

Angelique ignored me and pulled the strap free. 'Go,' she whispered, and slapped the horse's rump.

Amethyst's head jerked up, teeth bared, eyes wild, and the horse bolted for the ramp.

Angelique wrapped her arms around herself and watched it disappear into the swirling snow.

'I can't bear the thought of her being reduced to the life of a carthorse,' she said. 'I still remember Lord Orson riding her during cavalry displays. They were so beautiful together.' Outside, the wind's howl grew to a roar, sending more ice daggers smashing to the ground.

I squeezed her wrist. 'We've gotta get out of here.'

She stared out at the raging blizzard. 'We can't inflate the balloon in that.'

I glanced around the loading bay. 'We could inflate it in here – it's big enough – then tow it outside to launch.'

'Could work,' she said.

'We don't have any other option,' I replied.

We hauled the burner pack to the middle of the loading bay, dragging the envelope with it.

Pulling the canvas taut, I positioned the mouth of the balloon towards the burner.

Angelique flicked a switch and the flame ignited in a whoosh. I held the envelope as it rippled and swelled with heat.

She darted back to the sled and threw me one of the flight helmets. Grabbing the harness, she started clipping it on.

I took the control bracelet from my pocket and tossed it back to her. 'It's fully charged.'

A clang rang out behind us.

'What's going on in there? Open this bloody door,' a muffled voice said. The door handle banged against the jammed spanner.

'Looks like we have company,' I said, as we pulled our flight helmets on.

The scout balloon started to rise, tilting the blazing burner pack upright.

Angelique crouched underneath and clipped her harness into it. 'Okay, let's get out of here. Tow me towards the exit.'

She took a bouncing step as a loud clattering came from behind us. I spun around to see the ramp swinging upwards to close. The view of the snowy world outside began narrowing.

'Crap, they're trying to trap us in here,' I said.

'Hurry!'

I grabbed the front of Angelique's harness, pulling her and the balloon towards the exit. The balloon swelled and her steps bounced higher. She lifted completely from the ground. I focused on the exit just ahead, but too late spotted the low girder. With a gentle shudder the top of the balloon snagged on it.

God, god, god. My heart raced.

'Quick, pull me backwards,' Angelique said.

I tugged her by her legs, but the balloon had caught on a protruding bolt.

'Harder,' she said.

I leant back, feet scrabbling on the ground. With a rip, the craft pulled free.

'Is the balloon okay?' I asked.

Angelique looked up past the burner jet. 'It's a small tear. We should get away with—'

A thud boomed out. I spun round to see the ramp had slammed shut in front of us, muting the roaring wind to a sigh.

I stared at Angelique, her face draining of colour.

'We're trapped,' she whispered.

The shouts grew louder beyond the closed door. It shook and a second bang thundered through the bay.

'Sounds like they're using hammers now,' I said.

The door vibrated with a fresh blow and several rivets popped out around the rim.

I tightened my grip around Angelique's legs and the balloon began to rise towards the ceiling of the loading bay.

'It's over,' she said.

'It can't be – not like this.' I stared up at the floating balloon and my brain whirled. An idea broke out from my scrambled thoughts. 'Start up the Vortex.'

'Are you insane? We're too close to the ground. Remember what I said about materialising underground?'

The door thundered again and one hinge broke free. The door tilted forward and hands appeared around the edge.

'We're as good as dead if we stay, anyway.' I heaved her by the legs, back down to my level, and clipped myself onto the front of her harness.

The door groaned, tipped forward and clattered to the ground. Angelique's arms locked around me.

The air hissed and a bolt whistled past my ear. 'Get us out of here!'

'Working on it.' She reached up and pulsed the burner.

The balloon surged upwards into the vaulted space and began to slowly rotate.

Duke Ambra stood in the doorway, chiselled face framed by his flowing white hair. Soldiers fanned out around him with their gas crossbows pointed at us.

Ambra grabbed a weapon from the nearest man and aimed it at us. 'Not as poetic as reducing you to ashes in the flame room, Princess Angelique, but shooting an escaping prisoner will just have to do.' His mouth hooked into a sneer and he looked through the brass sight of the weapon.

The lights flickered and turned red.

The engineer I'd seen earlier rushed into the loading bay. 'My Duke, the reactor has been sabotaged. The control rods have been left exposed and the reactor is going into meltdown.'

'You did that too, Dom?' Angelique asked.

'Not intentionally, but hey I'll take the credit if it's going.'

She laughed. 'You're so obviously a Cloud Rider.'

I knew she meant it and that made it an even bigger compliment.

Angelique called out to Ambra. 'If I were you, I'd be more worried about saving your own worthless hide and evacuating your ship.'

'You!' he bellowed. 'This was your doing?'

She shrugged and slammed her fist onto the ruby button in the control bracelet.

Electrodes sprung outwards from the band over our heads and began arcing with blue plasma.

'Shoot them down,' Ambra screamed.

Angelique reached up and yanked the burner lever. The flame burned bright over our heads and we hurtled upwards towards the ceiling of the loading bay, arrows swarming in the air around us.

The Vortex whine grew into a howl and the room began to blur behind a wall of spinning cloud. Below us in the canvas cathedral, transport crates tumbled around scattering soldiers. One huge barrel smashed into a man and pinned him to the wall. His blood sprayed like a fountain into the wind. I pulled my gaze away.

The twister tore through the bay, and the massive arched beams started to buckle around us as if they were made of tin. Above, a great gash appeared in the fabric roof. Then the bellow of a wounded animal screamed inside my head, as snow swirled down into the loading bay in ribbons of white. Pain spasmed through me and rage heated my blood.

In a rush I understood what I was hearing – *Hyperion*'s AI, crying out, as the ship was torn apart.

Duke Ambra raised his crossbow. I stared at him as he started to disappear beyond the twister wall. The ship's cry blotted everything else out in my mind. His finger twitched and the arrow hurtled towards me. I closed my eyes, bracing for its impact.

Nothing happened and the howling gale dropped to silence.

More frozen seconds, and the *Hyperion*'s bellow disappeared from my mind. I opened my eyes to see the loading bay had vanished behind the opaque cloud gyrating around us, and beyond the darkness of the void.

My adrenaline ebbed away. 'We've made it into the wormhole,' I said into my helmet's speaker. Only crackling silence filled my headphones. Why wasn't Angelique answering?

Then I noticed her arms hanging limp by my sides.

'Are you okay?' I twisted in my harness to see Angelique's head slumped to the side.

The crossbow bolt had buried itself in her shoulder. A thin stream of blood trickled around the wound, and my mind stuttered. 'Angelique, just hang in there.'

We sped down the shimmering tunnel, the minutes stretching on. The blood roared in my ears and fear tightened its grip on me. At last, a puddle of darkness at the end of the tunnel rushed towards us, and rock began to flicker through the spinning walls.

The smell of damp earth filled my nostrils.

I yanked the burner lever and blue flame leapt upwards. The twister walls began to evaporate and translucent stone strata started sliding past.

The air began to thicken and a weight grew heavy on my chest. I fought the searing pain – my flesh, fusing with the rock. I kept my hand clamped onto the lever as weakness washed through me. The burner flame started to splutter, and I gagged. Heat burned through every fibre of my body and I tried to take a breath, but no air would come.

We were materialising underground and suffocating.

CHAPTER TWENTY-FOUR
CONTACT

The impossible weight of rock pressed harder, a fist squeezing the life out of me. Clay filled my mouth, and warmth flooded away from my body as it turned to stone.

I didn't want to die like this. We'd be buried alive and no one would ever find our grave.

Light started to grow. Above us a night sky flickered into view. We just needed to hang on a moment longer.

Come on…

With a rush we broke free of the ground and the sweetest air I'd ever tasted flushed the searing pain from my body. I stared out at the gentle rise dropping away fast beneath our dangling feet. Around us a moonlit landscape shone without a trace of snow to be seen.

Euphoria surged through me. The scout balloon twisted to the side, Angelique's head slumped against my shoulder. No!

I craned my neck round and pressed my thumb to her wrist. A faint pulse met the pressure of my grip.

'Just hang in there,' I said into my helmet mic.

She remained as still as the stone tomb we'd escaped.

The roaring flamer, an artificial star in the sky, raised the balloon fast. On the horizon a twinkling necklace of red and gold car lights headed in an endless procession along the freeway, and below us the grid of fields started falling into a familiar pattern.

There it was, our house back where it should be, nestling behind the diner and the hangar at the end of our field.

I grabbed the control bracelet on Angelique's arm and pressed the starter button. The engine coughed into life behind us. I slid the throttle wide open, grabbed the steering lines, and we hurtled forward.

'It's going to be alright, Angelique.'

Only static filled my ears.

I banked the balloon hard to the right and we sped towards the diner, tightness burning my muscles.

Despite the roar of the engine, the diner seemed stuck in the distance. I pressed my thumb hard against the throttle lever and pulsed the burner to maintain our height. A familiar tingle itched through my scalp and the murmur of *Athena*'s song surged into my mind, her greeting full of joy. At the same moment, a point of light appeared in the middle of our field, swinging left and right.

Reaching up, I tugged the release valve and air hissed from the canopy. I turned towards the beam, now directed straight up at us like a searchlight. Closing, I saw the figure clearly. Jules was holding a big flashlight with one arm, the other frantically waving to us. Mom, Bella and Harry ran from the house.

We passed overhead and I pulled the throttle back to idle. Dropping into a tight turn I killed the engine. The prop stuttered to a stop. Whoops and shouts drifted up from below.

'Angelique's hurt,' I shouted down. I saw Bella stumble and Mom steady her.

The ground swept towards us and my pulse hammered. Dad had taught me to land, but I'd never done it by myself – this would be my first solo and there'd be no second chance. I had to time this just right.

Taking a big breath, I closed the release valve and tugged on the burner lever. A bolt of flame cast a blue glow onto the grass skimming by. I braced my legs and gave the craft a final blast of heat. The meadow rushed up.

I'd left it too late, and the ground smacked into my legs. We sprawled onto the grass and Angelique flopped on top of me. Caught by a gust of wind the balloon leapt forward and started to drag us both through the field. I clawed at the ground to hold on, as blades of grass stung my face.

'The release valve,' Bella shouted, sprinting after us with everyone else.

I yanked the second lever and the balloon envelope collapsed with a sigh. We slid to a stop and I punched the release button on the harness. Rolling out of it, I scrambled over to see that Angelique's face had gone grey. God!

I grabbed her in my arms and buried my face into her neck. Her body twitched and I pulled back.

Behind her visor her eyes fluttered open. 'That was one of the worst landings I've ever experienced.'

I almost laughed, and eased the helmet from her head. 'I thought you were...' I couldn't even bring myself to say the word.

She shook her head. 'I can't be, because this arrow hurts like the fires of hell.'

'I bet.'

Bella dropped to Angelique's side. 'Oh, my beautiful daughter.'

Jules, Mom and Harry reached us. Angelique tried to smile towards her mother but grimaced instead.

Mom looked at the arrow shaft and gasped. 'How?'

Bella turned to her. 'There'll be time for explanations from Angelique and Dom later.'

Angelique struggled to sit up. 'But you need to know you what happened – Hades may come after us at any moment.'

Bella pushed her gently back down. 'I'm sure Dom will tell us everything. Right now, the priority is for me to deal with your injury.'

Angelique reached out her arm to me. 'Okay... But, Dom, please take the Tac.'

'Okay.' I pulled up the sleeve of her flying suit and started to unbuckle the device's strap. The watch face remained dark and I strapped it onto my wrist, its brass back still warm from Angelique's body.

Harry rubbed his neck. 'Looks like it needs major surgery to me.'

'Bella's a doctor, Mom,' I said.

Mom stared at her. 'It's been one revelation after another with you since they disappeared through that twister.'

Bella cast her daughter a smile. 'Harry, can you please carry her to the house?'

'You got it,' he said.

'I just need to grab my medical pack from *Athena*.' Bella set off at a run towards the hangar.

Harry gently slipped his arms under Angelique and lifted her.

'I'll get the bed ready,' Mom said. She squeezed Angelique's hand and rushed ahead to the house. We followed with Harry carrying Angelique.

'You scared us to death, guys,' Jules said.

Angelique grimaced again. 'It was all my fault.'

'No, it wasn't,' I said. 'The release valve on the balloon got stuck.'

Jules gave me the weirdest look. 'The thing is, Dom, it was me who had to tell your mom what happened and that you might not be coming back. Can you imagine how awful that was?'

'I'm sorry, Jules, I really am.' Caught in the middle – I really didn't envy her that.

But Jules didn't look at me. 'Not as much as I am. After that, I made Bella tell everyone the truth.'

'And she did?' I asked.

Jules nodded.

The distance in her voice cut me up. What had happened to the friend who'd only a moment ago stopped me losing it when I'd been alone on an enemy ship? Seemed now she'd just been waiting to see me in person so she could make it perfectly clear how pissed she was with me.

'So everybody knows now?' Angelique asked.

'At first we thought she was mad, with her talk of parallel worlds and all,' Harry replied.

'It's all true,' I said.

'We gathered that when she showed us the Vortex drive.'

Angelique looked up at Harry. 'Does that mean you're going to tell your world about us?'

He shook his head. 'Don't worry – the Hawks have agreed to keep this quiet. Bella was pretty persuasive.'

'She is,' Angelique said.

'And we've all been pitching in with the repairs,' Harry said. 'The airship's nearly fixed.'

'Oh, that's incredible news,' Angelique said. 'And you should know that if it hadn't been for Dom, I'd be dead now. He saved my life.'

Jules gave me a sharp look. 'Really?'

I shrugged.

'He was a hero,' Angelique said, voice trembling. Her emerald eyes fixed on mine. 'You are an extraordinary person, Dom.'

My throat clenched.

'Okay, young lady, less yakking and more getting better,' Harry said.

'Yes, sir.' She winced.

'And for god's sake keep still,' I said.

Angelique managed a vague nod and her eyes fluttered shut. Harry strode ahead with her.

'Jules—'

'I don't want to hear it.'

'Why are you so angry at me?'

'You think I'm angry?' She swallowed, and shook her head. 'If that's what you think, then you don't know me at all. Oh, Dom.' She sounded like she was about to cry. 'Forget it. I'll see you later.'

She spun round and headed off after Harry, shoulders slumped.

Confusion filled my head. What the hell was going on with her?

...

Inside the house, Bella, with Cherie helping out, had been operating on Angelique. Meanwhile, I'd paced the porch waiting with Mom and Jules, and had told them everything.

Mom blocked my path and kissed me on the forehead.

'What was that for?'

'For getting home safely. That's what really matters. And you were so brave.'

'Yeah,' Jules said. 'A real life hero.' But she didn't look at me and stared out into the dark.

Seriously. What was her problem? She was starting to really mess with my head. I frowned at her over Mom's shoulder.

Jules avoided my gaze and jutted her chin towards the hangar. 'I best go and supervise the Sky Hawks' repairs before they break anything.' She stalked off towards it.

'Did you have that talk with Jules?' Mom asked, watching her go.

'Yeah, I did. And I thought things were cool between us.'

'You might want to rethink that then.'

I sighed. 'Mom, at the moment all I can think about is Angelique. If she—'

'Hush now, you've done everything you can. I'm sure Bella knows what she's doing.' She ruffled my hair.

'You're not mad at me?'

'Tried that but doesn't seem to work that well with you, does it?'

I pulled a grimace. 'Guess not.'

'You really are just like Shaun.'

'Am I?'

She smiled and nodded. 'In a good and bad way.'

Footsteps approached from inside the house and I suddenly found it hard to breathe.

Please, god, let Angelique be alright. The door opened and Cherie peered out at us.

'Dom, I thought you'd like to know that your friend's awake. She wants to see you.'

It felt like the weight of a car had lifted off me.

Mom beamed. 'You see.' She gestured towards the door.

'How is she?' I asked Cherie.

'All I can say is Bella is one hell of a doctor, and they have some very fancy gizmos in their world.'

I pushed past her into the house and headed up the stairs to my bedroom. Through the open door I saw Bella bent over her daughter, both of them bathed in gentle orange light cast from a glowing Chi stone held to Angelique's bare shoulder.

Bella looked across and smiled at me.

Angelique's eyes slid open. 'Dom...' Her voiced sounded full of sleep.

I knelt by the bed. 'You had me worried there for a moment.'

She gave me a slow blink. 'All better now...' Her words trailed away and her eyes began to close.

Bella reached over and took the shimmering stone from her shoulder.

I stared at the round wound, a fraction of the size it had been, and beneath it, a purple bruise spreading its petals like a dark flower. The mound of cotton pads stained red on my bedside cabinet was the only real clue to just how bad the injury had been.

Bella held up the stone and its orange light faded. 'The flesh has knitted back together so she won't lose any more blood, but there's still going to be deep tissue tearing. That will take a while to fully heal because the injury was so serious.'

Angelique blinked at me again. 'But I'm alive, thanks to you...'

Her eyes closed and her head lolled to the side. She let out a long sigh.

I looked down at Angelique's hair, spread out like a golden lake on the pillow. 'But she's going to be okay?'

'Most definitely, although her shoulder may be a bit stiff for a while.' Bella placed the stone back into a red-lined velvet box and closed the lid. 'Come on, let's leave her to rest.'

We walked to the door and I glanced back at Angelique, curled up in my bed. The knot inside me began to loosen. She really was going to be alright.

Something vibrated and chimed on my wrist. I pulled my sleeve up to find the Tac swarming with white lights. Bella stared at it, and took a deep breath.

I felt sick. Was this it? Had our time run out?

'Another Hades' ship?'

'Let's find out,' Bella said, rushing for the stairs.

...

A jet of steam vented from the Eye. Around the gondola the Sky Hawks had their faces pressed to the portholes, Jules among them. Mom was inside the cabin with me. Everyone was silent, waiting for me to speak.

Athena's voice deepened to a quiver inside me and the transparent globe began spinning. It was close, very close. Contact, just two parallel planes above ours.

Bella's eyes flitted to mine as I kept my hand on the dome. 'Anything?'

I shook my head. 'I can't make it out. It's really blurred.'

'We have to know, Dom. They could be here within hours.'

I felt sweat trickling down my spine and frowned, trying to make sense of the vision.

'Look,' Mom said, pointing.

The white light in the glass sphere had started to change; tiny pinpricks of green swirled inside the luminous flock.

Bella put her hands together. 'It can't be.'

The globe blazed to life, lit with the jade sparkles.

'Another Cloud Rider's ship?' I asked.

Bella pressed her fingertips to her lips and nodded, eyes wide. 'I wasn't sure I would ever witness this again, Dom. This is only the second trace we've picked up in over a year, and the first was the *Poseidon*.' Her expression seemed to be struggling between laughing and crying at the same time.

'Are you sure?'

'Can you try to get a visual confirmation before they enter the Vortex.'

I nodded and shifted my perception. Within a moment everyone had become ghosts and *Athena*'s song grew to a throbbing crescendo. A vision formed in my mind, this time in sharp focus: a twister thickening around a green airship with two large props spinning fast at its rear.

Athena's song focused into a word. *'Apollo.'*

I opened my eyes and the cabin became solid again. 'A green airship, two large propellers, called the *Apollo*.'

'Oh, with the gods' blessing, there is only one ship in our fleet with that configuration, and yes it's *Apollo*,' Bella said, shaking her head and smiling. 'A day of miracles. And it hardly seems possible, but this means that Lord Orson must be alive.'

'Hang on a minute, Angelique saw his horse Amethyst on Ambra's warship and said that meant Lord Orson had to be dead.'

'My daughter must have been mistaken.'

'Maybe it was just a horse with a similar marking,' Mom said.

Bella nodded. 'Yes, that's the most likely explanation. Somehow, and gods know how, *Apollo* must have escaped the battle.'

I guess that was possible and I turned the thought over in my head. 'Hang on, if he did escape, doesn't that mean your husband could be alive as well?'

Bella clasped her hands together and nodded, eyes brimming with tears and unable to speak.

Mom pulled her into a hug. 'Oh, that's wonderful news.'

But I caught the sadness in Mom's voice. How could she not be thinking of Dad, wishing that we could have a

miracle happen to us too, for fate to somehow bring him back.

I gazed at the glowing green sphere, trying not to think those kinds of thoughts. 'What about the Pacifier? Thought you said your ships were stuck dead without a Navigator to guide them.'

'Going by this demonstration, our scientist chief Tesla, must have succeeded in developing the counter-measure,' Bella said.

'Tesla, that's an usual name,' Jules said.

'I suppose it is,' Bella replied. 'I never really thought about it before. Anyway, look.' She pointed at a lone glass sphere bursting into light at the bottom of the navigation computer.

I peered closer. 'What does that mean?'

'*Athena*'s just turned her homing beacon on,' Bella replied. 'Only another Cloud Rider craft with the correct cypher book could make her do that.'

'Great…' A strange emptiness filled me up and I found myself staring at my hands.

But if this was such good news, why did I feel like someone had just pulled my guts out?

Chapter Twenty-Five
THE MESSAGE

I rubbed my aching back. Roddy had turned up an hour earlier with the repaired engine strapped to the back of his truck. The cuts on my fingers were testament to the tough work it had been helping him and Jules mount the engine back into its pod.

Now at last we were nearly done.

Jules had been checking the oil hose connections, but whenever I tried to talk to her, she seemed to shrink away from me.

Above us the airship canvas billowed and the burner's roar reverberated through the hangar. Bella's face was lit green by the cockpit displays inside the gondola.

Athena was finally starting to look like an airship again – something designed to fly high and free. Images of cloud tops scudding beneath her kept appearing in my mind, her song growing louder and happier.

I tried to break the silence for what seemed like the thousandth time with Jules and nudged her. '*Athena* can't wait to get flying again.'

For the first time since I got back, Jules met my gaze and held it. 'That must be weird hearing her in your head?'

I shrugged. 'It's kinda cool when you get used to it.'

She actually smiled at me. 'I bet.'

After the tension between us, her smile felt like the sun had just come out inside the hangar.

'Can you pass me a spanner,' Roddy said, his head buried in the pod. 'I'm nearly done here.' He waggled an outstretched hand towards us.

'What size?' I asked.

'Biggest one in there – these bolts are massive.'

I rooted through the bottom of his toolbox and found a spanner that looked big enough to have bolted together the *Titanic*. I passed it to his waving fingers.

Roddy grasped it and the spanner joined his head inside the pod. 'This'll do it.' He made a groaning sound and metal squealed.

I peered through a gap in the hatch at the polished engine. 'Need anything else?'

'Nope, I'm good. You guys can have a break.'

Jules whispered, 'Dom, can we talk?' she said, her voice catching on the last word.

My throat tightened. 'Yeah, of course.' Here it came, like I knew it would.

I followed her outside, the growing gold band on the horizon heralding a new dawn.

Jules turned away from me and gazed towards it. 'Dom, I'm sorry for all the attitude since you got back.'

'I've been trying to work out why you've been so pissed at me. I thought you'd be pleased to see me.'

'Oh Dom.' She turned to me and her eyes shone with tears. 'You don't get it, do you?'

I gently took her shoulders in my hands. 'Then walk me through it, Jules, please.'

She held herself. 'I saw you nearly plummet to your death, Dom. Then I had to listen in whilst you risked everything on the *Hyperion*. Can you imagine how worried I was? But I had to keep myself in check, holding it together for your sake?'

So Jules wasn't pissed at me. Quite the opposite – worried sick. 'That must've been tough.'

She nodded. 'And since you've been back all I've heard is how big a hero you've been and it sounds to me' – she took a shuddering deep breath – 'like you were always meant to be a Cloud Rider.'

Is that what this was all about?

'Just because it turns out I'm descended from one, doesn't mean I've got what it takes, Jules. I've not been brought up for that way of life like Angelique has. I certainly didn't feel heroic, most of the time I was scared to death.'

'That doesn't mean it's not what you should be doing and I don't want to get in the way of that. But it's also tough watching someone I really care about nearly fall to their death, then having to listen in, feeling powerless to help as they risked their life in a parallel world.'

'But you did help, Jules. If it hadn't of been for you I would've lost it.'

'I'm glad I was some help.'

'You were much more than that. I needed you and you were there for me. And I get it, I really do. I wouldn't exactly be thrilled if you tried something similar.' That was a hell of an understatement. I would've been terrified for her.

'So, you…' she stared at the ground, 'you care then?'

'That's a stupid question, you know I do.' This also sounded like one of those – either/or – questions. Maybe this wasn't about me staying or going. Maybe she was really asking me to choose between Angelique and her, even though that was a moot point now they were leaving without me.

She raised her eyes and gave me a faint smile. 'Glad to hear it.'

'And I certainly wouldn't have worked out how to recharge the Psuche gem—' I stared at her. I'd forgotten all about it till now. I stuffed my hand into my pocket and withdrew the crystal. It sparkled like a fallen star in the growing light.

'My god, the message,' Jules said, the cloud lifting from her face.

I closed my hand around the gem and focused my mind. *Storm Wind*'s song swelled and *Athena*'s song wrapped around it in welcome. The ship AIs started to sing to each other.

I shut my eyes and Alex's face filled my head again. 'Take a ship and you will find *Titan* hidden in…' – I tensed, waiting for the location – 'Floating City. I unearthed old dock records indicating this was the last place the ship birthed and there is no mention of him departing again.'

'Floating City – *Titan*'s there.'

'You've got to let Angelique know at once,' Jules said.

I smiled at her. 'Look, if it hadn't been for you we would never have found that out.'

She stood taller, eyes brightening. 'I really did make a difference then?'

'To me you always do.'

'Really?'

'Really. And we'll continue this conversation later, okay?'

'Okay.' She dipped her head and headed back into the hangar.

I watched her go, feeling that we'd just wandered into somewhere there wasn't a map for in our friendship. But we'd work out where that place was together. Right now there were other things I had to deal with.

I ran towards the house and some crows took to the air in the distance, silhouetted against the growing light.

...

Angelique looked pale when I entered the bedroom. Grimacing, she struggled into a sitting position.

'How are you feeling?' I asked, perching on the edge of the bed.

She frowned and rolled her shoulder. 'It feels like I've been wrestling a shadow bear and losing, but I'll live.'

I smiled. 'That's the key thing after all.' I took out the Psuche gem and held it flat on my palm. It shone in the room, its light bathing our faces with blue light. 'I know where *Titan* is.'

Angelique's eyes widened. 'You do?'

'Alex said it was docked somewhere called Floating City.'

'Of course – why didn't I think of that? Floating City is the perfect place to hide a ship as big as *Titan*.' Angelique tilted her head back. 'This might be the breakthrough we've been looking for.' She dropped her gaze back to mine, face soft. 'Oh, Dom, I owe you everything. You've been such an amazing friend to me. Better than I deserve.'

'Don't say that.'

'It's true though. My life as a princess has always been about manipulating people, about status – it's what I was brought up for.'

I thought of the in-crowd at school and how desperate I'd been to be one of them. I nodded.

'And now it's all about survival. I'm... I'm too used to seeing people just in terms of how they could be useful to me.'

'Such as me?'

'I'm sorry, Dom.'

So Jules had been right, Angelique had been playing me. And even though Jules had been certain about it, she'd just let me get on with it, knowing I had to make my own mistakes and had to work Angelique out for myself. I'd been forced into a position where I had to pull through for the Cloud Riders, whether I'd felt a hero or not. It was hard not to feel everything that had happened on the *Hyperion* had just been a test – a test that I'd passed.

But was it really so bad to be the hero? Yes, Angelique had nearly made me forget about everything that was important to me. But at the same time she'd offered me a possibility of adventure, and wasn't that what I'd always dreamed of?

I gritted my teeth. Why was I being so stupid? Angelique was sitting here admitting that she'd been manipulating me, and deep down I knew I was still tempted to join her. But I had used my Whisperer ability to locate *Titan*. No, I'd done my bit. I'd done more than enough for the Cloud Riders already.

I frowned at her. 'Well you can stop with the act now. Your friends are on their way and that changes everything, doesn't it? You don't need me now.'

'But, Dom, you don't understand. Yes, maybe at first you were a bit of a game to me, another boy to wrap around my finger. But you quickly became so much more important. Then you showed me what you're really capable of on the *Hyperion*, not to mention you having the unique Whisperer gene. Imagine what we could do together, the life we could lead. You were born to fly – I saw it the moment you took control of that scout balloon. It's so obvious to me now that you're descended from a Cloud Rider. Now I know it's you I want, Dom, no one else.' She struggled upright.

Was this real or another one of her games?

I couldn't think of anything to say.

She pressed her face into my shoulder. 'Don't break my heart.'

Had she really just said that? It felt like the world was shifting under my feet. 'Oh, come on.'

Her face turned into mine, evaporating the remaining distance, and her lips pressed against my mouth, hard and hungry. For a moment, I kissed her back, remembering what I'd felt on the dance floor, back when she'd been playing me. Then it had been the most natural thing in the world.

But this just felt wrong.

I pulled away and stared at her.

'Be with me, Dom.'

I looked down, trying to think, trying to make sense of this.

'Because there's also something you need to know, something we've kept from you all so far,' Angelique said.

'More secrets, huh?' Frustration boiled up inside me. 'Are you actually capable of ever telling the truth?'

'You don't understand. We only kept this last thing from you because we wanted you to live out your lives in happy ignorance.'

'Ignorance about what?'

'Of the consequences if the Cloud Riders fail to stop Cronos.'

Ice crept under my shoulder blades. 'Go on...'

'He plans to eventually dominate each dimension of any worth, and that certainly includes your resource-rich world.'

I stared at her. What was she saying?

'One day he will arrive here with an invasion force.'

My imagination filled with images: our skies filled with red ships, our cities burning, the people taken prisoner and worse. I tried to marshal my thoughts. 'But with all the military this world has, surely we can deal with a few airships?'

'All your weapons would be useless against just one of their warships,' Angelique said.

'But why? Surely a missile—'

'Would be neutralised long before it had a chance to detonate... and that includes your precious nuclear weapons. With the AI controlling the gun turrets and with the Vortex drive at its disposal, a battle-class vessel can deal with any threat your world can throw at it.'

'Jesus. How long have we got?'

'It could be thousands of years before a full battle group is detached here, maybe less, but hopefully long after you and your friends have died of old age.'

That didn't give me much comfort. The knowledge that the world I knew was going to be destroyed… I wanted to howl, to lash out. Instead, I just bit my lip.

'But I can promise you this, Dom – whilst there's still breath in our bodies, the Cloud Riders will fight them. And I want you by my side in that war.'

My head reeled. I needed time to think. I stood up, steps unsteady, and headed out.

'Dom?'

'I need some air.'

I shut the door behind me and leaned against it, feeling like someone had punched me in the chest.

Chapter Twenty-Six
ARRIVAL

I stood watching with everyone else, the circle of angry purple clouds boil outwards across the sky. The hairs on the back of my neck bristled.

Another Cloud Rider ship really was going to arrive in a few minutes, a ship that had navigated its way between countless realities to end up in our backwater in Oklahoma. Somehow, Twister Diner had become the centre of this and every other universe.

I turned over what Angelique had told me. Had that changed everything? Was I going to go with the Cloud Riders after all? But the more I thought about it, the more I felt that Angelique had yet again been pulling my strings. If I looked at this with a cool head, our guests were about to be reunited with fellow Cloud Riders. Then they'd find *Titan* and somehow that would tip the balance in the war – and could even result in peace. Whatever Angelique said, I didn't have to tag along for the ride. She might want me there, maybe. But need me? No.

Harry emerged from the Battle Wagon, a video camera clutched in his hand.

'What a sight,' Mom said, shaking her head.

'Oh, it'll get better,' Angelique replied, leaning into Bella to support her. She'd insisted on getting up from her sickbed to welcome the visitors.

The dark wave of cumulus extinguished the sun.

Cherie stuck her head out of the vehicle. 'The pressure drop is right off the scale. This is going to be one big mama.'

'We'll be okay here, right?' Jules asked.

Bella smiled at her. 'We're at a safe distance from the wormhole, and the twister created by the Vortex won't last long.'

I watched the gyrating cloud curl tighter, its gnarled fingers crunching into a fist. A crack of thunder shook the world and a massive funnel spiralled towards the earth. In a swirl, dirt rose from the ground to meet it and become part of the dance.

The twister grew huge, spanning the distance between two barns a good couple of miles apart. The edge of the storm rushed over our heads, and stinging rain began to pelt down. The storm chasers cheered and hollered like it was Christmas and the Fourth of July all wrapped into one.

Shielding his video camera with his hand, Harry flipped a screen out and zoomed in until the spout filled the monitor. 'Oh, she's going to be a beauty.'

The storm edged towards us. With a screech, three distant silver grain silo towers crumpled, unravelling like apple peel into the sky.

'To think that's the gateway to another universe,' Jules shouted over the wind's shriek.

I leant closer and moved my mouth to her ear. 'I wish we could explore those other worlds together.' More than anything I wanted to share that with you, Jules. But I already knew that wasn't possible, she'd never leave her dad. And it felt like I'd decided to stay. So why was I kidding myself with thoughts of leaving?

I caught Mom watching us and she looked back to the twister.

The flecks of amber in Jules' eyes seemed to glow in the storm light as she stared at me. 'Do you, Dom?' She smiled and wove her arm through mine. 'Yeah, maybe you do after all.'

I tried not to jump at the physical contact, so unlike Jules. I expected her to take her arm away at any moment. But the arm stayed.

She was seriously brilliant. She was always there for me, no matter how much of a dumbass I was being. At every twist and turn she'd come through, and when it mattered I could count on her. Always.

I felt a glow growing inside me. This felt right. When I thought of how Angelique's kiss had been, hard and demanding, I shivered.

I suddenly found myself hoping Jules never found out about that.

The wind howled and Jules tucked into me. I could get used to this new Jules. The glow inside became a sun. This felt more than right, it felt damned great. I began to picture us together... When Angelique and Bella had gone, our lives would go back to normal and we could start … well, dating, being a real couple.

I gazed at her.

'What?' she asked.

'Oh, nothing,' I said, grinning. 'Tell you later.'

A long, loud whistle from Harry brought me down to earth and Jules and I blinked at each other. The twister had closed the distance and begun tearing up great chunks from our field. The dance of destruction, hypnotising like always. This would never get old for me.

The spout sparked with arcs of blue light and Harry shook his head. 'Just look at that son of a bitch – an F5 I swear.'

I spotted the flash of white and the nosecone of an airship appeared in the twister. I tried to make out the details of the craft through the swirling storm wall. 'Harry, could you zoom in a bit more?'

'Yeah, sure thing, bud.' He thumbed a control on the camera and the view got closer of the craft, edging out of the Vortex. I spotted multiple fins radiating from the nosecone and charred metal domes along its flanks.

Angelique clasped her hands together. 'It's *Apollo* all right. You can tell she's been in a serious fight – all her main weapon batteries have been destroyed.'

I called over to her. '*Apollo*'s a different design to *Athena*, then?'

She nodded. 'He's much bigger, but not as fast as her of course.' I could hear the pride in her voice. '*Apollo* is cruiser class.'

Bella squeezed Angelique's hand. 'Let's pray Lord Orson has news of your father.'

Athena's song grew in my mind and I heard *Storm Wind*'s much fainter song in the background, echoing the notes. I patted the crystal in my pocket.

Angelique smiled at me. 'You'll probably hear *Apollo* answer back in a moment. AIs are real gossips when they get together.'

Athena's voice became singsong in tone and washed over my whole body, a sea breeze on a tropical beach.

'She sounds so happy,' I called back.

Angelique laughed and clung tighter to her mother. 'Doesn't she.'

Jules squinted at me, a frown creasing her forehead. 'It's like your own secret language.'

'Huh?'

The airship drew close enough to see two people in the cockpit of the gondola. Bella waved both arms up at them.

Jules bit her lip, nodding at me. 'It's so clear now. I can never be a part of this, even if I did leave and travelled round all the universes with you. It just won't happen. Let's not pretend any more, Dom. It's just going to be even worse when you go.'

'What are you talking about? I decided to stay—'

'I can see the truth in your eyes, the truth you're not telling me.'

I couldn't believe how wrong she was getting this and I just stared at her.

She pointed at the airship. 'Dom, haven't I always known you better than you know yourself? You'd rather be up there rather than stuck in Oklahoma with us – be leading a life of adventure instead…following in your dad's footsteps. You don't need to go with them any more, but you still want to.' Her face hardened, and suddenly all the warmth had gone from it. 'And I guess it has its benefits, I suppose.' She jerked her chin at Angelique.

'Jules, you're way off the mark here.' But I thought about kissing Angelique, and my face flushed. And in a horrible way maybe she was right: I did want to be up there, flying, exploring. But not if it meant leaving. Not that.

She looked into my eyes, and shook her head. 'I don't think I am.'

A boom of thunder smashed the air around us. The twister began to evaporate, and the ship surged towards us. The wind's scream started to die, and the whine of the two large propellers became audible. Jules had stepped away from me, and was swallowing hard, right on the edge of tears.

Harry pursed his lips. 'There's a hatch opening under the gondola.'

Jules would have to wait. I crossed to Harry for a better look of the video screen. Two bomb-bay type doors were opening and a long brass tube began lowering from it.

'What the hell is that thing? Have you got any more zoom left?' I asked.

'Sure, if I use a bit of digital.' Harry pushed the knob and the gondola filled the screen. *Athena*'s song became urgent in tone, rapid, higher-pitched, the notes cutting through me like splinters.

'*Apollo*'s not responding,' Angelique said. She started towards me, eyes widening. She could feel it too.

Something was wrong.

The others stood around us, grinning and clapping, oblivious to the telepathic warning cry we'd both heard in our heads.

'There's steam coming from that thing now,' Harry said.

My eyes snapped back to the camera's screen. In the cabin window I saw… No, it couldn't be. Not here. Not in my world.

But it was. Duke Ambra's face, framed by white hair.

I stared at the image, blood going cold. Beneath the airship, cogs started turning the metal rod towards us, gas venting along the tube's side like dragon's breath. A massive arrow exploded from the tube and hurtled towards us.

'Take cover,' I shouted.

Everyone scattered and Angelique dropped into a crouch. The air hissed and the projectile blurred towards Bella.

No time to shout out a warning.

She turned towards the sound, the javelin-sized arrow skewered her through the chest, and she jerked backwards.

'No!' Angelique screamed.

I stared at the red-feathered bolt pinning Bella to the ground, blood bubbling up through the wound like a red spring.

Bella stared up at her daughter, face draining of colour. 'They tricked us…' She coughed and a ribbon of blood dribbled from her mouth.

Angelique bent over her. 'Shhh, don't try to talk, Mama. We'll get the Chi stone and you can heal this.' Her voice trembled.

Bella managed to smile and shook her head. 'Not something this serious, my love.'

'Please,' Angelique whispered.

Jules exchanged a silent look with me. We both knew this pain, knew it too well, had stood at funerals and seen it in each other's faces. I wanted to grab her and hold her, but now there was a gulf between us, with Bella and Angelique in the middle of it.

Bella raised an arm and stroked her daughter's golden hair. 'Be brave, my beautiful girl, for me, for your father – for our people.'

'Don't leave me alone.'

'You'll never be alone.' Bella placed her hand onto Angelique's heart. 'I'll always be in here, part of you.' She shuddered. 'Be kind to yourself...to others...and I pray one day you won't have to be a soldier any more.'

Tears curved down over Angelique's cheeks. 'Don't talk like this, Mama… I love you so much.'

Bella's smile was so full of affection it was unbearable to watch.

'And I will always love you,' Bella said. A racking cough shook her body and her face creased in pain. 'Goodbye, Angelique.' Her eyelids fluttered and her body arched up. With a sigh, she slumped back to the ground and her head tipped to the side.

'Mama!' Angelique shrieked and threw herself across Bella's body.

A squeal of cogs came from above us. 'Watch out, he's about to fire again!' Harry shouted.

I glanced up and saw gas venting from the gun barrel. Without even looking, I knew where it was aimed. I leapt across and shoved Angelique aside. She sprawled away from Bella. A second arrow smacked into Bella's chest, her body jerking like it been given a shock.

Angelique twisted from my grip and she fell on her mother.

'Everybody into the hangar now,' Harry yelled, pulling Mom away with him.

Faces drawn and staring at Bella, the Hawks started to fall back with him. Cherie slammed the hatch of the Battle Wagon closed and its engine revved into life.

Jules leaned over Angelique. 'Help me, Dom.'

We each put a hand under Angelique's arms.

She tried to shake us off. 'Leave me alone!'

My back tensed for the burning stab of an arrow. 'They'll shoot you if you don't move.'

Angelique turned her face up to mine, eyes liquid. 'I don't care any more.'

'Please...'

Lines etched across Angelique's brow and she stared straight through me.

The Battle Wagon roared forward and it circled round until it was between the closing airship and us.

Cherie threw open the door. 'Get your butts in here!'

Jules clasped Angelique's shoulder. 'Come on.'

She flinched away.

I placed my hand under Angelique's chin, forcing her to look at me. 'Bella wouldn't want you to throw your life away like this.'

She blinked slowly, eyes widening, and finally she seemed to see me. 'Yes...' she whispered, voice cracking.

I heard the air hiss, the Battle Wagon clanged and an arrow bounced off.

'Will you frickin' come on!' Cherie screamed.

Cradling my arm around Angelique, I pulled her to her feet. Above us, the engines of the massive airship hummed louder. We stumbled into the Battle Wagon.

Cherie floored the accelerator and we hurtled forward towards the open doors of the hangar. We hung onto handholds as she swung the Battle Wagon left and right, wheels squealing to keep their grip. Things crashed around us, a pair of binoculars swung and shattered against the steel plate.

Jules flinched as the armour shell rang like an anvil. Another arrow ricocheted off and tumbled past the windscreen.

'You'll pay for that!' Cherie shouted up at the roof.

The vehicle screamed into the hangar and Cherie slammed on the brakes. We lurched to a halt and someone threw open the hatch. In moments we were out and Harry was heaving the hangar doors shut. The drone of *Apollo* reverberated through the hangar and passed overhead.

Angelique got out and wandered in a daze towards *Athena*. She slumped onto the step of the gondola.

My mind filled with *Athena* singing to her, thoughts so full of sadness that it made my insides ache.

'What are we going to do?' Jules said.

Angelique rocked back and forth, arms wrapped around her chest. The sound of her sobbing wove into *Athena*'s lament.

I stared at the people in the hangar: at Mom, Jules, Angelique, Roddy, Harry and Cherie...the Hawks, all converging instinctively around *Athena* as though she might defend them.

It's all up to you now, Dom...

I grabbed Roddy's arm. 'How long till the engine's ready to fire up?'

'Five minutes.'

'Good.' I knelt before Angelique.

She blinked and focused on me. The others watched silently.

'I know this is real hard but you've got to pull yourself together.'

'But it's too late, Mama's gone,' she said.

I rubbed my thumbs over her wrists. 'It's never too late. It's all down to us now.'

'Us?' Angelique clamped her head in her hands. 'But Ambra will be coming around to land with his Shock marines. They'll slaughter everyone.'

'Then I'll buy us some time for you to get *Athena* into the air and jump. He'll follow you. We've got to save all these people, Angelique.'

'But how?'

The tempo of *Athena*'s song changed in my head, pitch rising, a feeling of hope creeping into it.

I scanned the hangar over the heads of everyone, looking for something...anything. My gaze skimmed past Dad's old ultralight.

The idea rushed into my mind.

'I need the scout's crossbow.'

She gave me a questioning look, but stood shakily and disappeared into the cabin. I grabbed Dad's bomber jacket and hauled it on.

Angelique reappeared with the weapon and handed it to me.

'How do I operate it?'

'Like this.' She turned a valve on the crossbow's side. It started hissing, moisture beading along a network of fine copper pipes running its length. She handed it to me. 'What are you planning?'

I gestured towards the ultralight and felt the balance of the weapon in my hand. The needle of the gauge on the top of the stock climbed towards the green. 'I'll keep Ambra distracted long enough so that you can launch.'

Mom gasped. 'You can't seriously be suggesting that you're going to fly that old thing?'

'It's what Dad would do.'

She bit her lip. 'Dom, no!'

'I have to, Mom.'

Her shoulders slumped and she blinked fast.

Jules closed and grabbed my arm. 'But—'

'We'll all be killed if no one does anything, and I'm the only one who can fly it.'

Jules' mouth became a broken line. She nodded.

Harry thrust a phone into my hand. 'At least take my cell so we can stay in contact with you, son.'

'Okay.' I shoved it into my pocket.

I turned to Cherie. 'If this doesn't work, get everybody into the Battle Wagon and make a run for it.'

'You've got it, bud.'

The whine of *Apollo*'s propellers grew louder and I dashed over to the ultralight. Leaping into the cockpit, I began buckling myself into the harness.

'Don't you dare get yourself hurt,' Mom said.

I gave her my best attempt at a reassuring smile. I scanned the control panel, pulse racing. How the hell did Dad start this thing?

I spotted a handle just under the dash. The image of him yanking on it flashed into my memory. I grabbed hold and pulled. The prop spun, but the engine didn't catch. Desperation swelled inside me. I tried again, but the same thing happened.

God!

Jules bit her fingernails, watching me. 'Isn't it a bit like one of those mower engines – don't you have to turn the gas on first?'

I tipped my head back in the seat. 'Of course.'

Her eyes darted along the aircraft. 'Here's a valve.' She twisted it. 'Try now.'

I reached forward and yanked again. The prop swung and the engine spluttered. It roared into life, filling the hangar with its throbbing bark. My throat unwound.

Mom, grim-faced, kicked away a wedge from under the front wheel.

The roof clanged and an arrow thudded through it into a hay bale.

'Okay everyone, take cover in the Battle Wagon,' Cherie shouted. The Hawks surged towards the vehicle.

'That means you two as well,' I said to Jules and Mom.

They both nodded, the fear in their eyes cutting me.

I set my jaw, opened the throttle and the ultralight leapt forward under me. Pushing the steering pedals with my feet, I taxied the small plane towards the doors.

I passed *Athena* and concentrated my thoughts. 'You look after her, you hear me?'

Her song grew louder, brighter in my mind, determination creeping into her tone.

Angelique raised a fist salute and I nodded back. We understood each other.

Jules rushed ahead of the ultralight and heaved the doors open.

Through the opening I saw the canvas belly of *Apollo*, less than a hundred feet up and descending fast into the field.

This was going to be real close.

Heart hammering, I straightened the wheel, centred the stick and stared straight ahead. Sucking in a deep breath, I pressed the throttle wide open.

Chapter Twenty-Seven
DOGFIGHT

The ultralight bolted forward and swept out into the field. A crosswind buffeted the plane and I had to fight to keep the wings level. It bumped over the grass and gathered speed. A shadow raced over me and my world grew darker. The airship became a canvas ceiling fifty feet above, blotting out the sky.

I watched the airspeed indicator climbing to ten knots, twenty, thirty...and I hauled the stick back. The nose came up and the little plane jumped up into the air.

Levelling out, I sped directly under *Apollo*'s gondola and spotted its gun barrel venting more steam.

There was a ripping sound of fabric and an arrow tore a hole through my right wing. I banked hard to the left in a climbing turn and skimmed through the top leaves of the oak tree, and over the grey rooftop shingles of the house, into clear air.

Instinct kicked in, and I understood exactly how far to push the ultralight. I didn't have to think – I knew how to fly this baby. Dad had drummed it into me, lesson after lesson, until it was branded into every sinew of my body, and now that memory rushed back.

The time had come to dance with Ambra.

I pulled the ultralight around in a sweeping arc to face *Apollo* head on. Ambra and the pilot stared at me through the cockpit window. Now to really get his attention.

Hoisting the crossbow with my right hand and closing, I aimed the weapon.

In response, *Apollo*'s gun barrel swivelled towards me.

A duel in the air. Bring it on.

Breathing out, I settled my aim and pulled the trigger. A hiss of steam, and blue flame vented from ports on the stock.

The bolt flew away, flat and true. It smashed straight into the cockpit window, shattering its glass into a mosaic.

A speck streamed from *Apollo*'s gun and a javelin projectile shot past me by less than a foot. The ultralight bucked and the sound of splintering wood came from behind me.

Hanging onto the joystick which juddered in my hand, I banked hard to the right and skimmed over *Apollo*. I swivelled in my seat and saw my broken prop splutter to a stop. Crap!

Dad's voice filled my memory.

'If you need to make a forced landing, you have to maintain airspeed so you don't stall and drop out of the sky.'

I dropped the nose, just like he'd taught me, and spotted the hangar doors opening. The Battle Wagon emerged, pulling a rope taut behind it.

My hope leapt. Connected to the other end of the rope, the nose of *Athena* edged out. They'd done it. The green airship cleared the hangar, all props spinning fast, burner sparking blue, and began to rise from the ground. Her song echoed through my mind with a roar of defiance.

Another javelin hissed past me and arced towards the ground. *Apollo* was closing on my tail. Ambra's face was framed in the broken hole of the cabin window, shouting instructions to the pilot.

I just needed to keep them distracted a bit longer. I pressed the stick to the side until I faced *Apollo* head on.

The little aircraft began to drop fast, no longer an ultralight without its engine, but a heavy hang-glider. The throb of the enemy's prop grew louder.

I spotted a projectile speed up towards *Apollo*'s cabin and smash into its gondola's hull. I traced the line of vapour down to *Athena*, still climbing: a weapon similar to *Apollo*'s, now deployed beneath her cabin.

Apollo's rudder slammed hard over and the massive craft yawed round towards the smaller *Athena*. Angelique was trying to save me. Hell. This wasn't the plan.

Athena's props scrabbled to gain height. *Apollo* would destroy *Athena*. No question. At least twice her size and with the advantage of height.

I had to do something.

Instinct took over. I pushed the ultralight's stick forward hard, trying to build my airspeed, and dived towards the rear of the enemy craft.

My plan that had seemed so sensible on the ground looked totally lame now. What could I do against such a vast ship? I hurtled towards the rudder until it seemed to fill up the whole sky. Angelique's words flashed into my mind.

'*Apollo*'s steering was stuck after being rammed...'

My heart slowed and a strange calm filled me up. I dropped like a meteor and the wind whistled past. The rudder, the size of a house, sped towards me and I shut my eyes. I knew I had no choice. My time had come. This would be for Jules, Mom, Angelique, for everyone down there.

The ultralight struck the rudder and my body slammed forward, spots of light splintering my vision. The stench of aviation fuel filled my nose. Unseen things ripped and shrieked around me, and the world became a blur of smudges.

I blinked and my head slowly cleared. What had happened?

The sky and ground tumbled past like a mad carny ride; my crossbow plummeted away towards the ground, end-over-end. The whirling slowed.

I was suspended from my harness, staring down towards *Athena* several hundred feet beneath me. My ultralight had been hooked like a fish on a line, and hung down the side of *Apollo*. The tether of fabric connecting me, the remains of the airship's ripped rudder, had knotted around the rear axle of my plane and stopped me plummeting to my death.

With a tearing sound, the ultralight lurched down on its fabric rope. The harness bit into my chest and I found myself level with *Apollo*'s gondola.

Ambra stared out at me from the shattered cockpit and bared his teeth in a snarl. He rushed to the cabin door, heaved it open, and levelled a crossbow at me. 'I'm going to kill you, boy!'

Blood roared in my ears. Down below, *Athena*'s nose pitched upwards and her song grew louder in my head. Points of light started to converge in my vision.

The scene rippled. Then I saw the ultralight hanging from *Apollo* and myself in the harness. In a rush I understood: it was what *Athena* could see happening up here.

Angelique's words appeared in my head. 'If you can hear me, Dom, release your harness now.'

I tried to talk, but no words came.

The image of me zoomed in. I could see my own face etched with fear.

'Trust me, Dom.'

The image disappeared and I found myself back, dangling in the harness. The view of the cabin was no longer visible below, but *Athena* was levelling out beneath me.

Mouth dry, mind whirling, I glanced across at his leather-gloved finger still tightening on the trigger. What had seemed a minute had been a few seconds.

'Goodbye, boy,' he said.

I thumped my fist down hard onto the catch of the harness. The straps snapped away and I dropped like a skydiver. Ambra's howl was lost in the screaming air.

The green canopy of *Athena* hurtled towards me and I slammed into it with a bone-jarring crash. With a rush of canvas and sky, the air exploded from my lungs, *Athena*'s envelope yielding like a trampoline under me. I grabbed handfuls of fabric and the bounces slowed, every sinew in my body screaming with pain.

'Are you alright?' Angelique's voice came from beneath the sweep of the airship.

I sucked in enough air to speak. 'Yes!'

'Hang on.' *Athena*'s nose dropped towards the ground. 'I'll land as quickly as possible.'

I hooked my hands around a webbing strap and rolled onto my back. The sun blinked out, and I found myself staring up at *Apollo*, its rudder jammed hard over, circling down towards *Athena*.

'Ambra's going to ram us!' I shouted.

'We're not going to make it to the ground in time,' Angelique called back. *Athena* began levelling out again, and a crackling sound grew over the throb of the engines.

'What are you doing?' I called out.

'The only thing we can do, the trick you taught me: deploying the Vortex as a weapon.'

On the airfield below us, specks of people jumped out of the scarlet Battle Wagon and scattered like seeds across the brown parched grass. Somewhere down there, I knew Jules and Mom would be standing and watching what was happening, fear filling their hearts.

Apollo sped towards *Athena* and energy started crackling around our airship. The air howled and the twister thickened. An arrow sped from *Apollo* and disappeared from my line of sight beneath the gas envelope. A scream filled my mind and *Athena*'s song stopped dead.

'No!' Angelique cried out.

My stomach clenched. What had happened?

I spotted Ambra leap from the doorway of the gondola. His dark figure plummeted into the maelstrom and disappeared like an evaporating shadow.

He didn't stand a chance from that height.

Then my world was gone, lost in swirling cloud. The air started to thin in my lungs and knots of pain exploded in my body.

'Come on!' Angelique shouted. 'You'll suffocate out there without a flight helmet on.'

Body drenched with sweat, hanging onto the webbing strap, I began to descend until my legs dangled over the edge. I took my full weight and my arm muscles burned. I lowered myself hand-over-hand, bracing my legs against the canopy. The envelope curled away back beneath me towards the gondola, and my head began to spin.

Angelique stood in the open doorway, staring up at me, face ashen. 'Dom, you can do this.'

I glanced down for a second and saw the field fading to black through the bottom of the spout.

A heavy sleep started to build within my limbs.

'Keep your eyes open,' Angelique yelled.

My head jerked up and I stared at her through the white light dancing across my vision. Lungs burning with cold fire, muscles screaming, I swung out and my legs hung over the abyss. I clawed my fists around the webbing, gritted my teeth, and lurched towards Angelique.

She leaned out, one arm anchored around a pole by the door, the other reaching towards me. 'Just a few more feet.'

Blue lightning flickered through the twister walls and the world beyond became dark. The fog crept into my mind and one hand tore free. Outside the spout I could see dark crow-shapes starting to swirl like vultures sensing death. They called to me in my mind and a chill entered me, numbing all thought. Their whispers filled me with emptiness and all I wanted to do was let go.

'Dom, don't you dare give up. Look at me.'

I blinked and saw her green eyes burning into mine, fingers straining towards me.

My right hand quivered, grip breaking free.

'Dom!' Her gaze held mine, a tug pulling at my chest. *Athena*'s song reached deep inside my skull, pushing the ice away.

'You can do this...' The thought was clear – a woman's lyrical voice.

The idea caught like a flame and ignited in my mind. I brought my left hand up and swung forward, let go, and crashed into the side of the gondola.

Something hard locked around my wrist. Pain exploded through my arm and my eyelids flickered open.

Angelique, jaw clenched, had her hand clamped around mine. 'Try, damn you!'

My feet dangled over the oblivion sucking at my body like a deep black ocean.

Angelique's eyes sparkled with the reflection of the lightning and she sobbed.

Athena's song thundered louder in my head.

'You will not die…'

Angelique's mouth hadn't moved, and I knew I was hearing *Athena*'s true voice clearly for the first time.

Adrenaline and determination burned through every fibre. My other hand shot up and gripped Angelique's. I hooked my legs up onto the edge of the doorway.

She grabbed the back of my shirt and hauled me inside.

Someone was retching. It took me a long moment to realise it was me.

Nausea and exhaustion closed in around me. The sound of a door being slammed shut came from a long way away. Cool hands pressed against my face, and my thoughts spilled away into silence.

Chapter Twenty-Eight
ATHENA

Warmth, slow and deep, crept through my body. Something cold was on my forehead. I opened my eyes and tore at the plastic thing clamped to my mouth.

Above me, knots in the wooden panels – like dark eyes in the curved roof – watched my struggle.

My mind snapped awake. 'Where—' I coughed the words caught in my swollen throat.

'It's alright, it's just an oxygen mask,' Angelique's voice said.

A hand moved under my head and a pillow slid underneath. My body felt like one big tangle of aches and bruises.

'Here, drink this.' A sparkling glass of water lowered into my line of sight. Angelique's head loomed over mine, green eyes circled with lines. She lifted my head to the lip of the glass and cool water trickled down my sore throat.

I focused on my surroundings. I was lying in one of the gondola's bunks, with furs and blankets piled up over me. Outside, I could see the tops of golden clouds gleaming against an orange sky. The three props spun slowly, their hum vibrating through the mattress beneath me.

Angelique peered into my face. 'How are you feeling?'

'Like I've gone one-on-one with a guy wielding a baseball bat.'

She gave me a crooked smile and sat down on the edge of the bunk.

Beyond her I could see the open Eye. *Athena*'s glowing globe had risen to a higher position among the other glass planets. 'So we made the jump okay?'

'Yes...' Her head dropped forward and her face crumpled.

Ignoring the pains shooting through me, I struggled to sit upright and drew her into a hug.

'I'm all alone now, Dom—' She broke into sobs and gestured towards the Eye.

I looked over and saw an arrow had skewered it. I suddenly became aware that *Athena*'s ship song was quiet. 'Is she okay?'

Angelique shook her head. 'She's been critically injured. That arrow shorted the energy matrix around her and overloaded her Psuche gem. I've shut down most of her non-critical system but it's looking really bad.'

'How bad?'

'Unless I can get her to a Master Technician to fix her, she won't make it.'

'Then that's exactly what we'll do. Where's the nearest one?'

'In Floating City.'

'But that's perfect, you're going that way anyway.'

Angelique shook her head spilling fresh tears. 'You don't understand. That last jump took everything *Athena* had. We can't jump again. We're stranded here and *Athena*'s going to die.' She started to sob again.

Her hurt swept all my words away and *Storm Wind*'s call softly echoed the sense of desolation radiating from her. An image of Mom filled my head. I scrunched my eyes up and wrapped her tighter in my arms.

So that was it, the end of my great adventure. Stuck on an alien world and never seeing home again.

I stared through a porthole at the sun, setting into an ocean. Far below, icebergs glittered like diamonds in an iridescent green sea. A three-mast ship, its yellow sails bowing forward, threaded a fine silver wake through the ice field. Another new world. It filled me with a fresh sense of wonder.

I held Angelique until her crying grew quieter and her grip loosened on my back.

She pulled away and dabbed her tears. 'Sorry...'

'Never be.' I took her hands in mine. 'You know Bella would be so proud of you.'

Her eyes searched mine.

I massaged the back of her fingers with my thumbs. 'You saved everybody from Ambra.'

'*We* saved everybody. I'm just glad he's dead.'

I rubbed her white knuckles and nodded. 'But how did he get hold of *Apollo* in the first place?'

'Something must have gone wrong with the self-destruct, allowing Hades to capture it. And gods knows what they did to *Apollo*'s AI...it shouldn't be possible for Hades to take control of one of our ships. But whatever they did was enough to convince *Athena* that they were a legitimate Cloud Rider vessel. Then she led them straight to us by turning on her homing beacon. I was too happy to even think it might have been a trap. Gods, I've been such a fool.'

Her hands trembled in mine.

'You mustn't beat yourself up. I'd have done the same if I'd lost everybody I knew – leap at any hope.'

She nodded, spilling a tear.

There had to be a way to save *Athena*.

'Use me,' Storm Wind's voice said in my mind.

Angelique stared at the light blazing from my pocket. I stuck my hand in and pulled out the Psuche gem. Aqua light flooded the gondola.

'Place me with my sister.'

I stared at Angelique. '*Storm Wind* just told me to place his Psuche gem with *Athena*'s.'

She rushed to the Eye and gripped the rail. 'Of course. I've only heard of it being done a few times, but he should be able to piggy-back her systems and fly the ship.'

'At last some good news.' I sat up and discovered a whole new set of bruises at the base of my spine.

Angelique gestured to my medal. 'May I?'

'Of course.' I opened the pendant and handed Storm Wind's Psuche gem to her.

Angelique took it from me and knelt by the Eye. She scooped away the blue coals to reveal Athena's faint crystal glowing beneath them. Very carefully, she placed Storm Wind's Psuche gem next to Athena's.'

At once his voice magnified ten fold in my mind. I sensed his awareness spreading around us, a sense of joy as he merged with the airship. Athena's song faintly echoed his in welcome.

Angelique face relaxed a fraction. 'It's working. 'A gentle chime came from the cockpit. 'Perfect timing. It's been twelve hours, but the Vortex is now fully charged.'

I stared at her. 'I was out that long?'

'You got a bit too close to those shadow crows in the wormhole. They have that affect on people.'

I shivered, remembering the sense of emptiness that had made me want to let go.

'Luckily you weren't exposed for long, so you'll be fine.' She smiled at me. 'Come on let's go and get Jules, then we can get your mission truly under way.'

I swung my aching legs off the bunk and stood up, gritting my teeth. Through the cockpit's window, the sky had deepened to dark ruby, the sun sinking into the horizon. Studying the instruments, sitting in the captain's chair, Angelique looked very small and alone.

'What?' she asked, angling her chin towards me.

'Part of me will always wish I'd gone with you. You know this is tearing me in two, right?'

'I know...' She gave me a sad smile. 'And you mustn't feel guilty about wanting to stay home. I guess if I had somewhere to call home, I'd want to stay there too.'

I sighed. 'Okay...but what will you do once you drop me off?'

'Without any other Navigators left, it will be down to me to find *Titan* and the rest of our ships to mount a counter attack.'

'Couldn't you just stay with us and hide?'

'That's not in my nature, Dom, and someone has to stand up to Cronos. Anyway, I need to draw any Hades' ships away from your world. When I drop you off it will be goodbye. You'll never see me again.'

It sounded so final. I cleared my aching throat. 'Right.'

'You would have made a fantastic Cloud Rider, Dom.'

'That means a lot, coming from you.'

Angelique smiled and pressed a throttle forward. The engines roared up to a loud howl. She nodded towards the brass handle by the door. 'Would you care to do the honours?'

I limped across and took hold of the Vortex lever.

'Just give me a moment,' Angelique said. She closed her eyes and *Athena*'s glass sphere in the Eye flared with green light.

A familiar tug pulled on my chest and the combined ship songs began to build as Angelique became almost invisible.

I locked my hand harder around the lever.

'Okay, on the count of three,' Angelique said, her voice echoey. 'One...two...three.'

I pushed the lever down. Electrodes spiked out in a ring around the gondola and blue lightning started flicking between them. The scream of wind cried up around the ship and the smell of ozone built in the cabin.

Angelique gave me a ghost-like smile. 'Let's get you home, Dom.'

Chapter Twenty-Nine
RETURN

Our twister evaporated and there was the diner, several miles away in the night. Angelique banked *Athena* towards the building, glowing in the darkness.

But the light was too orange, too bright.

I grabbed Angelique's spyglass from its wall mount and peered through it. Flames flickered from the roof of the diner. My gut twisted.

Angelique gasped. 'Look!' She pointed towards the far horizon.

A small twister was forming around a red balloon, Vortex energy flowing around it in cables of blue plasma. The craft disappeared behind the building spout.

'The scout ship,' I said. But who? 'Nobody could have survived that crash. I saw Ambra leap to his death.'

Angelique stared at me. 'He did what? Quickly, tell me what was he wearing?'

'Black overalls—'

'As in a Fly-Glide suit?'

I gaped at her. Oh damn, she was right. Something vibrated in my pocket. I shoved my hand in and pulled out Harry's phone.

Cherie Calling lit up the display. I stabbed the accept call button.

'Dom, help us!' Cherie shouted.

'The fire—'

'We're trying to get to Sue – she's trapped in the diner. The fire trucks are on the way but by the time they get here it'll be too late.'

I let the phone flop in my hand. The fire was turning from orange to crimson, the burning spikes growing higher.

'Mom's trapped in there,' I said to Angelique. 'We've got to land.'

She didn't break eye contact from the twisting twister, pulsing with light on the horizon. 'But Ambra's jumping and if we—'

'I don't frickin' care – we've got to get down there and help.'

Angelique blinked. 'Of course.' She spun in her seat, back towards the ship's wheel. 'But we can do better than land.'

'How exactly?'

'Use the ballast tanks – in an emergency we can dump our fresh water supplies to gain height and there's a good couple of tons in the storage tank.'

'Let's do it.'

Angelique pressed the throttle hard forward and the engine's note barked higher.

Cherie's voice scratched from the phone speaker. I shoved it to my ear. 'Cherie, tell the others that we're going to dump water straight onto the fire.'

'Okay, but for god's sake hurry.'

I shoved the phone back into my pocket. 'Angelique...'

'I know, I know.' She pushed the ship's wheel forward and *Athena*'s nose dropped at a steep angle towards the ground. The air whistled past the cabin, my stomach plummeting with the dropping ship. In the middle of our field I spotted the wreckage from the *Apollo*, twisted struts sticking up like gnarled, black trees.

A flash of lightning in the distance and Ambra's twister unravelled and spilled away to nothing in moments.

He was gone. Escaped. And how long would it be now till he returned with a flotilla of Hades' craft to settle the score?

I fought the panic rising up through me and concentrated on the diner. That was all that mattered right now.

Angelique scowled after him and gestured towards a blue lever set into the roof above the cockpit. 'When I tell you, pull that.'

'I'm on it.' I braced my legs as the angle of the floor steepened, and grabbed the handle.

The diner was framed in the centre of the windshield, the target of our dive-bombing run. The fire fizzed and crackled in two places, one at the rear of the kitchen and the other by the front door. The only two exits from the building. I imagined Mom inside, trapped, screaming... The sweat greasing my hands made them slip on the handle.

'We're coming, Mom, just hang on,' I whispered, wiping my palms on my jeans, I gripped the lever tighter.

Angelique gave me a sharp look and pressed the throttle hard against its stop. The rev counter climbed into the red-zone.

We were close enough now to see the Hawks throwing buckets of water at the flames, and Harry spraying them with our garden hose.

Storm Wind's song strengthened – my friend trying to comfort me in the one way he could.

'Get ready, we'll only get a single shot at this,' Angelique said.

The oak tree sped under the gondola, the field rushing past.

The flames leapt, tongues licking the sky. I tightened my grip. The Hawks turned towards *Athena*, faces lit like red masks. We hurtled towards the fire, an arrow speeding towards its target. If Mom died...

The view of the diner filled the windshield.

'Now!' Angelique shouted.

I yanked the handle. Rushing water exploded beneath the gondola and atomised into a silver cloud. The nose of the ship flew up. I stumbled and rolled towards the back of the cabin and struck the rear bench seat. In a screech of wood, the diner's roof scraped the hull and *Athena* shot into the starry sky.

'Hang on – I'm reversing the engines,' Angelique shouted.

She yanked a lever and the side engine pods rotated the blurring props backwards. *Athena* started to groan and creak as the ship shuddered and slowed its ascent.

I hauled myself up and looked through a clear diamond panel in the rear stained glass window. Behind us I saw the cloud we'd created settling onto the diner, the flames guttering and dying.

Angelique pulled us round in a steep banking turn. 'I'll get us down as fast as I can.'

Storm Wind's song and *Athena*'s weaker accompanying voice grew louder and I clung onto it, trying to push away the nightmare crowding my thoughts. Mom was all the family I had. First Bella, now Mom? She had to be okay. She just had to be.

The airship's angle steepened and the engines rotated back into position. We began to accelerate. Hanging onto the grab handles, I edged my way forward to join Angelique in the cockpit, a chill creeping up my neck.

...

We ran towards the Hawks clustered around the rear door of the kitchen, hanging off its frame, its screen burned away to nothing. I shoved past everyone with Angelique and they watched us with grim faces. The stench of smoke filled my lungs and I coughed. I clamped my hand over my mouth and tried to breathe.

Mom's immaculate kitchen had been transformed into an alien landscape of blackened metal and charred wood. Dark vapours whispered from the debris and filled the room with smog. Three shadowy figures loomed from the gloom.

Harry, Cherie and Roddy came towards us.

I grabbed Harry. 'Mom?'

He gave me a desolate look that made me want to collapse.

'I'm so sorry, Dom. No one could have survived this heat.'

I stared at him. 'Mom...'

Angelique wrapped her arms around me.

'Mom...' I repeated. Thoughts crashed in my head. I blotted out *Storm Wind*'s voice trying to weave through the pain. I was right back at Dad's funeral. Grief rushed into me.

Roddy stepped up to me and forced me to look at him. Tears had streaked the soot on his face. 'Let's get you out of here.' He placed a hand on my shoulder.

This wasn't happening, wasn't real, it couldn't be. This was a parallel world, not my own... That was it: Angelique had brought us to the wrong dimension. I turned to her, but I saw the pain in her eyes, the twist of her mouth.

No. This was real. All too real.

My world and Mom was dead.

Something deep inside tilted, broke. The pain exploded from me, rising like fire, and I screamed. I shook off the hands trying to hold me.

'Mom,' I shouted. 'Mom, Mom, Mom.' Tears burned my eyes.

Angelique hung onto me. 'It's okay, it's okay.'

'No it's not! This is all my fault. If I'd broken contact with that scout, Bella and Mom would be alive and you'd be long gone.'

Pain flickered through her face, but she tightened her grip on me. 'No, Dom, you can't blame yourself for this. Ambra is the one responsible. Ambra killed both our mothers!'

Her fingers bit into my arms. I welcomed the stinging pain. I needed it. Anger hotter than my grief burned through me. 'I'm going to kill that—'

A faint thud stopped my words dead.

Harry looked around the kitchen. 'Did you hear that?'

A pulse of hope. It couldn't be.

'Mom? Mom, are you there?' I shouted.

Another thud from somewhere in the corner. Hope bloomed inside me.

We raced over and pulled aside a shelf that had toppled over, spilling charred and bent pans across the ground. Hidden behind it was the door of the walk-in freezer.

A muffled shout came from it. 'Is anybody there?' Mom's voice called out.

Harry whooped.

I leapt at the door and heaved at the warped handle, ignoring the heat burning my hand. The door squealed open and cold air gushed out.

Mom flew into my arms.

I hugged her, arms clasped around her back. The world stopped. I was never going to let her go again.

Hands guided us outside and we clung onto each other, me supporting her shaky steps. Someone draped a blanket around Mom. She was alive. She really was alive.

Gradually, the outside world came back into focus. I became aware of the Hawks still damping down the diner with buckets of water. In the back of my mind, *Storm Wind*'s whale song had become a gentle lullaby.

'Mom, I thought you—' My throat closed up.

'I would have been if I hadn't shut myself in the freezer.'

'But I don't understand how the fire started,' Harry said.

'I do,' Angelique said, appearing with two brass balls in her hands. Each sphere was perforated with small holes. 'These are Hades' incendiary bombs. Ambra must have set them off to cause a diversion.'

I stared at her. 'Are you saying Ambra deliberately set that fire so he could escape with the scout ship?'

Angelique nodded. 'That's exactly what I'm saying.'

Something hardened inside me – a fierce ball of heat. Ambra had crossed the line and had threatened my family and friends somewhere they should have been safe.

'Jules, Jules,' Roddy cried out. He ran towards us. 'Has anybody seen her?'

'Last time I saw her she was heading into the hangar,' Cherie said. 'Think she needed some alone time after Dom and Angelique disappeared into the twister.'

'Where the scout balloon was stored?' Angelique asked.

The world tilted again.

I ran. I ran faster than ever in my life, and flew into the hangar.

Empty. Not a sign of Jules. People swarmed around me, shouting, peering into every corner.

I ran to where we'd stored the scout ship and skidded to a stop. The tarp we'd covered it with was stained with blood.

Oh god.

Then I saw it. A note laid on top.

I grabbed it and stared at the words:

'Princess Angelique, I have taken her prisoner. Forty-eight hours. Hells Cauldron.'

My insides turned to stone. Jules gone, my Jules. Taken by that swine.

The image of Jules alone with Ambra flooded my mind and I felt like I might shatter. I hadn't even had the chance to tell her how I felt. I knew now, really knew, that I loved her. And now she was gone.

Angelique appeared by my side.

Not daring to speak, I thrust the note towards her.

She scanned it and gasped. 'Ambra's using her as bait.' She took hold of my shoulders and stared at me fiercely. 'Somehow I'll get her back, Dom, I promise.'

'Jules, Jules, where are you...' Roddy cried out.

I started to lift my hand to beckon him over.

Angelique yanked my arm down. 'Don't. We can't tell him anything.'

'What do you mean? We have to.'

'He'll insist on coming with me. But you know as well as I do he's not a soldier and this calls for cool heads. That's the last thing Roddy will have right now.'

Roddy screamed Jules' name outside, an animal cry on the night air, receding into the distance.

'I'm sorry but I need to go, Dom,' Angelique said. 'The longer I leave it the further away Ambra is getting. He's in a small craft and I still have a chance of catching him before he reaches Hells Cauldron.'

I tried to speak but couldn't. I felt numb. Couldn't hold my thoughts together.

Angelique took my arm. 'Will you see me off?'

I stared at her.

'Dom?'

I nodded.

We slipped outside and crossed the road. In the distance, flashing blue lights sped along the road towards the diner.

We headed across the adjacent field, carving a path through the dried out corn, towards the green outline of *Athena* just peeking over the trees.

Sirens blared behind us. A hiss of brakes and the ears of corn were lit up by strobing lights. I didn't even bother to look round.

Chapter Thirty
DEPARTURE

'What are you doing?' Mom called out.

She and Harry walked towards me as I held onto *Athena*'s tether. The corn rippled in patterns from our prop wash. Inside, Angelique huddled over the controls, adjusting the burner's flame roaring into the canopy. She looked up.

Mom gazed at me. 'Well?'

'Angelique's heading off to rescue Jules.'

They both stared at me.

'You mean that Ambra guy took her?' Harry said.

'We found a note.'

He clenched his fists. 'Goddammit.'

I blinked back the sudden tears. 'Oh, Mom...'

She flew to me and hugged me. 'That poor child.'

Grief swarmed my head. I couldn't think. 'I don't know what to do, Mom.'

Emotions played across her face like clouds across the sun. She placed her hand onto my chest. 'What's your heart telling you?'

'It's...' I tried to concentrate. What was it saying? I saw it in the tears in Mom's eyes. I saw the smoke still billowing up from the diner. The ball of heat began to burn brighter inside me.

I was going to make Ambra pay for everything. The time to fight for Jules, Mom, my friends, and my world, had come.

'I'm going after her,' I whispered.

She pulled me into a hug and trembled in my arms. 'Dom, I love you so much.'

'I love you too.' I blinked back my own tears. 'Just tell Roddy what's happened. Tell him we'll save Jules, whatever it takes.'

'I know you will.' She pulled away and held my face between her hands, her eyes sparkling. 'You remind me so much of your dad. This is exactly the sort of crazy thing he would do. That's why I loved him so much.'

I nodded and swallowed down the stone in my throat. 'Harry, can you hang onto this?' I said, passing him the tether.

'Sure thing, bud.'

I clambered up into the gondola. 'Angelique, I'm coming with you.'

Angelique turned and stared at me. 'But what about all you said?'

I crossed to her and grasped her hands in mine. 'Jules means everything to me – I can't just stand by and do nothing.'

Angelique slowly nodded. 'Now that I do understand.'

I could see the fire burning in her eyes again. She sat a little taller, jaw set hard, and I drew energy from her strength.

She rubbed my arms. 'If anyone can find a way to rescue her, we will.'

'We will,' I repeated.

I crossed back to the doorway. 'Harry, can you and the Sky Hawks look out for Mom, whilst I'm away?'

'I don't need any fussing,' Mom said.

'Oh, I think you do, Sue,' Harry replied. He nodded towards me. 'The Sky Hawks aren't about to abandon your mom at a time like this. We'll do anything we can to help.'

In the distance, the whoosh of fire hoses mingled with the cicadas' song. We looked towards the diner in silence for a moment, at the fine mist of smoke and water visible over the trees.

Mom put her hand on her hips. 'We'll rebuild the Twister Diner. It'll be better than ever – you wait and see.'

'I bet it will, Mom.'

Harry peered up at me. 'You go and kick Ambra's ass for me.'

I nudged his shoulder with my fist. 'You got it.'

He unclipped a leather pouch from his belt and shoved it into my hand.

'What's this?' I asked, turning it over.

'Open it and see.'

I unbuttoned the leather case and withdrew a set of pliers, with loads of extra blades and attachments folded into the handle.

'It's a Leatherman multi-tool. It was your Dad's. I was going to give it to you when you turned eighteen. There's something on there for nearly every job. It might come in handy,' Harry said.

I smiled at him. 'Thanks.'

'There's something I want to give you too.' Mom took off her Saint Christopher from around her neck and pressed it into my hands.

I swallowed down the lump in my throat. 'Thank you.'

'It will keep you safe on your travels,' she said, smiling up at me through her tears.

'That will be good where we're headed.' I glanced in at Angelique. 'What was it called again?'

'Hells Cauldron,' Angelique said, tapping one of the dials.

Harry scratched his neck. 'Sounds lovely. Make sure to send us a postcard.'

I forced a laugh. 'I'll do my best.'

Mom took my hands in hers. 'Your dad would be so proud of you, Dom.'

'I hope so.'

She smiled. 'I know so.'

The engine roared up behind me. 'Think that's my cue.'

I slipped the Leatherman into the pocket of the bomber jacket.

Harry dipped the rim of his baseball cap. 'Safe voyage, son.'

Angelique gave the burner a blast. Harry put an arm around Mom and the two of them began backing away.

I pulled the door closed and felt a bolt of excitement mix with my fear.

Mom and Harry raised their hands in farewell. I waved back and Angelique pushed the throttle forward. *Athena* rose, propellers humming, her song growing in my head, and we accelerated into the sky.

The ground fell away fast, and our house, the diner and the hangar, my whole life, became small enough to blot out with the palm of my hand. I turned away and looked up into the night sky full of stars, feeling my heart soar with the climbing ship.

Angelique spun her chair towards me. 'Time to make the first jump. We've got a long trip ahead of us and we need to start putting a plan together.'

I nodded. As we ascended, the patchwork landscape of Oklahoma spread out before us, its endless fields stretching away.

I kissed the Saint Christopher and hung it on the window frame. Placing my hand on the Vortex control, I braced my feet. 'Ready when you are, Captain.'

'May the gods protect our souls.' She placed her hand on the Eye, and *Athena*'s glass planet flared with light. She looked over the top of it at me.

Energy surged through my chest, and *Athena*'s and *Storm Wind*'s song filled me with joy. I tightened my grip on the handle and got ready to start the Vortex drive.

– To be continued in Breaking Storm –

ACKNOWLEDGEMENTS

There are so many people who have helped me on my journey to publication. I wish I could name you all, but you know who you are.

I must specifically mention a few people without whom I'm certain that I wouldn't have reached this magical moment. The first is Kathryn Price at Cornerstones, one of the most talented editors I have had the pleasure to work with – but what a taskmaster. When I produced a draft that I was convinced was the best thing I'd ever written, Kathryn pushed me to do better. I still hear her voice in my head when I write – telling me about show now tell; about pacing; about not over-writing a piece. You, Kathryn, continue to be an inspiration.

I like to think of the wonderful Lee Weatherly as my industry mentor. Lee spotted some spark of potential in me a number of years ago during a writing workshop, then helped to foster that spluttering flame of self-belief and became my guiding light over the years. You are the best, Lee. I must also mention Jack Ramm at Eve White Literary Agency whose belief in Cloud Riders has been constant, thoughtful and insightful. He's been a complete pleasure to work with.

Of course, special acknowledgements must go to the fantastic Three Hares publishing team. Cloud Riders feels like it's come to its true spiritual home. Many thanks Helen Bryant, for your guidance (and patience) and Yasmin Standen who has enough energy to spin the planet. Thanks also to Jennie Rawlings, whose cover design is stunning. And, if you have seen the book trailers for Cloud Riders, you'll have heard the fantastic score by my best friend, and man with a heart of gold, Martin Severn. What would I do without you, Mart?

Finally, I want to thank my partner, Karen, and my son, Josh, who've put up with the continuous naval gazing, the vacant stares and the gnashing of teeth that being an author involves. You guys are superstars and I love you to bits. I certainly couldn't have got here without you.

Thank you all for your support on this wonderful journey. Despite its twists and turns, I wouldn't have missed it for the world.

Printed in Great Britain
by Amazon.co.uk, Ltd.,
Marston Gate.